Wicked Women

Dreda Say Mitchell

Big Mo Crime Series Book 3

First published in 2021 by Mitchell and Joseph Ltd

www.dredasaymitchell.com

Paperback format ISBN: 978-1-9164202-9-8
e-book format ISBN: 978-1-9164202-8-1

Book cover Stuart Bache at Books Covered https://www.bookscovered.co.uk
Formatting Polgarus Studio https://www.polgarusstudio.com
Editing: Emmy Ellis https://studioenp.com

Praise for Award-Winning Author Dreda Say Mitchell

'As good as it gets.' ***Lee Child***

'Great book written by a great girl.' ***Martina Cole***

'A truly original voice.' ***Peter James***

'An exciting new voice in urban fiction.' ***Guardian***

'Zippy, twisty plot… and a bevy of memorable supporting goodies and baddies.' ***The Sunday Times***

'An exciting new voice in urban fiction.' ***Guardian***

'Thrilling.' ***Sunday Express Books of the Year***

'Awesome tale from a talented writer.' ***The Sun***

'Fast paced and full of twists and turns.' ***Crime Scene Magazine***

Amazon Readers Love The Big Mo Crime Series

'Top class.'

'Little Mo captures your heart.'

'Absolutely fantastic read.'

'You must read this book.'

Prologue

1971

'Go! Go! Go!' Rita screamed.

Rita's red Biba tunic dress, ample cleavage and white go-go boots flashed in the back seat as she bundled into the car. She slammed the door of the Ford Granada with such force the bodywork rattled. Upfront sat Brother Bertie in the driver's seat and Ruddy. They shared a shocked look. They'd been waiting to pick her up, as arranged. So what was all the racket about?

That's when they noticed she was tightly clutching a small black sack in one hand and in the other a pistol. An old Browning. Rita appeared less like a lady of the night who'd spent an hour with a client and more like a bank robber who'd just fled the scene of a crime. All she needed was a stocking over her head and a bag with 'swag' on it.

Ruddy asked, 'What's a working girl like you doing with a shooter?'

The other woman didn't hear her, too preoccupied with searching anxiously through the rear windscreen. Twisting urgently back to them, Rita started shouting the odds again. 'Are you deaf? I said go! Go! Go!'

Brother Bertie didn't like her attitude. In normal circumstances he would've told her where she could shove it. However, she was a mate of Ruddy's, and he'd do anything for his friend. He got the engine into gear and proceeded down the street towards Park Lane.

Rita was not happy with Bertie's footwork on the accelerator and told him as such. 'I mean, get a move on, mate. I'm a tart who's late for her next job, not an old dear in a wheelchair going to the Darby & Joan. Give it some welly!' She squinted with intense suspicion at him. 'And who the heck are you anyway?'

She prodded Ruddy below the shoulder with the gun. 'Ruddy! I thought I asked you to pick me up. Who's this bloke?'

Ruddy answered, 'This is my friend, Bertram. Brother Bertie.'

Rita skinned her teeth. 'Brother? 'Ere he's not one of them religious types. Can't keep their hands to themselves. Unless their paying, o' course.'

Ruddy continued her explanation. 'I don't drive, you know that. So I had to find someone to pick you up.' Over her shoulder she peered meaningfully at the gun. 'What the heck did you bring that along with you for? I told you the geezer I asked you to service is perfectly harmless.'

'Perfectly harmless? He's a man, ain't he?' Rita sneered, tucking the shooter away. 'You don't meet many harmless men in my line of work. Or in any other line of work come to that.

I always take a shooter with me for awkward moments. And talking of men, tell your mate, Brother Whatnot here to step on it. He's plodding along like a Sunday afternoon driver.'

'He's doing us a favour.' Ruddy was getting the nark. 'I've asked him to take it easy. With you being on the game, you're well known to the coppers. I don't want Bertie pulled over and have to answer nosey questions from the rozzers about what you're doing back in your glad rags.'

'You mean they'll think he's a pimp?'

'Exactly.'

Rita eased back, muttering, 'If we get pulled over, that'll be the least of his problems.'

Ruddy was getting suspicious. What was going on in the back seat? Rita was on edge like a dog that hadn't been for walkies in ages. What was the deal with the gun? And what was in that bag that she was clutching like the crown jewels? What really pissed off Ruddy was that this was only happening because she done a good turn for a poor bloke.

She'd been cleaning the flat of a man she only knew as the 'Colonel'. He was in his mid-forties, ramrod straight and every inch the soldier. Although he could afford to live in the West End, as time went by he had fewer and fewer possessions. In the end his place was hardly worth cleaning there was so little in it.

The day came when the Colonel explained, tears welling up in his eyes, that he could no longer afford to pay Ruddy to clean his home. 'I'm broke, my dear. It's the card tables, Ruddy. I can't stop myself. It ruined my father and now it's ruining me.'

Poor bollocks. Ruddy liked a shuffle herself so understood exactly where he was coming from. So she carried on cleaning his flat for nothing. The Colonel would be sunk in gloom, in one of his few remaining antique chairs while she ran the broom round his feet. One day she asked him whether he'd ever considered getting a lady friend. Wouldn't that put some flash back in his fire?

'No respectable lady would consider a gentleman like me. I'm not a good catch unless I conquer the cards.'

Ruddy cosied up to him. 'There's more than one way to skin a cat, Colonel. There are ladies out there who will provide such a service for a small fee.'

The Colonel was horrified. 'I couldn't consider that. It's sordid. Besides, I can't afford a small fee.'

Later than evening, Ruddy bumped into her old friend Rita in the Docker's Return boozer in the East End. Rita had been on the game for a few years and already had a number of posh clients up West.

Ruddy didn't hang around putting her proposition to her friend. 'I need you to do a freebie for me.'

Rita arched a curious brow. 'Didn't know you batted for the other side, sweetheart.'

Ruddy wondered whether Rita might be a little too fruity for the Colonel but pressed on. 'Not me. I've got a friend who lives where the other poshos do. Perhaps you could call on him and put a few more hairs on his chest.'

'For nuthin'? Are you pulling my bobtail? I ain't the welfare.'

Ruddy got up close. 'You owe me. The number of times

I've bailed you out. Look on it as compo.'

Rita thought about it. 'He's got no readies?'

Ruddy shook her head. 'He ain't got sixpence to scratch together.'

Rita thought some more. 'Fair enough. I'll show him a good time. But you'll have to pick me up after the job.' Her nose wrinkled. 'I don't take public transport when I'm knackered.'

Ruddy's mind came back to the car.

Rita got angrier and angrier about Bertie's driving. 'I ain't got all day. You're like a pissed cabbie who's forgotten the knowledge.'

Holding on to her temper, Ruddy turned to her friend. 'What's the matter with you?'

She got no answer because Rita was gawping in alarm out of the back window.

'I don't believe it. They're onto me already.' She spun round, took the shooter out and pressed it between Bertie's shoulder blades. Growled, 'You need to get me out of here, Graham Hill style. If I'm caught by the law, there's going to be blood, and I don't care who it belongs to.'

Ruddy was horrified. A police car was trailing.

'Is she joking?' Bertie wasn't too anxious; this wasn't the first time he'd found himself looking down the barrel of a gun.

'She never jokes about things like that. You better put your foot down.'

Bertie drew breath and yanked up the handbrake. The car violently skidded sideways to the other side of the road.

Pumping the engine, he threw the wheel. The car jerked forwards, accelerated the other way, past the police car. It tore down the road. A siren wailed behind them. The coppers did a three-point turn and set off in pursuit. Bertie violently pulled into the oncoming traffic's lane.

Rita shrieked, 'Are you crazy? Dicked in the nob?'

Bertie and Ruddy shared a look and howled with spontaneous laughter. They loved a bit of high jinks every now and again. Bertie urgently pressed the horn, warning the oncoming cars they'd better get out of the way. Vehicles scattered, some forced to mount the pavement. He did a hard left into Berwick Street. It was filled with mobile stalls and carts left from the day's trading in its street market. They were parked on either side of the road, allowing traffic to still flow down the street.

Bertie slammed on the brakes which threw Ruddy and Rita akimbo across the car. He jumped out. Ran back up the street, pushing and scattering over carts and stalls in the road behind them. The cops screeched to halt in front of the obstructions. Bertie hot-footed it back to their motor and took off at high speed. In the rear-view mirror, he saw angry police kicking at the overturned carts.

Rita was warming up to Bertie. ''Ere, Ruddy, your fella's good. There's plenty of teams out East who'd pay good money to hire him as a wheels man.'

When they reached Chinatown, he parked up on a pavement. Ran into a restaurant and, shortly afterwards, he emerged with a waiter who opened a gate into a small courtyard. He drove in while the waiter closed the gate. All around, Soho echoed to the sound of police sirens.

Rita seemed to have calmed down. 'Good job, mate. Now what? We wait until the plod get bored?'

An unhappy Bertie turned around. 'My friend, Ling, will let me leave my car here for a few days until I can organise some false number plates. In the meantime, I'd suggest you think about getting the bus home.'

Rita nodded. 'Fair enough.' As easy as you please, she dropped her pistol into her black bag. Opened the door. 'Pleasure doing business with you. Thanks for the ride.'

With that, she disappeared into the crowds on the street outside and the warm evening air.

It was past midnight when Ruddy finally got home, but she didn't go to bed. She was plunged into unease. She knew Rita. She gave new meaning to the word shady. Ruddy couldn't get it out of her head that Rita had been up to something at the Colonel's. In the morning she'd give him a little tinkle to find out how things had gone with Rita. He got there before her. He rang just after eight. 'Ruddy, I've been robbed.'

Chapter One

2006
Thirty-five years later

Jimmy Southpaw's steely gaze swept over the sombre crowd gathered in the graveyard. 'It's been years now since my Robbie was laid to rest. But I tell you this. The pain hasn't lessened with the passing of time.' He thumped his heart with feeling.

Excruciating grief tore him up. His insides were a raw open wound. *Robbie's gone! Robbie!* Even six years on, Jimmy still couldn't get over the sorrow of his firstborn boy having been taken from him. Swallowing deeply, Jimmy fought hard not to sob his guts out. It would be taken as a sign of weakness if an upright man with his reputation lost his bottle in public.

Jimmy Steele was a living East End legend to some and to others a notorious, fearsome gangster. The kingpin of the infamous Steele family, until his retirement five years back. Known by his nick, Southpaw, on account of the lethal left-handed punches he'd wielded to devastating effect as a youth in the ring. He was a big and powerful man who had flexed his muscles to climb the criminal underworld ladder.

His heir and eldest child, Robbie, had burned to death in a fire in a police station six years ago. Robbie Steele breathed his last inside a cop shop! The East End was still reeling from the shock of that. Apparently, there had been nothing of Robbie left. Imagine that a father with nothing left to bury of his son.

Jimmy's hollow voice carried on the chilly wind. 'Let's remember what a top banana my kid was.'

Jimmy couldn't stop the tidal wave of cruel sadness, the crippling toll that his son's death had taken from finally crashing down on him. A guttural noise cracked from the back of his throat as he choked up.

'Stay strong, Granddad Jimmy,' Mo, his granddaughter whispered for their ears only. Her arm supported him on one side, while her younger half-brother supported him on the other.

His granddaughter was the pride of Jimmy's life. Twenty-four years old, a feisty firecracker, who wore her twin Jamaican and white-English heritage with pride. She had smooth, glowing brown skin, curly hair that bounced against the tops of her shoulders and intelligent steel-grey eyes that were replicas of her Granddad Jimmy's. Maureen Watson, known by most as Big Mo, was his heir and had been running the Steele family concerns like she was born to it for the last five years. She might be small in stature but she was a giant of a figure in London's underworld, well on her way to consolidating her lifelong ambition of being London's reigning Queen of Crime.

Mo had only learned that Robbie was her father after his death, so this ceremony that honoured his memory was very emotional and important to her. When Jimmy had chosen his son's wrong-side-of-the-blanket granddaughter to be his heir, that had provided another shocker for the East End. Then again, it was twisted family drama that kept the East End gossip vine on its toes.

Jimmy's remaining son, Harry, and Robbie's widow, Kristal placed their palms on his back, adding their strength to help get him through this traumatic day. Sometimes Jimmy thought the antics of his family would be the death of him, but it was at times like this, when they presented a united loving front, he was truly grateful for them. Harry was based in New York now running the family concerns on that side of the pond. He'd be flying back later today.

Straightening his backbone, feeling the ground more solidly beneath his feet, Jimmy proudly stepped away from the helping hands. He tugged the silk rope, and the white sheet covering the memorial fell away. Robbie Steele was immortalised in a white marble sculpture ascending to Heaven supported by a group of angels. The angels wore the shirts of Robbie's favourite footie team, Arsenal. The crowd broke into spontaneous applause, although truth be told, there were those who were disappointed, whispering and bitching behind their hands:

'Fancy putting two wings on the boy. He looks like a schoolkid in a nativity play.'

'Two angels taking Robbo to Heaven? It should have been two blokes with horns and pitchforks taking him down to the other place.'

'That statue must have cost a fair bit of poke. The scrap value of the marble alone must be worth a couple of drinks. Jimmy Southpaw wants to be careful, someone'll bring a forklift up in the middle of the night and have that away.'

'Not unless they want a memorial of their own, they won't.'

Jimmy stared at the memorial, silent and alone, lost in in his own thoughts and memories until he noticed Nico Sinclair standing at a respectful distance. Nico was tall, olive-skinned with the type of looks and slick fashion sense that left both women and men gawking at him on the street. He was also one of South London's Premier League Faces. Not a man to cross. His sister, Kristal, was Robbie's Steele's widow. Family was everything to Nico.

Nico approached Jimmy. They had business to discuss. They walked away among the gravestones. Jimmy checked that they were a safe distance from prying ears before asking, 'You all booked up for your holiday abroad?'

Nico nodded. 'All sorted. I've rented a villa up the coast from Marbella. I'm flying out in a couple of days.'

'You taking anyone with you? You'll need someone to keep an eye on the place while you're out 'n' about. Know what I mean?'

The South London gangster hesitated. 'I'm taking another guy as cover. It'll be more plausible if it's two blokes on the razz renting a place.' His voice lowered. 'Obviously, he's not in the picture about what's really going on.'

Jimmy's seasoned face considered the younger man. 'I hope he's reliable. Who is he?' Noting Nico's tightening lips, Jimmy put him bang on the spot. 'What's his name?'

Nico let out a lengthy sigh. 'Damien.'

'My grandson?' Jimmy looked like he was on the verge of heart failure.

His disbelieving gaze zeroed in on his twenty-three-year-old grandson in the distance. In the last five years, Nico had taken his nephew under his wing. Grudgingly, Jimmy had to admit that the relationship had transformed the boy's life. For starters, he wasn't such a mummy's boy anymore. And the kid didn't walk around with that strange angle to his head that had always put Jimmy in mind of some weirdo. It turned out that Damien had nearly been deaf in one ear since he was a nipper, hence leaning his head forward with this good ear to hear. It was Nico who had sussed the problem and got a top-flight doctor from up Harley Street to put the lad straight. Another plus on his grandson's side was he'd shed untold pounds and looked as fit as a butcher's dog these days. Mind you, despite maturing under Nico's expert eye, that boy was still prone to behaving like a prized plum some days.

'Are you off your trolley?' Jimmy showed his displeasure. 'A lot of words spring to mind when Damien's name is mentioned, but reliable ain't one of them. If that little plonker totals a bar and gets arrested by Los Copos, that could royally mess things up.'

Nico got the nark. 'Damien's more mature than you give him credit for.' He was always sticking up for his sister's son. 'He'll do what he's told.'

Suddenly the strain of the day caught up with Southpaw, his skin to sagging. 'Don't let me down here, Nico. I'm relying on you.' There was almost a pleading in his voice. Jimmy never begged anyone. 'I don't want my bird to suspect anything and fly the nest. We might never find him again.'

'Which birdie is that then?'

The men were taken unawares by Mo's arrival. Neither of the men noticed Mo walking towards them. They fell silent and widened the distance between them. Mo looked from one to the other with suspicion. She was no fool, guessed that something was going on.

Her brow arched with meaning, her body tensing. 'If this is something to do with the business, it goes through me first.'

That's my girl! Jimmy thought approvingly at her adamant stance. That's what he'd taught her to do. Always ensure that Tom, Dick and the Devil Himself knew that she was head honcho of the family firm.

Nico answered, calm and chilled as per usual. 'Chatting about old times. Old friends. Old lovers.'

Mo coloured slightly at the last. There had always been *something* between her and this gorgeous hunk of a fella. Her secret truth was she adored him. Had loved him for years. However, Nico was known for his loyalty and devotion to his wife, so Mo kept it at a flirty-flirty level. A man with a ring on his finger wasn't her style. Besides, she had her own love thing going on these days.

She turned to her grandfather. 'I've got to go.' She took his hand and squeezed.

He was disappointed. 'Not joining everyone for a drink to remember your own ole dad?'

Mo was brisk. 'It's business. Something I've got to sort tomorrow. And you've always said business comes first.' Thinking about the business she had to attend to made her blood boil.

Mo strode through the crowd, casting wistful glances at the memorial to her old man which now towered over the neighbouring graves. They said in the books that a man's soul could only depart this world when it was at peace. And she was sure her father's spirit wouldn't be at peace until how he'd died in the first place was resolved. And it never had been.

Robbie was the only guy who'd died in that police station fire. Strange that. They decided an electrical fault in the crumbling building was to blame. What burned and hurt her most of all was that she knew Robbie had been murdered. Someone had deliberately set the cop shop on fire so her father burned to death. Year after year Mo had followed lead after lead in a desperate bid to unveil the truth, only to end up in dead ends. As for the two cops who'd picked Robbie up that night, Mo couldn't find them anywhere. It was as if they'd vanished off the face of the earth.

'Bit syrupy, ain't it.'

The unexpected sarky statement took Mo unawares, dragging her from her thoughts. Leaning against a nearby gravestone was Kristal, her stepmother and Robbie's widow. She was a bottle blonde wearing a LBN that accentuated her superb 1950's hourglass figure and generous boobs. No doubt she'd spent hours earlier at the beauticians getting her slap sorted along with a few shots of Botox. For Mo there had been a time when meeting Kristal had been close encounters of the evil stepmummy kind. But in the last five years they had reached a truce. Basically put, they weren't at each other's throats.

Mo knew Kristal was pointedly referring to her dead husband's memorial. Known for having a gob on her, the other woman continued having a snide. 'And Robbie was never big on the Ten Commandments, especially the seventh, which is how you came to be born.'

Mo let the personal dig fly over her head. The problem with her stepmother was she was about as subtle as a flying brick. Kristal kept up her sanctimonious chat. 'Frankly, I can't see your ole man approving. He'd have preferred being portrayed literally riding shotgun at the wheel of a fast motor.'

Mo didn't bother giving sourpuss Kristal the time o' day and was on her way. And that's when she noticed something no one in the assembled gathering had. A hooded shadowy figure hiding behind a tree.

Chapter Two

Stalking forward, Mo was on a mission to find out who it was. And if it was an enemy, God help them. The Steele family had collected a legion of rivals over the years; it was only to be expected. You had to watch your back in this criminal life. Foes plotted and planned, biding their time for that right moment to stick it to you, good and proper, in your back. And what better moment than when a family's guard was down, gathered to honour its dead. That's why Mo's minders were in attendance today. Josh, who was also Barker's, Granddad Jimmy's right hand's nephew, and Delilah, her cousin who never left home without her lethal twin machetes she carried in a rucksack on her back.

After a subtle signal to her protection to follow at a discreet pace, Mo casually made her way to where the uninvited guest lurked in the shadows. In the back of the waistband of her trousers was a gun. It wasn't any run-of-the-mill shooter. It was black with a gold handle. It had belonged to her father, Robbie, his personal weapon gifted to him by his father. And now it had been passed down the line of Steele men to her, a woman, the new head of the family. Mo didn't want to have to use it on such a solemn occasion. However, if an assault was launched, she wouldn't hesitate to blast all-comers to Kingdom come.

Whoever it was got wind they'd soon have company because they did an about turn and, head down, hot-footed it away. *Think you're gonna leg it? Not on your life, buster.* Mo picked up speed. A flick of her finger was the signal for Josh and Dell to tighten the net around the perimeter and keep an eagle eye out for any other unwanted parties; this could be an ambush. The thought of it, on the day Mo was remembering the father she had never known, sent rage ripple through her.

The person started running. Mo did the same. Josh and Dell reached the exit, barring it. Their prey was trapped. The intruder backed up like an animal caught in a cage knowing they were beaten.

Mo called out, voice ice-cold and deadly. 'What business have you got here?'

The person's shoulders stiffened. They didn't cower as most would, faced with the fury of Big Mo Watson. They refused to turn around. *It's like that, is it,* Mo grimly thought. Josh and Dell strode forward, crowding in on the stranger with the intent of dragging them before Mo. But the strangest thing happened; their steps faltered and slowed the closer they got. Finally, they stopped dead.

'What's going on?' The muscles in Mo's neck strained with her demand.

They didn't answer, instead backed away. *For crying out loud!* Mo stalked forward, her hand easing on her shooter.

She didn't hesitate when she reached the person; she yanked the hood down. The person swung to face her.

Mo staggered back. 'Mum?'

Sitting opposite her daughter at the table, Precious Watson dashed a stray tear away. Aware things could turn explosive, Mo had bundled her mother off to a nearby caff before anyone else twigged that Robbie's former lover had shown her uninvited face at his memorial service. Major league ructions would have gone on if Kristal had clocked her. Probably have been the advent of World War Three. Mo shuddered. And Granddad Jimmy wouldn't have been best pleased either. Mind you, that was a two-way street because Precious despised him with a passion. Why that was, everyone was keeping schtum from Mo.

Even tears couldn't detract from what a stunner Precious Watson was. Lovely and lush brown skin, tall and willowy with the type of looks that had both men and women gagging in the streets. Precious had only ever given her daughter snippets of the story of how she had become Robbie Steele's lover on the side. What Mo couldn't figure out was why her mum would go with a man wearing a ring on his finger. Going with a married man was not Precious Watson's style. Mo and her mum had fallen out in spectacular fashion about the whole Robbie saga five years back. Mo had desperately wanted to know about him, and her mother stubbornly refused to tell. Four years they didn't speak. If they saw each other on the street, it was a strictly walk-on-by arrangement.

The situation had crushed Mo, broken her heart. Her mum meant the world to her, and the fact that they weren't speaking had cut her to the core. Her mother, with the support of Brother Bertie, had brought Mo up single-handed. Yeah, they'd had their ups and downs, but that was only natural being a child and a parent. Mo loved her mum, it was that simple. In the end she had been the bigger woman and made amends. When Precious had laid eyes on her girl on her doorstep, she'd wept with joy and embraced her daughter so tight Mo thought she was being squeezed to death. The best death a person would have ever had.

'Turning up today, I never meant nuthin' by it.' Her mum's terse voice drew Mo back to the present. Precious' shattered gaze implored her daughter and only child to understand.

'I know, Mum,' Mo quietly conceded.

'I just needed to be there. It was my right.'

'I know that too.' And Mo did. The particulars of what had happened between Robbie Steele and her mum, Mo didn't know. What she did know was how much her mother had loved him. Even though they hadn't been an item since Mo was a baby, when Robbie had passed, Precious had fallen apart.

A brief small smile temporarily pushed the misery from the older woman's face. 'When I told him I was pregnant with you I thought it was game over.' Bitterness, thick and unforgiving, entered her tone. 'Then again, he never told me he had a missus all nice and tucked up indoors waiting for him. I was so in the dark.'

Mo shook her head with years of frustration and confusion. 'That's what I don't get, Mum. The East End is one big gossip vine. Radio Back Fence Chat FM. There must have been talk that Robbie was already taken. I don't get how come it never reached your ears?'

Precious' gaze ducked away but not before Mo saw the flash of something twisted in her eyes. Regret. Was that what she saw? Was that what her mother had felt after all these years? Wished none of this had gone on? Wished that Mo had never been born?

'I cherished you from the first day I knew you were growing in my belly.' Precious' words were fierce. How had her mum known what she was thinking? Her mum raised her head and covered her hand with steadfast conviction. 'Robbie did too. You should've seen his face when he cradled you in his arms. But things… were complicated.'

'Kristal?'

Precious glanced into the distance, the hiss of her breath audible as she pulled in a lungful of air. 'I hated it that Robbie shared his home with another woman. Hated the fact that another woman lay, her body entwined with his at night.' Her gaze flicked back with a force that pressed Mo back in her chair. 'One day I woke up and realised that I was the other woman. And then that fucking man, Jimmy Southpaw —'

'What?' The urgency Mo felt to know more pushed her closer. Something had happened between the Steele and Watson families that no one would speak about. 'What did Granddad Jimmy do?'

Precious' chair scraped back. She leapt to her feet, anger jutting her jaw. 'I've told you not to mention *that* man in my presence. As far as I'm concerned, you've only got the one grandfather, and it's my dad.'

Oh! Here we go! In any other situation, Mo would've disdainfully kissed her teeth, but in the Caribbean community, the gesture was a no-no between a child to her parent. A sign of disrespect. Instead, she twisted her mouth with extreme displeasure. Mo had such love in her heart for her mother's father, Brother Bertie, but she also adored Granddad Jimmy too.

Mo called her mum out. 'Why do you hate Granddad Jimmy so much?' A nasty grunt was the response she got to that. 'What has he ever done to you?'

Precious' features contorted, ugly and pinched. Then she reined it in and lengthened her spine. 'I'm going away for a while. A couple of weeks away with my girlfriends up north including a spa break.'

Mo stood and took her mum in her arms. Her mum was hurting, and as much as she wanted answers to her questions, she did not want to add to her pain. It was her turn to squeeze tight.

After she kissed her on her cheek, Precious whispered, 'It's time you knew what went on in the past. When I get back, I'll tell you everything. *Every last bit of it.*'

Chapter Three

The office door to Birdwhistle & Son Solicitor's in Stratford was flung violently open.

The receptionist, a woman well into her sixties, squealed, eyes ballooning in fright. Robbed of speech in the tiny reception area, she could only watch as a small woman waltzed inside like she owned the place. The newcomer wore Jackie O shades and a wide-leg grey trouser suit that had been tailored to perfection to fit every curve and line of her body. The only slap she wore was a touch of blueberry-coloured lippy which heightened the glossy brown of her skin. A tanned waist-length leather jacket hanging off her shoulders finished off the go-getter poise of a woman about town. And a woman who most certainly meant business.

Despite appearances, the solicitor's was no father-and-son business but a one-man-and-his-dog outfit located above a pizza takeaway at the top of a sleazy back-door staircase where the stench of cat piss got stronger the closer you got to the top. The receptionist looked way too nicely turned out in her navy skirt suit, black flats and glasses for a back-alley practice like this. Her jaw slackened when one of the most gorgeous men she'd ever clapped eyes on and a woman with a rucksack on her back followed close behind.

Trying to regain her composure, she coughed nervously and asked, 'Have you got an appointment?'

As if she was on a catwalk, the woman took her time strolling on her cube-heeled Dior black ankle boots closer to the desk. She eased off her sunglasses, revealing the most piercing grey eyes that the other woman had ever seen. The shade was a combination of tough-as-nails steel and see-through glass. Only one woman had eyes like that in London's underworld, eyes that she'd inherited from her legendary hardman villain grandfather, Jimmy 'Southpaw' Steele. Big Mo Watson.

This visit was the unpleasant task Mo had put off doing yesterday after Robbie's memorial. Mo's leisurely gaze took in the deplorable condition of the office, her mouth drooping with disdain. *What a dump!* Turning back to the receptionist she scoffed, 'An appointment? You don't look like you've had one of them since England won the World Cup.'

Mo shifted her gaze to the door behind the receptionist. Benjamin Birdwhistle. That was the name typed on a white piece of paper lopsidedly taped to the door. With a controlled shimmer of her shoulders, her jacket fell into her hand which she neatly handed over to the gobsmacked receptionist.

When Mo skirted around the receptionist's desk, the woman began babbling, 'You can't go into there—'

Josh distracted the receptionist, capturing her attention with, 'Why don't you make us all a lovely cuppa Rosie Lee, sweetheart, while my boss and your boss have a little intimate chinwag. Mine with two sugars, thank you very much.'

Mo found Benjamin Birdwhistle mid-snort through a line of coke. He didn't even hear her enter. Her mouth twisted with disgust at the state of his office. Papers everywhere, including the floor. The place looked like it hadn't had a lick of paint since the year 1066. And the filth… Mo promised herself a good ole scrub-up when she got indoors. How the mighty have fallen. Until six months back, Benjamin had been one of the most promising young lawyers at an upmarket city law firm that had catered to the needs of the rich, the minted rich and the occasionally off-the-books clients. Her grandfather had fallen into the latter category and had been a client of the most senior partner for decades. Robbie had been assigned another brief.

Only when Mo gingerly parked herself on the edge of the green plastic chair opposite did Benjamin realise, he had company. With a strange wheezing, his head jerked up like a puppet.

Benjamin Birdwhistle was a man in his thirties, but a life devoted to the hard stuff had put years on him, leaving his skin a patchwork of white and red blotches. His chestnut hair would soon be a thing of the past. Mo's disdain grew. She didn't have a problem with folk having a tote or sniff – each to their own – but in her experience drugs bunnies were unreliable. Trust a secret to them and you might as well blare it out to the world with a megaphone. They'd sell you down the river in exchange for money for their latest fix. Or worse yet, to the coppers for a lighter sentence.

Benjamin Birdwhistle nearly did it in his pants when the fog in his brain cleared enough for him to recognise who had joined him in his sleazy office. Ashen-faced, he stammered, 'Miss Watson, what an unexpected and charming pleasure.'

Getting a visit from a member of the notorious Steele family could mean one of two things: they were going to put some business your way or you were in for the kicking of a lifetime. At least it wasn't that bonkers Kristal Steele. His stomach churned when he recalled the run-in he'd had with her when her husband was still alive. He'd survived the encounter only by the skin of his teeth. In contrast, the word was Big Mo was tough but fair. No unnecessary bloodshed... If possible.

Mo casually crossed her legs, her hooded steely gaze sinking into him. 'How's business, Benjy?'

Cold sweat beaded along his brow; his Adam's apple bobbed convulsively. 'I can't complain. I'm so pleased that I started my own firm. You wouldn't believe how many clients I have.' He talked himself up, tugging the lapels of his jacket to bolster his confidence. 'There are so many people in this community who need my help.'

'I bet there are,' Mo shot back tartly. 'I can imagine the cases you get around these parts to plead before His Worship. GBH. Breaking and entering. And...' A piece of paper below her nose caught her eye. She picked it up and read it. 'And, it would seem, a Mrs Gladstone who would like you to sue the council after her cat got stuck in the rubbish chute.'

Mo let the paper fall back onto the desk. 'See, that's the strangest thing, Benjy. Me and this Mrs Gladstone have got something in common. It's reached my ears that you're treating me like a grade A pussy.'

'What?' His vocal cords strangled the word. His skin turned pasty, the sweat a slimy sheen on his forehead. 'Whoever has been telling you this is speaking utter rubbish. Has got the wrong end of the stick.' And the solicitor meant every word of it. 'You've never been one of my clients.'

Mo let him stew in his discomfort for a while before dropping the killer blow. 'But my father was. Robbie Steele. When you worked for that swanky firm in town.'

'And God rest his soul,' the solicitor dramatically and rapidly shoved in. He dipped his head as if in silent prayer respect for the soul of Jimmy Southpaw's eldest son. In reality, his feverish prayers were for himself. Slowly he raised his head. 'What a sad day it was when he left this world.'

Mo leaned forward, uncrossed her legs. Time to get down to business. 'Then explain to me why folk are whispering in my ear that you're going around town desperately trying to sell documents that belonged to my dad to the highest bidder?'

Outwardly, Mo was the picture of calm, but inside she seethed with white-hot fury. How dare this rat-faced scumbag try to hawk property that belonged to her father. Robbie Steele was a touchy subject for Mo. She'd only got to know about him after his tragic death. Even after all these years the image of her dad struggling to breathe, gasping and choking his last in a police cell messed her up.

The solicitor squirmed in his seat, his hand flashing in the air. 'That's outrageous —'

'I tell you what's outrageous; your bollocks and bullshit I can smell from here,' Mo growled. 'Before you got kicked out on your jacksie from that firm in the city, you nicked important, confidential information that belonged to my dad. Stuff about his businesses.'

Mo stabbed her finger at him. 'The way I hear it, you've got a serious gambling habit. Got a mountain of debt owed to the wrong people. So somehow you've got to come up with the readies before they pay you a nice friendly where they do interesting things to the bones in your legs —'

Terror-stricken, Benjamin Birdwhistle bolted out of his chair and ran into the small en suite bathroom. Dell and Josh were inside the office in a flash, her cousin Delilah already unzipping her bag to take out the lethal machetes she was known for.

When Mo walked into the bathroom it was to a view of the guy's backside as he tried to get out of the window. *What a proper prick.*

Mo motioned to Josh, arching her brow. 'It looks like our friend, Benjy, needs some air to clear between his ears.'

The solicitor squawked for his life when Josh grabbed him. Instead of pulling him inside, Josh hung him by his ankles out of the window. Josh rocked him so that his skin scraped along the brickwork.

Mo leaned out, taking in the view. 'They say that this whole area is going to be redeveloped for the Olympics coming in twenty twelve.'

Mo adored East London. This was her manor. It was good to hear there was going to be a significant injection of cash around here. That a place like Stratford, which, let's be honest, most people just passed through or came to get the Central Line outta here, had potential.

'Whatever they do, I hope it doesn't kill the ole East End. Talking of killing…'

The solicitor shrieked when Josh dangled him dangerously by one leg. 'Please! Please!'

Mo watched with grim satisfaction. He deserved that and more. Josh hauled him back in and slammed him against the wall. Mo had resumed her seat, Dell standing behind her.

'Now,' she announced, tone harsh and deadly, 'I want my dad's things.'

Wide-eyed and scared, Benjamin confessed, 'It's in the safe.'

Josh let go of him. The solicitor fell over himself to open a safe, situated behind a cupboard. He didn't hang around, handing Mo a bulging brown envelope. Just feeling something that belonged to her dad had Mo tingling. Get so emotional. Anything belonging to Robbie was so precious to her.

While Benjamin cowered, Josh matter-of-factly enquired, 'Do you want me to administer a couple of slaps?'

Standing, Mo shook her head. But she left the solicitor with a warning. 'You want to thank your lucky stars it's me here today. If my Granddad Jimmy had got wind of your dirty tricks you'd have probably ended up as a concrete block at the Olympics.'

While Dell drove with Josh upfront, in the back seat, eagerness and curiosity had Mo rapidly going through her dad's papers. For five minutes straight she flicked through them, trying her best to make sense of it all. None of it made sense. Exasperated, she rested her head back. There must have been a reason that piss-poor, low-rent brief had tried to auction Robbie's possessions for a song on the black market. Mo didn't have the time to look again now. She was due in court. Mo stared down hard, one last time at the pile of papers in her lap, her brain buzzing away.

What am I missing?

Chapter Four

'Your Honour do not let the seemingly outward innocent appearance of this young girl deceive you,' Eddie Harvey, prosecutor for the Crown gravely pronounced in plummy tones before the judge inside Court Room Number Three.

'The defendant is in fact a hardened criminal with a record that goes back to when she was almost in the cradle. There is no saving someone of her ilk. She is already on the road to Holloway Prison.'

Criminal almost since the cradle. How bloody dare you! This jester was looking for a backhander to bring him down to size. Balling her fists against her bag which held Robbie's papers, Mo had to restrain herself as she watched proceedings from the gallery. The teenager in the dock was one of her success stories of the kick boxing gym she'd opened three years ago. Mo had named the place Southpaw's in honour of her Granddad Jimmy's youthful life as boxer with a lethal left hook. Mo might be in the business of ducking and diving, nevertheless, that didn't stop her from feeling a keen obligation to steer as many of the next generation as possible towards the path of the straight and narrow.

If that lawyer knew the life journey the young girl, he was laying into had been on, he wouldn't be so quick to condemn her. Poor kid, no one in her family had turned out to support her. Then again, that was a blessing. The mother was a notorious druggie found most days, palm out, begging for a handout outside Bethnal Green Tube, and the father hadn't been seen since popping to the shop for a pint when the girl was a toddler.

Mo's boxing gym tried its hardest to give the kids discipline, even so, the seductive siren call of the underbelly of the East End was sometimes too hard to resist. Mo knew this all too well first-hand. The girl had succumbed to her mates doing a spot of five-finger discounting down the local supermarket and been caught red-handed.

Ten minutes later, when Mo took the stand as a character witness, Eddie Harvey wore a smirk of epic proportions which got her dander well 'n' truly up all over again. Normally she'd have wiped that self-satisfied smirk clean off his chops but bashing the prosecuting brief was not a good look in a court of law. She was here to persuade the judge to give the kid another chance. The poor girl was terrified, so Mo sent her a 'keep your chin up' smile.

'Your Honour.' Mo directly addressed the judge, dipping her head slightly in a gesture of respect. Then she turned her full attention to the court, her words strong and sure. 'I haven't come here to give you a sob story. That's the last thing this young lady needs. I'll tell you what she does need, though. A second chance. She knows she's done wrong.'

Mo stretched her neck. 'I will make it my personal

mission to ensure she stays on the right side of the law.' Mo levelled her beady gaze on her charge. Under Mo's intense stare, the girl squirmed uncomfortably. 'Believe you me, if she steps out of line, I will personally drag her up here, by her ear before you, Your Honour.'

It took the jury less than an hour to reach a guilty verdict, which was to be expected. However, the day was saved when the sentence was community service.

'I'm really sorry, Big Mo.' The teen hung her head in shame as Mo stood beside her in the courtroom.

Mo placed a gentle finger under her chin, lifting her head. 'Don't ever look down. Head up, eyes straight ahead. Always.'

The girl flung her arms with bone-crushing gratitude around Mo. 'I promise. On my life, I'm going to be like a saint from now on.'

She scampered off, and soon Mo found herself alone with Eddie Harvey, prosecuting counsel in the room. Casually placing his legal papers into his briefcase, he told her, 'Kids like her always come back. They can't help themselves. Criminality runs thick in their blood.'

Mo sauntered over to the cocksure bastard and got right into his space. 'That's a laugh,' she lobbed back. 'The biggest crims on this planet are you toffs who've made a bundle off the backs of the hard graft of the working man and woman.'

Arching a sardonic brow, it was his turn to get into her space. 'On their backs, are they?'

Mo's breathing juddered. She whispered, 'I know one working girl who likes it on her knees. Doggy style.'

The sound of their hot, heavy breathing fired up the straight-laced courtroom. Eddie swept Mo into his arms, their lips passionately locking in a hard kiss. They couldn't get enough of each other. Mo had been having a secret affair with the lawyer for eight months. Mo hadn't even let her bestie, Twinkle, in on her latest relationship. If Jimmy Southpaw got wind his granddaughter was sleeping with the enemy, a brief who put members of the underworld away, there would be the devil to pay.

When they met it had been bang! Literally. They had collided inside a restaurant, resulting in Eddie spilling his drink down his front. The liquid soaking into his shirt showcasing his pecs had got Mo hot all over. The attraction had been instant. So electric that they had found themselves doing more banging against the restaurant outside wall around the back. The sex had been explosive, leaving Mo breathless and gagging for more. Talk about knowing exactly how to press a girl's clit-activation button.

Eddie was in his early thirties with square-jawed good looks and hair that rivalled a golden field of wheat. Floppy, blond-haired poshos with lah-di-dah accents weren't her style. Give her a working-class man any day of the week. But this guy put the sex into sex-eee. Mo was obsessed. Addicted. The guy should wear a warning: Smokin' hot! Mo was in way too deep by the time she realised his job was trying to send people like her to prison.

Then Mo had committed the cardinal sin; she'd sorta fallen for him. It would never be total, the reason being, Mo's heart was taken by Nico who wasn't available. Mo wasn't the type to mope around on lost causes, so when Eddie came along, she threw herself into it, heart and soul. It wasn't just the physical thing between them, he also made her laugh, was a proper gent. Always considerate of her feelings and taking care of her needs. He made her feel all bashful and shy as if she was a teenager all over again.

Lately, Mo's yearning for her own family, her own small unit, had become overwhelming. She wanted to have a husband. Children. And Eddie would do perfectly. Nevertheless, she was going to wait until she was older. And by the time she was ready, Eddie would still be there at her side. Somehow, she'd figure out a way to smooth Granddad Jimmy's ruffled feathers when she introduced her lover to him.

Eddie smouldered in her ear, hot breath setting her skin on fire. 'You looked like you wanted to give me the tongue-lashing of a lifetime. I'm ready for your tongue on any part of my body.'

Mo nearly went into full-blown meltdown when his tongue did a delicious slooo-mooo circuit of her ear that left her tingling all over. His mouth was filthy. Mo loved every dirty second of it. That upmarket voice all mucky in the gutter had Mo nearly orgasming right there.

She wriggled out of his arms and got his shirt off.

'What are you doing?' His startled gaze urgently skidded towards the exit.

Naughty grin fixed to her mouth, Mo placed her finger against his lips. No one was going to disturb their fun and games. The guy who operated the security cams had been given a 'we'll say no more about it' little earner to ensure all the cams inside Court Room Number Three for the next hour were off. Mo drank him in. There was something super sexy about that tie hanging against his bare chest. She used it to lead him towards the front of the room.

Eddie stalled when he sussed where they were going. 'Are you crazy?'

By way of an answer, her palms thrust against his chest, tumbling him backwards. Straight into the judge's chair.

'Have you lost your mind?' His outraged words were not matched by the excited gleam in his eyes.

Air hissed between his teeth watching Mo raise her skirt and taking her time wriggling free of her panties. He adored the way the muscles bunched and bobbed in her legs, giving them the illusion of being the longest legs in the world.

Mo climbed on board, made quick work of his zip of his expensive trousers and, never taking her eyes off him, sank down. He groaned deep and rough, his head tipping back in ecstasy. Mo got such a kick out of giving him pleasure. Her hips swayed and shifted, her palms caressing his bare, flushed flesh.

Playfully, she breathed into his ear, 'What's the verdict, Your Worship?'

'Guilty as charged.'

Mo squealed when he reversed their positions. Now it was her turn to moan, clutching on to the arms of the chair for dear life. His fingers tangled in the spider necklace she wore. It was a gift from her cuz, Dell. It looked like a shoelace with a small spider attached with knots in its legs.

Dell promised that it would give her powerful protection against the badness in the world. Nothing existed as they got into it until they both shuddered in the judge's chair.

While Eddie sorted his clothing out, a business card tumbled out of his pocket. Picking it up, Mo examined it. It had a black background with fancy gold writing. It read:

Sixes and Sevens Gentlemen's Club.

Her brows shot to her hairline in shock. The only gentlemen's club she knew were places where the dirty ole mac brigade went to ogle naked ladies. Fuck me! Was her guy a dirty fella? Her displeased glance stabbed her lover. 'Is there something you want to tell me?'

'What?' He frowned and then saw the card in her hand. After a small hesitation, his lips curved into a heart-stopping smile. 'It's a stuffy gentleman's club I'm a member of in Mayfair. A very respectable place filled with upper-crust blokes with more money than sense.'

Mo turned the card over before handing it over to him. 'Sixes and Sevens? Where did it get its name from?'

Tucking the card back in his pocket, Eddie explained, 'Sixes and Sevens was some type of card game, I believe. It started life as a gambling club when it opened way back in the eighteen hundreds.' He wrapped his arms around Mo's waist.

'Are only guys allowed through its doors?'

He nuzzled the side of her throat. 'Once that was the case, but now women are members too.'

'I want you to take me there.'

Eddie's hands dropped from her body. 'Why? It's full of dull people —'

'What are you doing there then?' she countered.

'Being a member runs in my family. As a matter of cause, my father obtained membership for me when I turned twenty-one.'

Truth be told, Mo was sick to death of them running around in secret. She wanted to show off her man for the whole world to see.

She blurted out, 'You ashamed of me, Eddie?'

He didn't take that well. 'You know I love you.' Her heart melted. That was one of the things she adored about him, he wasn't ashamed of saying the L word, unlike so many other men. 'We just need to tread carefully. We wouldn't want your grandfather to find out about us through other sources.'

Mo remained frustrated and fucked off. Mouth set in a mulish thin line, she slung on her clothing and headed for the exit.

'Darling,' Eddie called.

She ignored his pleading. At the door she swung back around. 'If you're not embarrassed by me, prove it. Take me to the Sixes and Sevens Gentleman's Club.'

Judging by his closed expression, Mo knew she was facing a losing battle. Sucking back her hurt, she stormed out of the courtroom.

Chapter Five

Mo briskly entered Club Class with a purpose. She was going straight to her office to check through her dad's papers again. Nelly Furtado's 'Maneater' played on the big screen. The club was a hop, skip and jump from Leicester Square and one of the most popular night spots up West. And it was all Mo's. Jimmy Southpaw had gifted the club to his granddaughter and heir so that Mo had her own HQ. Sometimes Mo still shook her head in disbelief that this was all hers. She'd come such a long way from the hoodie-wearing teen tearaway. She so wished her dad could see her now.

Mo's plans derailed when she caught sight of her best friend, Twinkle's, face. Mo stopped dead with choking dismay.

Twinkle managed the bar and was bustling like the rest of the staff getting the club ready for the ravers tonight. Her bestie looked terrible, absolutely god-awful terrible. Twinkle was tall, usually with face-popping freckles and hair so red it glowed like a halo of sunshine around her gentle face. The glow was non-existent today, her hair limp and lacklustre, her freckles dull dots marking her skin. Mo dragged in a shattering breath. Her bestie resembled someone who hadn't slept in a week. What the heckin' hell was going on? Although Mo marched forward, resolved to get answers, her inner voice reminded her that she had business to see to. In this instance, Robbie's documents.

She'd give Twinkle a couple of minutes, tops, and then be on her way. The reality was, all Mo could think about was her father. Robbie.

'You spend the night with James Bond and couldn't leave his loving arms this morning?'

Usually, Mo's cheeky crack would have tickled Twinkle's funny bone, leaving her sporting a grin that was as wide as from here to Trafalgar Square. Instead, her lips were compressed, her gaze fidgety, lashes blinking like crazy. Mo winced when Twinkle grabbed the head of her walking stick to join her on the other side of the bar. For the rest of her days, Mo would feel unforgiving guilt about what had happened to her best friend. A life-changing fall meant that Twinkle would always walk with a pronounced limp, needing the support of a walking stick. In her heart, Mo had convinced herself Twinkle's predicament was her fault.

Reading the guilt on Mo's expression, Twinkle ground out, 'Will you leave it out.' She struggled with her breathing with something that looked like fury glazing her eyes. 'Stop treating me like some stray pup from up Battersea Dogs' Home.'

Her voice was loud enough to draw the stunned attention of the staff working nearby. You didn't go around shouting the odds at Big Mo. The ferocity of Twinkle's tone knocked Mo for six. Growing up in the East End wasn't easy, sometimes the only way to make it through with your marbles intact was to develop a hard-knocks exterior to survive. Not Twinkle. She was a soft soul who cared about the feelings of others.

Colour flooding her cheeks, Twinkle sucked back her temper 'Sorry, Mo. Dunno what's the matter with me lately, I'm all out of step.'

Concerned, Mo peered closer. 'It's not that bloody ole girl of yours? I'll swing for her if she's started up on you again.'

Twinkle's mother, Sheena Brodie, was a notorious brass the length of the East End for running a very unsavoury home that catered to the very basest needs of men. For years she'd cruelly verbally abused her daughter, including spitefully telling Twinkle from an early age that she wished she'd never been born. *You shoulda kept your legs shut then,* Mo had wanted to scream at the bitch. In the end, after Twinkle's terrible accident, Mo had stepped in to read Sheena Brodie the riot act and got her bestie a job down Club Class to keep her away from the evil clutches of a woman who had not one drop of maternal blood in her hardened veins. Mo had wanted to set Twinkle up in her own place near her duplex overlooking the river in Wapping. Twinkle wouldn't hear of it; she was going to stay with her mum through thick and thin.

Twinkle stammered, 'Actually, have you got a bit of time now. I was hoping to have a word —'

Mo cut her off. 'Time is something I haven't got. We'll sit down and talk soon. Promise.'

Stumped by Mo's dismissal, Twinkle mentally shook her head with such sadness. A stranger, that's what it felt like having a gas with Mo these days. It was like they weren't on the same wavelength. When had she and her best friend drifted apart? They had been so tight once. Mo was her sister from a different mother. Feverishly, she recalled the days when she would have confided all her woes in a heartbeat to the girl who was the most important person in her life.

Twinkle would have told her about the pain she was in right now. It crucified her leg and hip, shredding her to pieces. White-hot fire viciously shot through her body, making her tremble from her head to her very soles. She would have told her how the pain seemed to be with her most times these says. How some nights she lay in bed wishing that death would just take her to end the agony. She'd have told Mo that the painkillers that the doctor had been giving her for years no longer worked. How the last doctor she saw up the surgery had made her feel like a timewaster. And Twinkle couldn't live like that anymore. That's what she wanted to talk to Mo about. Her decision.

Now, Mo was too busy, and Twinkle understood why that was. However, it didn't make it any easier to swallow that these days, Mo seemed to be a best friend in name only. The simple fact of the matter was Mo wasn't plain Maureen Watson anymore, she was Big Mo, East End hardman Jimmy Southpaw's appointed heir, which meant she had a reputation to carve out in these here streets of London.

Expanding the Steele family empire, both legit and under the table, was her number one priority. Cement her rep as the Queen of London's Underworld.

Twinkle struggled to stop her shoulders slumping in dejection. Instead, she carefully wrapped her arms around Mo in a tight, loving embrace. 'We'll go on holiday together soon, eh? Just me and you. A Caribbean cruise. Lazing on the deck in the sun, a couple of hottie guys serving us cocktails and anything else we fancy.'

Mo whispered, 'East End Girls Forever.'

'East End Girls Forever.'

That was their special phrase, their pick-themselves-up during trying times. And an incredibly trying time was coming up for Twinkle. But she kept it to herself because it was clear her bestie had no time for her.

Mo couldn't seem to get out of Twinkle's arms fast enough. She dismissed the other woman's problems. She didn't have the headspace. She needed to focus on going through her father's papers. Mo was convinced that she must have missed something. Head already filled with her dad, without saying another word, Mo left. She didn't even notice how Twinkle bit her lip almost white, bracing against the pain.

When Mo reached her office, she slung her jacket on the powder-blue sofa, walked across the room and plonked herself down in the exec chair behind her desk. She spread her father's documents carefully in front of her.

What did I miss?

Unlike in the back of her car, Mo took her time

searching. The first set of papers were bank accounts. Despite thoroughly checking them, she couldn't find out who the bank accounts belonged to. Were they Robbie's? Probably, she concluded. *Never put all your bank accounts in one basket*, was what Granddad Jimmy had taught her. He'd explained that the family enterprise held a piddling bit of cash in bank accounts in your usual high street financial institution. That way, if the taxman came a-calling you pointed him in the direction of these accounts. He's happy, everyone's happy. The real family assets were stashed away in accounts under dummy names and behind the names of shell corporations.

Was that what Robbie had been planning on doing? Getting ready to squirrel away some of his ill-gotten gains in foreign banks? Mo leafed through the next documents. It took her a while to identify that they concerned investments. Investments. Bank accounts. That link made sense.

'S. Sapphire' was written on a small piece of paper. S. Sapphire? What was that? Who was that? Mo parked it for safekeeping at the back of her mind. Next up was a folded piece of paper, which she carefully opened out. It was the drawn plan of a building with four floors, the third floor ringed in red. Why would her father have this? On the roof of the building were seven chimneys. That's odd, Mo thought. Why the heck would anyone record how many chimneys a building had? The middle chimney stood out from the others. Its shape was more rounded with a painted black stripe round its middle and another just below the top. It was a dead ringer for a ship's funnel.

Scowling and turning the paper over, Mo discovered a drawing of the same distinctly shaped chimney. Mo leaned in, peering closer. For some reason her heart was kicking up a storm against her ribs. A series of short red arrows pointed downwards along the chimney. Partway down the chimney the word 'bricks' was written. Next to that was a drawing of a square box.

Mo couldn't get her head around this. None of it made sense. The information ran rings in her head.

Funny-shaped chimney.

Arrows going down.

Bricks

Box.

Slowly a picture started forming:

Arrows indicate for someone to go down the chimney. Stop at the bricks. Loosen bricks. Behind loose bricks is a square box.

Square box? Square box? Square… A safe?

Fuck me! Harsh, uneven short spurts of air pumped out of her. Had her father, Robbie Steele, been planning a heist? Was that why he'd needed the bank accounts? To stash the stolen loot away?

But what had he been planning to steal?

Frantically, Mo turned the papers every which way but found nothing to lay bare what he'd been planning to rob. Even the location of the blag remained elusive because the building had no name.

Mo slumped back. This looked like a blinder of a job. An easy one too, if access was by way of a mere chimney. Due to her small stature, the one thing Mo had excelled at in school was gymnastics. The logistics of getting on a roof and going down a chimney should be right up her street. *More like right up my roof!*

An incredible idea flashed into her bursting mind.

Wouldn't it be something if she carried out this job in honour of her dead father. *And how are you go to achieve that? Eh? Go around London like some numpty, staring up at roofs looking for odd-shaped chimneys?*

Big Mo Watson wasn't the type to let anything slip through her fingers, particularly anything associated with the father she'd never known. Maybe she could ask Granddad Jimmy if Robbie had been planning a job. She dismissed the idea almost as soon as it arrived. Best leave Granddad Jimmy to his retirement and golf.

Mo suddenly went rigid. She knew exactly who to ask. And groaned.

Knowing she didn't have a choice, Mo got on the blower. 'We need to meet.'

Chapter Six

A wave of light-headedness threatened to turn Mo's world upside down when she got out of the back seat of her motor. Her vision blurred, ears buzzing, eyes squeezed tight. Somehow, she managed to grab on to the handle of the car, slumping against it. Her laboured breathing puffed out horribly, like the noise of a dodgy car engine.

Dell and Josh were beside her in an instant. Mo heard the fear in her cousin's voice. 'What happened? You all right, girl?'

Josh tutted. ''Course she ain't all right, you plank. Let's get the boss sat back down, and when Big Mo's nice 'n' comfy we can ask her about the particulars.'

Usually, Dell wouldn't take any lip off her working other half, coming straight back with an arched put-down. Even after all this time the relationship of her bodyguards was characterised by verbal bash-ups, although over the years Mo had noticed that there was less bite in it. It was all part of the shtick of their relationship. This time, though, Dell tried to do what he asked.

'Stop fussing, will you.' Mo's strong command froze

their gentle ministrations. She didn't want it to come across that she didn't appreciate them trying to sort her out, plus given it was their job to keep her safe they were proceeding in the correct manner. Mo hated fussing. She was independent to the core. She wasn't ending up like some of these bosses who wanted their hands held every bleedin' two minutes.

All she needed was to get some air into her lungs. Opening her mouth, she took in London's less-than-fresh air. In and out. There! She was starting to feel her old self again. But lately, she'd been feeling lousy. This morning she was so whacked out she could hardly roll out of bed. Probably dog-tired is all, she convinced herself. What I need is a week on the beach, sun warming my skin, pina colada in one hand, Eddie in the other. Cautiously, reopening her eyes, Mo sighed with heavy relief that the world wasn't moving.

They were in Hoxton. Back in the day, way back in the day, this had been one of the poorest parts of the East End. Now it had hooked up to its money bags City cousin, the area of Shoreditch, and – voila! – had transformed into one of the buzziest hangouts for young professionals and arty types. Come night-time it turned into twenty-four-hour party people. Mo had a nose for making money and had scented there was a killing to be made here, buying and doing up properties. One of those she bought off an old tailor, a relic of the rag trade that had once existed nearby on the Commercial Street and Petticoat Lane. The old sweetheart hadn't wanted to go, but when Mo showed him what she was willing to pony up he'd had his bags packed that night. Or in his words: *'If a fool's going to pay me that I'd be a fool not to take it.'*

East London was so near the City its downtrodden streets and lived-in houses were being spruced up and sold on to professionals who worked in town.

Josh and Dell escorted her towards the coffee shop she owned, its upstairs doubling up as a studio and three-bed for a couple who were artists who turned a blind eye when Mo needed to use the third bedroom for 'business'. Mo heard the raised voice before she opened the door.

Gimme strength! She groaned because one of the voices was unmistakable, that of the person she was meeting. Her stepmother, Robbie's widow, Kristal Steele. Life wouldn't be life for Kristal if she wasn't creating and stirring up a cauldron-sized worth of drama. And from the sound of the particulars, she was having a right royal go at someone.

Kristal, face full of fury, was giving the manager a scathing dressing-down. 'You call this tea, do ya?' She jabbed a sunset-orange talon with displeasure at her cup. 'More like something you dredged up from the Thames.'

The manager's back stiffened, his hands fluttering in the air. 'Madam, I can assure you that this is the Assam tea that you ordered.'

'Arse and what?' a scandalised Kristal lobbed back. 'Arse and ham tea? Are you taking the piss, sonny?'

'Kristal,' Mo loudly interjected, rescuing her manager. The poor bollocks probably had no idea that he was a hair's breadth from having his throat wrapped and squeezed.

Kristal looked like she always did, dressed to impress. She showcased a low-cut ribbed tank top that displayed her premier league feature, the twin globes of her boobs. And capri jeans with metallic slingback heels. She appeared more like she was off on her travels in the South of France than the East End. Mo noted how Kristal's lips twisted the closer she got. There had been a time when meeting Kristal had been close encounters of the evil stepmummy kind. Kristal had made no bones about how she couldn't stand her. Despised her in fact. Mo wasn't heartless and had some sympathy for her. Some. It couldn't have been easy to find out her ole man had a wrong-side-of-the-blanket daughter, who was a mere year older than their own son. And if that wasn't enough, to add salt to the wounds, her father-in-law, Jimmy Southpaw, had chosen Mo to be his heir over Kristal's son, Damien.

Kristal had tried to take her down, and Mo had had no choice but to assert her authority and put her stepmother back in her pram. That had been five years ago now, and since then they'd reached an amicable truce; basically they weren't at each other's throats anymore.

Mo briefly lay a reassuring arm about her manager's shoulder. 'Don't stress yourself. Consider it sorted.' Beneath hooded lids, Mo surveyed the faces of the clientele who were doing a piss-poor job of pretending not to gawk and listen. 'And get everyone a bevvy of their choice. On the house.'

Hearing her words, Kristal arched a curious brow. 'Is this your place then?'

Sliding into the seat opposite, Mo nodded with pride. 'A

few others too, including the club around the corner that I got for Damien to add to his portfolio.'

Kristal's lips pursed with her approval. Her feelings for her stepdaughter might be a bit touch 'n' go sometimes but she couldn't fault the way Mo looked out for her half-brother. His having a different mother never entered the equation. Blood and family, that's what mattered.

After ordering a coffee, Mo got down to business. 'Did Robbie ever talk about a job he was planning on doing?'

Kristal's expression shuttered as it always did when Mo mentioned her father's name. Kristal would never admit it, but what Robbie had done bringing another kid into the world while she'd been desperate to get pregnant had hurt her badly. So badly.

Kristal checked her out beneath her false lashes. 'Job? Whatcha mean by job?'

Mo didn't beat about the bush. 'I have reason to believe that he was planning a robbery, a heist of some kind.'

The other woman's features screwed up in confusion. 'Robbery? Of what?'

'That's what I thought you'd know.'

Expression cagey, Kristal picked up her tea. 'You've got the wrong end of the shovel there, babes. Robbie didn't believe in dirtying his hands, know what I mean?' Licking the moisture from her painted lips, she placed her cup back down. 'I mean, that's what you've got the help for, ain't it.' Her canny gaze intensified. 'Where are you getting all this from?'

Mo was guarded. She faced a dilemma:

Should she tell Kristal? Versus shouldn't she tell Kristal?

Mo wanted to open up to her, but the honest to goodness truth was could she trust her father's widow? Betrayal seemed to be Kristal Steele's middle name. Mind you, in the last five years she hadn't given Mo any trouble.

Her decision was taken away from her when Kristal archly informed her, 'Did you get this from Robbie's stuff that wanker solicitor was trying to barter on the streets?'

Surprise lit up Mo's face. 'How did you know about that?'

Kristal chuckled sly. 'Wouldn't you like to know. It's not just you who has eyes and ears around every street corner —'

'And on reception desks,' Mo tartly cut in. 'That old bird of a receptionist of his gave you the nod and the wink after my visit?'

Colour flooded Kristal's face that she'd been caught out. 'Mable is a friend of the family.' Her voice turned serious. 'What did you find in Robbie's papers?'

Mo knew there was no point in withholding the truth from her stepmother. Dropping her voice for their ears only, she revealed what she'd found out. 'What I can't figure out is what he was going to lift and where he was going to do the lifting.'

Kristal shook her head, clucking her tongue. 'Oh! You mean *that* job.'

'What do you mean *that job*?'

Kristal shook her shoulders, leaning back. 'Robbie was always going on and on about some blag out West that he was going to do. It was his last big job before he focused the business on legit concerns —'

'Why would he want to go legit? Didn't he enjoy the under-the-table business?'

Kristal drained her cup. 'Who knows what was what with Robbie.' Sourness tugged her lips. 'One minute he swore I was his princess and the next he's getting some other woman up the duff.'

Mo let out a long, weary sigh. 'Are you going to always blame me for existing?'

Kristal provocatively glanced back. 'Dunno.' Her expression softened. 'The reason Robbie never went through with the blag was his dad told him to drop it.'

'Why would he do that?'

'Didn't ask. But Robbie stopped jarring on about it.'

Mo continued. 'What or who is S. Sapphire?'

Kristal's expertly manicured finger ran the length of her neck. 'Sounds like a necklace that should be sitting right here.'

Mo asked, 'What was he planning to steal?'

Kristal's shoulders lifted. 'Couldn't tell you. What I can tell you is I'm late for an appointment up at the spa. I'm having an all-over body chocolate peel.'

Mo followed Kristal to her feet. Then she slapped her hand over her mouth, swaying. She was going to lose her dinner.

Kristal urgently shouted at a waiter, 'Oi! Penguin! A glass of water over here, pronto.'

Her stepmother waved Josh and Dell back to the bar area and got Mo sat back down.

The refreshing coolness of the water eased Mo's nauseated, deathly feeling. Eyes swimming in tiredness, she glanced up at her concerned stepmother. 'Thank you. I've been feeling like the back end of a goat lately. Nothing a little TLC and some feet-up time won't cure.'

'Whatever you say, babes.' The other woman's casual response didn't match the keenness of the stare she fixed like superglue to Mo.

Mo wasn't really listening. All she could think about was her plans to do Robbie's last big job was dead in the dust.

Concealed behind the tinted windows of her racy Merc, Kristal took out her mobile. 'It's me. If a little sparrow gets in touch wanting to tweet-tweet in your ear, let me know.'

Chapter Seven

'So who owns this joint then?' Mo posed her question to Eddie as they sat at a table in the very elegant dining room of the Sixes and Sevens Gentleman's Club in Mayfair.

Eddie had finally relented and taken Mo for dinner there. And the place didn't disappoint. It was like something out of the National Trust. Wood panelling and pastel wallpapers. Soft light shooting in from huge windows and skylights and furnishings that your bum sank into. The waiting staff wore bright-red jackets with gold trim and buttons along with three-quarter-length thigh-hugging pants that Eddie had explained was the same livery clothing that had been worn by the workers here when the club first opened in the 1800s.

Talking of clothing, Eddie had outdone himself with his sharp dinner suit, the jacket of which was lined with a distinctive silky blue material. Mo's heart pinched every time she gazed starry-eyed at him. *He's all mine. All mine.* She couldn't believe it. Tonight was their first step in public together, and Mo was going to ensure it wouldn't be their last. Mo got no answer to her question. Eddie's mind seemed to be working overtime, his eyes darting around the room like a sparrow who suspected a cat was about to pounce.

So Mo tried again. 'Who owns it? I know a few people in the club business myself, perhaps I've run across them?'

Eddie heard her this time, turning to her. He looked back to his usual laidback self, but he couldn't mask the anxiety in his voice. 'The food here is some of the best in town. The story goes that one of the reasons the club was a big hit when it opened was the owner installed one of the best French chefs. The club has kept up the tradition, including the current owner.' He pre-empted her, 'Who I do not know.' Some of his flash came back. 'Shall we order?'

Mo stared at him quizzically. 'Funny you don't know the owner, because everyone here seems to know you well enough.'

On arrival, staff members had greeted him with familiar smiles and nods. Eddie had mumbled back, hurrying her through the reception. Mo leaned back, nursing her brandy cocktail. There could only be one reason why her lover was behaving this way.

'Are you embarrassed bringing me here, Eddie?' She searched his face. 'Scared about what they'll think about you liking a bit of black?'

He was genuinely upset at that, mouth tumbling open, initially speechless. 'You should know me better than that. Our skin colours have got nothing to do with our relationship.'

Mo matched his movement forward. 'So what's up?'

A muscle beat in his cheek. 'The only thing that's up is my girlfriend asking lots of dumb questions.'

Mo looked at the man she loved, stunned, knocked back by his put-down. Then Mo remembered who she was, stiffening with deadly intent. 'You ain't talking to your charlady. Just because you're fucking me doesn't give you the right to screw me.'

An expression of regret softening his features, he grasped her hand. 'Forgive me, darling. I don't know what's come over me. I've had some tough cases lately.'

Mo got it. However, she wasn't going to end up with her fella thinking he had a right to treat her like dirt. At the first sign of any funny business, a woman needed to nip it in the bud. If she didn't, the guy started asking questions about who she was seeing, where had she been. The crack of his knuckles against your flesh swiftly followed. If the guy took no heed of your concerns the first time round it was time to turn your back and leave. And never go back.

A waiter arrived to take their order. He looked at Mo with curiosity as if confused by who she was before handing the wine list to Eddie with a sure smile.

Without perusing the list, Eddie merely muttered, 'We'll have the Chateau Crouton Eighty Four. And can you tell the waiter we'll have the lobster. And ask him to tell the kitchen to make it snappy.'

'Of course, sir.' The waiter hesitantly added, 'And by the way, sir, the sommelier is on the premises this evening. Perhaps you'd like to have a word with him…'

Eddie savagely cut him dead. 'Can't you see I've got a guest for the evening?' His voice had a brittle bite Mo had never heard from him before.

If the guy was peeved at Eddie's tone, he wasn't showing it. Perhaps it was all in a day's work here being spoken to like that by London's upper crust. Down East, you'd have got a slap for that kind of 'tude. Add to that, Mo disapproved of treating workers like they were crap beneath your shoe. Her people at Club Class were treated with class.

'What's a sommelier?'

Eddie sipped his drink like he hadn't heard her. Miffed, Mo waited in silence for their meal.

After they'd eaten, Mo said, 'I'm just going to powder my nose.'

Eddie quickly jumped in. 'There's a lovely bar nearby. Apparently, the ladies is all mirrors and Art Deco design.' Art Deco? What's that when it's a home? 'Why don't I get the bill and you can use the powder room there instead.'

But she couldn't wait. Truth was, her tummy was feeling rotten. Probably too much rich food. She didn't want to spoil their beautiful evening by telling him. Mo got to her feet. 'Back in a jiffy.'

She walked through the dining room. The place oozed old money. Not like those clubs Mo was used to where the boys all flashed their labels and made sure everyone saw their diamond-encrusted watches while dangling the keys to their sports cars through their fingers.

There were two attendants in the ladies, one of whom asked Mo if she needed any help.

'Nah! You're all right, babes. I know how to drop my own drawers.'

While she topped up her lippy in a giant gilt mirror, Mo

pondered Eddie's behaviour. She decided she'd had enough mystery for one evening. When she returned to her table, she was going to have it out with him and find out what was really going on.

But there was a slight interruption on her journey back. As she passed one of the tables, she heard a familiar voice:

'And I want chips, mate, lots of 'em with some of your best ketchup. Make sure you tell the bloke with the white hat at the cooker that I don't want the ketchup in a fancy dish with a spoon, bring the bottle.'

Mo rounded on the table in disbelief. 'Gramps? Ruddy? What are you doing here?'

Mo's jaw went south at the sight of her grandfather on her mother's side, Brother Bertie, and his best friend, Ruddy, sitting at a table in a member's club in Mayfair of all places. They were your typical old-timers usually to be found on his allotment who everyone in the East End knew. So what were they doing here? Then again, if Mo recalled, hadn't it also turned out they had been close friends with Nico and Kristal's uncle, legendary south London Face, King Ted? And her mum's father hated Jimmy Southpaw. Mo was beginning to think she was missing something about who these two were.

Bertram Watson was affectionately known as Brother Bertie because of his easy-going style and friendly nature. Indoors and out he always wore his pork pie hat and walked, in style, with a stick that had the Lion of Judah carved in its silver tip. Mo had a bond with her grandfather since the day he'd cradled baby-her in his arms. His friend, everyone called Ruddy, short for

Ruddy Nora. She wore her trademark, wobbly red beehive and a cinch-waisted mauve cocktail dress with petals cascading down the front. Ruddy didn't let her age get in the way of showing off a bit of leg.

Ruddy was the first to respond. 'Well, look who it is. Little Big Mo.'

'Baby-gal, seeing you has made the cobwebs disappear from my old eyes.' Baby-gal, that was his pet name for her since she was a child. Answering her earlier question, he added in his distinctive Jamaican accent that he refused to tone down for any setting, including Mayfair, 'We're members.'

'But it cost an arm and a leg and another arm to pay for membership.' Eddie had told her what that eye-watering fee was.

'Well, it would be, if we paid.' Brother Bertie chuckled.

Ruddy cackled. 'Can't see the social stumping up for these prices.'

They both creased up laughing while Mo tried to figure out how it was they were exempt from paying membership. None of it made any sense. And she never got an answer because at that moment an older, statuesque woman appeared in the dining room entrance.

An expectant hush fell over the room, everyone's eye turning her way. The woman deliberately posed in the doorway like a film star appearing at a Hollywood premiere. Or a prima donna making her long anticipated first appearance at Covent Garden Opera. What she wore was midway between a dress and gown. Silver, off the shoulder, clinging at the top, flaring at the waist. It looked like a one-off designed by a couturier. Her hair was unashamedly grey, styled in a short cut around her face with layers and playful flicks at the side. And she was tall. Was she fifty? Sixty? It was hard to say. Around her neck was a string of high-end pearls that dared you to guess their value. Everything about her dared you.

She held a leather lead to a Doberman Pincher whose coat was so sleek, it too could have come from a designer's studio. In contrast, behind them was a young woman wearing spectacles, with boring hair and even more boring clothes.

The elegant woman stepped into the room on heels that could make most dizzy staring at them. 'Good evening, diners! Are you all enjoying your meals?' She made the Queen sound like a stall holder down Whitechapel Market.

The diners all chorused in turn like schoolkids. 'Yes, Duchess!'

Duchess! And she looked the part. After a few more moments holding the limelight, the Duchess began slowly visiting the tables. Mo bid Gramps and Ruddy farewell and hurried back to her table. There was no sign of Eddie. *Fan-fucking-tastic*. He'd left her a note:

'Called back to the office. Trouble with a case. Call you later.'

Mo's temper flared. Mind you, she shouldn't be surprised. Eddie had been acting up all evening. Dumping her to make her own way home fit right in and seemed to be par for the course for tonight.

Mo was suddenly conscious that someone was standing over her. She found the Duchess peering suspiciously down on her. The Doberman was sat peering up at Mo with even more suspicion. The young woman stood quietly to the side.

The Duchess was polite. 'Good evening, young lady. And whomsoever might you be?'

Up close, Mo became aware of something about this woman she hadn't noticed before. There was a quality about her that chilled Mo to the bone.

The Duchess was trying to psyche Mo out, but Mo wasn't having it. 'My name is Maureen, Mo to my nearest and dearest. And *whomsoever* might you be?'

'I am the proprietor of Sixes and Sevens. People call me the Duchess. That's because I am actually a duchess. The wife of a peer of the realm, God rest his soul.'

Mo gestured at the dog. 'And what's his name? Is he married to a peer of the realm too?'

The Duchess' mouth grew pinched. 'That's Arthur. He doesn't take any nonsense and he's my constant companion.'

Mo stood. 'That must be embarrassing when you've got gentlemen company in your boudoir?'

The Duchess pursed her lips. 'So you've got a tart tongue, have you? And I'm sure that's not the only tart thing about you. I don't want to be vulgar, but perhaps you could tell me what you're doing on the premises? Only we have a very strict members-only policy.'

'I'm a guest of Eddie Harvey's. Although he's had to leave due to an emergency.'

The Duchess hesitated for a moment. 'I know all the

members of my club. I've never heard of an Eddie Harvey. I understand gaining access to these premises must be a Cinderella moment for you but I'm afraid the ball is over, Cinders. Perhaps to avoid an embarrassing scene, it would be better if you left. Arthur will show you the way out.'

She took Arthur's lead off, and the dog wagged his tail like a bouncer adjusting his bow tie.

Mo pointed her finger at the Duchess, drew close and whispered, 'You and I will meet again, Dutch. Be sure of it.'

As if her evening couldn't get any worse, the heavens opened up just as Mo was escorted outside the club. Shivering, she looked skyward before she got ready to hail a cab. But all thoughts of a ride home vanished when something on the club's roof seized her attention. Seven Victorian chimneys.

And the middle one was shaped like a ship's funnel with two black stripes.

Chapter Eight

Barely able to contain her growing excitement, Mo fumbled in her bag for Robbie's plan. Those plans stayed with her twenty-four-bloody-seven. Mo crossed to the other side of the street so she could see the building from all angles. She examined the layout of the building on her father's sketch. Glanced back across the street. Bingo! An exact match of the building. The seven chimneys and the middle sitting pretty on the roof were the clincher. It was definitely the Duchess' club that Robbie had been planning to raid before his mysterious death.

Yeah, fucking yeah! Mo was tempted to finish her jubilation by fist-pumping the air. But she didn't. At all costs she needed to maintain her cool. Stand discreet.

Carrying out her father's blag was back on. Any doubts she had melted away. Mo's thoughts ran to the Duchess. Drawing in the evening air, she imagined the expression on that gilded old hag's mug when she twigged her safe had been cleaned out. It would be worth coming back and being thrown out again just to see the gobsmacked horror on the posh tart's face. And it would put that mutt, Arthur's, snout out of joint too. That was a plus.

With purpose, Mo crossed the road again. Stepped up her pace down in a side street which ran along one side of the club. Mo's gaze ran the length of the building, sizing it up. The only way she was going to be able to do this job was to become familiar with the internal layout of the club. Figure out logistics. Then Mo would know the perfect way to pull off the heist. That meant, somehow, she had to get back inside the club. Now. Mo stepped back slightly. Her gaze intensely searched the outside.

'Gotcha!' Mo noticed a louvre window open on the club's ground floor.

Mo hauled herself up to peer inside. It was a toilet cubicle. Using her foot to springboard up, she squeezed inside and dropped onto the seat below. But as she did so, she noticed something strange. On the window's catch was a small piece of torn material. Blue paisley. Hold up! Wasn't that the same fabric that lined the inside of Eddie's flash jacket? The empty cubicle was still locked from inside which meant if Eddie had been in here, he hadn't left via the door. The penny dropped. Eddie had escaped out of the toilet window.

Mo was angry but also confused. What was going on in this place? Jimmy Southpaw banned Robbie from raiding this club. But why? Brother Bertie and Ruddy were members here, although two less likely members of high society it was hard to imagine. And then Eddie, initially, had raised a real hue and cry about bringing her here, and when he did, he got the collywobbles so badly, he'd legged it through a toilet window. Eddie's behaviour hurt her to the core.

What was going on?

Mo looked at Robbie's sketch again. The safe he was planning to access from the chimney was in a room on the third floor by a spiral staircase. She unlocked the cubicle and peered into the main room of the gents. The décor of the room was a wonder to behold. Mo had to give it to the Duchess, the old bird had class. Sparkling forest-green tiles and antique urinals and toilets with framed old-style posters, like Pears soap and one with the slogan, 'A penny a tinkle'.

Judging that no one was around, Mo silently slid out and was almost at the door when a strident voice caught her bang to rights.

'Excuse me, madam, this is the gentlemen's. You can't come in here.'

On a super-slow twist of her heel, Mo faced him. An irate attendant in an uptight uniform with a towel draped over his arm.

She gave him the Mo *long look* which had silenced better men than him. 'I can't come in here?' Her mock outrage was stated with her best fancy-pants accent. 'It was a simple error on my part. I'll be enjoying a drink with my friend the Duchess in a short while. Perhaps I'll ask her where I can and can't go in my *friend's* club.'

His response was pure horror. 'Of course, madam.'

Close call. No time to waste. In the corridor she headed for the main staircase. It was one of the most amazing spectacles she had ever seen. Grand and long, it seemed to wind on forever like Jack's beanstalk. Mo hurried up it until she found the smaller spiral staircase. Robbie's plan was right on point because next to it was a room. It had a sign on it:

'The Lady. D-Private.'

Mo briefly wondered if The Lady was the Duchess. 'D-Private'. Duchess private? Mo quietly entered, closed the door behind her and turned on the light. The room was noticeably more understated than the rest of the club. This room was dominated by a green Chesterfield sofa and a huge painting of a woman above the fireplace. The woman was striking and wore a cor-blimey purple dress that would get you noticed on a Saturday night out on the razz. Next to the painting was a sign that read: 'The Lady'. Ahhh! So this was The lady. Most importantly of all, the painting was mounted on the wall that was also the chimney breast. And behind it, Mo would bet her life was the safe with the Duchess' goodies inside. Frustration bit deep that she didn't yet know what those goodies were.

'I would never have taken you for a connoisseur of art.'

The cool voice shook Mo up. She spun around. The Duchess stood just inside the room. A narky Arthur was sitting next to her, sizing Mo up with a view to choosing which limb he was going to have off first.

The dowdy young woman who had trailed behind the Duchess into the dining room in a low, expressionless voice said, 'I'll get security.'

The Duchess waved her hand. 'I don't think that will be necessary.' She sounded relaxed, almost as if she was enjoying this unexpected encounter. 'I'm sure this young lady will be only too happy to explain what she's doing here. Especially in the light that she was escorted off the premises earlier. As a patron of a young offenders' charity, I always want to support little scrubbers like this when they're in trouble.'

The older woman took a step closer, ice forming in her hazel eyes. 'Who sent you?'

Mo's urgent gaze skimmed over the Duchess's shoulder to the door and planned her escape. Knocking this aging biddy over would be a doddle and was the least she deserved. The young woman looked like you could blow her down with a feather. It was Arthur who posed a problem. He appeared well up for a ruck.

Mo played for time. She manufactured a confused expression and put on a bewildering voice Eliza Doolittle would've been proud of. 'I'm just a poor girl from the East End, innit! Truth is, I come up here searching for my fella who seems to have done a flit.' Her face dramatically fell. 'I think he's ashamed to be seen with me. Mind you, he is one of my betters. A girl like me shouldn't aim so high.'

The Duchess drew closer. Arthur licked his lips. 'I don't think so. If you were a common thief, you'd have grabbed a silver spoon downstairs and run for it. Instead, you bluff your way into my establishment, and when you're ejected, you break in.' Her powdered nose was inches from Mo's face. Meaningfully, she added, 'And then you make your way to my private apartments and to find my safe with its family heirlooms —'

'You what?' Mo played it startled and too stupid to live. 'I touched your family's hairs? Not likely, missus, I've got me own hair, thank you very much. Admittedly, sometimes my hair does belong to someone else when I put extensions in or a weave.' Mo cooed. 'Ohh! I think a weave would be a proper treat on you. A modern-day Dusty Springfield.'

The Duchess let out a smile that dripped with poison. She leaned over and whispered something into the younger woman's ear. The woman left, giving Mo the opportunity she needed. And she took it. Mo stormed forward. Shoved the Duchess to one side and ran for it. But she didn't get far. A bony, vice-like hand gripped her wrist, snapping her back straight into the path of a fist. The power of the blow flew Mo across the room, crashing into a side table that collapsed beneath her weight. She lay there, winded, head ringing and pain throbbing in her cheek. Mo could believe what had just happened. Had someone three times her age put her down?

Arthur ran for cover under the Chesterfield, yelping and whining in fear.

The Duchess rolled up the sleeves of her silver gown. Advanced on a dazed Mo. By the arm, she dragged Mo to her feet. Mo realised that her summing-up downstairs had been right: there was something very chilling about this woman.

'I'll ask again.' The Duchess wasn't even flustered. 'Who are you and who sent you?'

Mo kept it schtum which earned a stinging right-hander that catapulted her onto the sofa under which was Arthur was cowering. Mo saw she was going to be beaten senseless. Where had this upper-class lady learned to brawl? Mo fought back. She hit back as the Duchess closed in on her, catching the other woman's face perfectly with a belter of a blow. It was like hitting steel. The Duchess barely flinched.

The flinty older woman yanked Mo to her feet. 'Are you going to tell me who sent you or is Lady Nice going to have to turn nasty?' She drew back her fist for a final punch.

'Duchess! What are you doing? You can't hit… er… Miranda!'

"Yeah! Miranda!' affirmed another outraged voice. 'She's our mate's grandkid.'

Brother Bertie and Ruddy stood staring on from the doorway in stunned disbelief. The Duchess had instructed her assistant, Jane, to go fetch the pair. Earlier, when she had entered the dining room, her hyper observant eyes had noted this young woman talking to them. Therefore, she had concluded they must be connected somehow.

Brother Bertie and Ruddy pulled the Duchess off Mo. Eventually, she shook them off. Raising her head, she gave a big smile as if the punchline to a joke had just been explained. 'Miranda? Downstairs she said her name was Maureen. Mo.'

Brother Bertie played dumb, not answering. Instead, he tore a strip off his granddaughter. 'What the backside are you doing up here? No one visits the Duchess' apartment without an invitation.'

Mo was pissed to the max for getting duffed over by some wrinkly. Then again, she suspected that the Duchess was far more than that. 'Like I told Dutch here, I was looking for my companion. Obviously, he isn't here, so I'll be on my way.'

Straightening her shoulders, Mo hit the door. Her face

was set in grim triumph. The Duchess might've slapped her silly, but Mo had managed to achieve her goal of having a good ole butcher's and snoop inside the room the safe was in. Now all she needed to do was verify what was inside. What these family heirlooms were. Her mind turned to the one other clue in her father's papers.

S. Sapphire. Mo still had to figure out who or what this was. Only one way to find out. Put the word out and see what turned up.

Brother Bertie and Ruddy shared an intense look. Then stared worriedly after Mo's retreating figure. And prayed that the Duchess believed them that Mo was Miranda, a friend's granddaughter from the East End.

The Duchess got down on her hands and knees and peered under the sofa. 'Arthur! Some guard dog you turned out to be. You're fired!'

Chapter Nine

There was going to be a murder this day! A very bloody one! Nico vowed later that day inside the bar at the airport. Nico was stylishly turned out as usual. The slim-fit dark-blue trouser suit and Italian calfskin shoes made him appear taller. Being suited and booted was his thing. Shame his whistle was going to be spattered with the blood of his nephew. He was going to slowly, *very slowly*, wring Damien's neck when he put in an appearance. The kid was already thirty minutes late. At this rate they'd miss the friggin' flight to Spain. If there was one thing that got on Nico's wick it was the Dossers R Us brigade. Lazy bastards who rolled up when they felt like it. What really peed him off was that he thought he'd taught his sister's boy better. Nico had pulled out all the stops, done his best to make up for not being in their life until five years ago and providing a father figure after Robbie Steele had met his maker.

Nico couldn't fuck about on this trip, too much was a stake. With that in mind, he plonked his bag down and took a seat. Damien had five mins, max, to show his face. After that, Nico was out of here.

The airport bar was chock-a-block with holidaymakers letting their hair down and enjoying themselves. On the other side of the bar a group of young lads, around ten in number, were already creating, getting their fun in the sun well and truly started before boarding the plane. At the rate they were knocking back the sauce they would be lucky to get through passport control much less anywhere near the plane.

All at once he caught the face of one of the merry band. *You have gotta be fucking shitting me!* Teeth grinding, Nico stood and crossed the bar. In the heart of the group he found Damien. His nephew was decked out in lairy shorts, T-shirt and designer pumps looking like a dead ringer for an extra on *Hawaii Five-O*.

'Nico! My man!' Damien held his arms high and wide, king of the party. 'Glad you're here, it must be your round! Get your wallet out, mate. Ha! Ha! Boys, this is Uncle Nic, the big geezer with the villa.'

There were jeers and derision from Damien's fellow drinkers. 'Villa?' One snorted. 'Crap club… We're all Arsenal here, mate. Where the hell is Birmingham anyway?'

That caused another bellyful of raucous laughter. Nico was not amused. He looked his nephew squarely in the eye. 'Word. You and me. In private. Now.'

Barely holding on to his temper, Nico headed for a quiet spot outside the bar, soon joined by Damien. His nephew wore that 'one fry short of a happy' mean expression he occasionally had.

His uncle got into it straight away. 'Who the feckin' hell are those pissheads?'

'My mates.' Then hesitantly added, 'And mates of my mates.'

Nico was desperately hoping there was a simple explanation here. 'And they're flying off to somewhere else?'

Damien was still smiling like he was already savouring the Spanish sun. 'Nah! They're coming with us. You said this villa is a big crib, so I invited them along. The more the merrier 'n' all that. They'll kip on the sofas and floor.' Damien's speech slowed as the light bulb in that brain of his finally pinged on that there might be an issue. 'It's not a problem, is it?'

Grating laughter and sneering in the distance got Nico's attention and back up again. One of Damien's *mates* was spraying another with a can of beer. For an instant, Nico closed his eyes, blotting everything out. He imagined himself back at home with his wife, Pam, and his kids, Annalisa and Victor. As snug as a bug sitting together with popcorn and crisps watching a flick in his specially designed movie room. When Southpaw asked him to do this favour, he should've gently blown him out. Made up an excuse. Anything.

With patience he did not feel, Nico reopened his eyes. Turned back to his sister's kid. 'There's no room for an additional coach party of legless freeloaders. Tell them the freebie's off.'

Damien was crestfallen. 'I can't do that. They've already paid for their tickets. I'll look like a right lemon. It's not like we're going anywhere on business, is it? It's just a holiday. Anyway, my granddad's paying, ain't he? He wouldn't mind.'

Mention of Jimmy and 'business' was like a nail scratching and squealing on a blackboard for Nico. He'd already promised Southpaw at the cemetery he'd get his job done, quietly and smoothly. Quietly? That was a laugh! He hadn't even left English soil and Damien was already making enough of a racket to wake not just the dead but the whole graveyard. Worse, Jimmy had warned him about his grandson being a liability and was only just reassured he was going along for the ride.

Nico had every intention of putting his foot down with Damien, but the words wouldn't come. His anger semi-died in a heartbeat. He had a weak spot where his sister's son was concerned. Despite knowing full well it wasn't his fault, Nico carried a bellyful of guilt that he hadn't been there to help bring the boy up alongside Kristal. Nico knew he was the only one the lad had confided in about how much he missed his father. But looking up to his father had also become a double-edged sword. It turned out the reason Damien had hidden the fact that he'd been losing his hearing in one ear since the age of eight was because he thought it would make him appear unfit to be a strongman like Robbie's son. In his book, his father's son and heir had to be tough and exhibit physical perfection.

Nico had taken him in hand, got his hearing sorted and put him straight that the only person Damien should look up to was himself.

A bag of peanuts landed at their feet accompanied by a bellow of, 'Come on, Damien, you booze-dodger! Get a round in!'

Kristal's son stared down at the nuts. 'Don't worry, Uncle Nic, I'll have a word with the lads. It'll be all right.'

But when they returned to the table, someone was already having a word with them. An irate father warning one of Damien's crew to knock the swearing on the head in front of his little girl before he knocked *him* on the head.

That got Nico's temper on the rise again because he imagined the git cursing a streak in front of his own daughter. Nico stepped in lively, cuffed the guilty boy around the loaf and apologised profusely to the spitting dad. 'Sorry about that, mate. Some people have got the manners of a donkey.'

He palmed the guy a tenner by way of an added amends. Then he grabbed one of the boys by the scruff of his neck, yanked him out of his chair and parked himself in the seat instead. He beckoned with his hands for his audience to gather closer.

'I'm going to lay it on the line for you boys. Damien had no business inviting you along on our happy holidays, but I'm going to overlook that on one condition. If any of you draw attention to my spell in the sun by boozing, fighting, tea-leafing or upsetting little girls or their fathers...' Nico paused to ensure they had their ears cocked wide open. 'I'm going to drop you out of an airliner at thirty thousand feet without a parachute.'

Some of the guys looked sick at that.

'Is that clearly understood? And if you've got any doubts about my willingness to do that, ask your mate Damo. He'll tell you what it's like.' The silence that followed suggested the message had got through.

But they couldn't keep it up. They knew better than to act up in front of passport control and armed coppers. They even managed to be reasonable in the departure lounge. But as soon as they trooped onto the plane and it was too late for them to turn back, it kicked off again.

Nico groaned when he heard one of the gang hassle a female flight attendant with, 'If you get lonely on the flight, luv, we'll be sat the back. Bring a couple of bottles and a friend with you.'

Nico delivered a savage kick to his leg that had him howling in pain. He was lucky Nico wasn't doling out a full-blown kicking because if there was one thing that made him lose his rag it was men trying to force their attentions on women. The thought of it had his stomach recoiling in repulsion.

'Sorry about that, miss.' God! Was that what he was going to do for the whole of this trip, apologise?

'I understand, sir. In the same way, I'm sure you understand that there are very strict rules about behaviour on aircraft.'

As soon as the flight hit cruising height, the boys were looking to hit boozing height. Nico did his best, but it was like herding a group of pissed-up puppies who hadn't been house trained.

'Oi, hostess. Fill her up, will ya? I get thirsty when I'm depressurised.'

'I'm sorry, sir, I am no longer serving you alcohol. You're intoxicated.'

'Intoxicated? You're having a buzz. You should see me sticking it to the Old Bill on a Saturday night. That's intoxicated. I'm as sober as that judge who gave me three months in a young offender's institution. Don't look at me like that.' A soppy grin tipped onto his face. 'You're proper lovely when you smile.'

The aircrew had had enough. One warned Nico, 'If you don't tell your young friends to settle down, the pilot has informed me that he'll land at the nearest airport where the police will be waiting to take them into custody. Apart from any legal problems that might involve, they will also be handed a bill for refuelling costs.'

Nico moved like human turbulence down the aisle, grabbed up one of Damien's boys at random and punched him very hard in the face. He pulled him up by his collar. Blood running down the dazed kid's face, Nico shouted, 'Any more trouble and I'll do this to every last one of you.'

Stunned silence gripped the cabin. Then satisfied applause erupted. Several members of the crew came by Nico's seat to offer their personal thanks. Ten minutes later, another flight attendant came over to do the same. 'Excuse me, sir, but the copilot would like a word.'

Nico just wanted to be left alone. Still, he put on his brightest smile. 'There's really no need for everyone to thank me for putting those boys back in their box. They've been a right show-up and I'm only sorry I brought them along in the first place.'

The woman was persistent. 'I understand, sir, but he's very insistent. He's waiting for you in the galley.'

Sighing, Nico got out of his seat. The copilot indeed was waiting for him. He was alone holding a piece of paper in his hand. 'Hello, sir, you're Nico, aren't you?'

'Look, mate, I don't need any thanks. Why don't you get back up front and make sure the main pilot's got his hands on the steering wheel?'

The guy half-smiled, then surprised Nico by handing him the folded piece of paper. The pilot explained, 'A member of the traffic control team on the ground back in England contacted us to pass this message on to you. I hope it makes sense. Enjoy your flight.'

Bemused, Nico found privacy sitting in the toilet to read the message.

A word to the wise. My sources in Spain tell me our guy had dyed his hair grey and uses coloured contacts. He's also grown a tash and goatee in an effort to disguise his appearance. With English punters he pretends he's Spanish, goes by the name of Miguel, and that he's just a barman not the owner, so be ready for that. Mind yourself, he's probably got local friends, know what I mean? And don't forget to put your hands on a satellite phone with a scrambler when you get there. I don't want any text messages or mails or any of those other methods that are about as private as a sandwich board in Oxford Street.

Don't fuck it up.

JS

Jimmy Southpaw.

Nico tore up the message and flushed it down the loo.

He had to hand it to the cunning East End Face. How many other guys would know how to pass on a message to an airline pilot mid-flight?

There was nothing friendly about Jimmy's reminder not to mess things up. Nico closed his eyes, conjuring up the image of the man who was his target.

Chapter Ten

Mo closed the door of her office and froze. There was someone in the darkness of her room. Twinkle had cleaned the bruises the Duchess had inflicted on her, and all Mo wanted to do was settle back and think of how to carry out the heist. Instead, her body coiled with sudden tension, the baby hairs on the back of her neck standing on end. Her blood quickened and ran cold. Whoever was fool enough to lie in wait for her in her private domain either thought they had the biggest nuts in town or had a death wish. No one, *no one*, invaded her private domain.

Never rush it. Always consider your next move, was what her Granddad Jimmy had taught her to do in such situations. Palm loosening slightly on the roundness of the door handle, Mo lightly sniffed the air. Tangy, spicy, scent of aftershave; defo a man. She used her ears next, tuning in to the sounds around. Her breathing was audible but so was his. Not as light as hers, however, neither was it heavy too. Her nose twitched; there was another smell in the air. Whisky.

Old-style aftershave + heavy breathing + whisky =

Relaxing, she flicked on the light. Turned around. 'Granddad Jimmy, why are you lurking in the dark like the Big Bad Wolf?'

'Just checking if you still had your wits about you.'

Mo playfully countered, 'Thought you could catch me on the hop? No chance.'

Two sets of twin steel-grey eyes stared back at each other. She noted that her grandfather was casually sitting in her chair. This rubbed her royally up the wrong way. He had stepped aside, making Mo the head of the family, so for him to lord it up in her seat of power was, frankly, taking liberties. He of all people should know better than to pull a stunt like that.

Truth be told, her blood was still running high due to the fact that for an hour straight she'd been calling Eddie without any response. Finally, he'd contacted her half an hour back with the story that he was still up to his neck in the legal case that had called him away from their dinner. Mo had wanted to tear a strip off him for leaving her cold in that club, but in the end, it had worked out to her advantage, giving her time to snoop and size up the building that Robbie, and now she, planned to rob.

Still, when she caught up with Eddie, she wanted an explanation for the lining of his jacket being on the latch of the toilet.

Mo moved across the room and wrapped her arms around Granddad Jimmy's neck in a deep hug. She adored this man. He had plucked her from nowhere and given her access to her biggest dream, becoming the Queen of Crime.

After pressing a deep kiss to his weathered cheek, she stood to the side of the chair. Deliberately, Mo rested a possessive hand on its back, signalling that he needed to get off her throne and park himself somewhere else.

Instead of moving, he settled his much larger palm over hers. 'The best thing I ever did was put the business into your hands.' And with that, Jimmy stood. He surprised Mo by not taking the seat opposite but placing his powerful body on the sofa. He patted the seat next to him.

Mo hesitated for a few seconds; something was going on here. For starters, Granddad Jimmy never sat on her sofa. She sat next to him, positioning her body so she could view his face.

Mo asked, 'Is something up?' Alarm sank its teeth into her. 'Are you ill?'

Blimey! He seemed properly rough around the edges. His colour a touch off. He'd appeared preoccupied lately.

Jimmy waved her concerns away. 'There's no worries on that score. I'm alive and kicking as if I was sweet sixteen.' His face creased into a ghost of a smile. 'Did I ever tell you about the time I took my first proper kicking?'

Mo tensed slightly. During her first years taking over the Steele family empire, one of the things her grandfather would give her a sorta *Jackanory* story time about were crucial incidents and moments in his life by way of teaching her important life lessons. He'd stopped doing that a long while ago. So why was Granddad Jimmy telling her a story now?

Mo kept her confusion to herself as she listened. 'I was

eleven and me ole mam warned me that Chicksand in Brick Lane was off limits. Apparently, the place was filled to the brim with roughnecks.' He chuckled. 'My poor mum might as well have saved her words cos I took not a blind bit of notice and me and a couple of mates sneaked over there.'

'Did you get caught?' Mo asked.

'Caught?' He guffawed. 'Caught, battered and booted to high heaven. Had bruises on me for six months. I learned a hard lesson. Always listen to the older folk. They've been around a lot longer and know the lay of the land.'

Mo had had enough of beating about the bush. 'What's going on, Granddad?'

His face fixed into an emotionless mask. 'There I was, playing a round of golf earlier with some old associates of mine when word reaches me about a touch of argy-bargy in a gentleman's club up Mayfair way.' His large hands rubbed against his thighs. 'Then, to my surprise, I hear that it's my Mo that has been carrying-on with the owner of said club. I sez to myself, someone must be pulling my plonker because the head of the business I set up would never be caught swinging her fists for the public amusement of others.'

He finished by directing a deadly gaze on her. Now, Mo understood why Granddad Jimmy was sitting in her chair. He'd felt the need to assert his authority. To remind her that the empire he'd ruled had been built brick by criminal brick by him. And that's why Mo could've kicked herself. She should've factored in that word would finally reach him about what had gone on. He might be retired but it didn't stop him from having an ear to the ground.

Tread careful. Granddad Jimmy is the number one master at reading faces. So she held tight to her surprise, keeping her features expressionless. 'It was nothing, a run-of-the-mill misunderstanding. Then I left.'

He never took his eyes off her, inspecting her face. 'Those bruises on your face look like you took a good hiding.'

'Like I said, it was a misunderstanding.'

'So you weren't casing the joint?'

'Casing the place?' Mo was the picture of puzzled innocence. 'Why would I be doing that at a posh-nosh club up West? A mate invited me there for a slap-up meal, a few bevvies at the bar, nothing more.'

Her grandfather carefully considered her expression of fake puzzlement before saying, 'I don't want you to go anywhere near the Duchess.'

'Why? Who is she?'

Jimmy turned his face, giving her his profile. 'Let's just say she's an ole family *friend*. I wouldn't want anything to put a strain on my relationship with her.'

Mo told him a half-truth. 'On the grapevine, word is she's got family heirlooms that I reckon is a stash of jewels that's the envy of some.'

So quick Mo didn't have time to react, Jimmy loomed over her, his big body blotting out the light, his eyes flashing a warning. 'Are you thinking of turning her place over?'

''Course not.' She held his troubled gaze. 'As I said, it was a simple disagreement.'

'Don't even think about trying to steal her gems. The Duchess is vicious and very, very dangerous.'

Chapter Eleven

'You mark my words, the girl's up to something,' Ruddy pronounced with authority the following week, sitting alongside Brother Bertie in his allotment. The whirlwind beat of Little Eva's 'Locomotion' played on his battered transistor radio.

The allotment was on the Isle of Dogs or the Island as it was known locally, the part of East London Brother Bertie lived and where he'd brought up his daughter, Precious, and her daughter, Maureen. Ruddy sat in a deck chair patterned with the Union Jack while Brother Bertie's was the Jamaican flag. They were on their second glass of his legendary home brewed Lord Have Mercy Rum Punch, the purest white rum steeped for a month in ganga he grew on a patch on the allotment kept well hidden from prying eyes.

Brother Bertie knew exactly who his friend meant by *'the girl'*. His granddaughter, Mo or Big Mo as she was called by many these days, due to her position in life. Inwardly, Brother Bertie shied away from his friend's words because he didn't want to believe that Mo was up to anything in connection with the Duchess' club. Doubt had plagued him since physically having to pull Mo out of a tangle with the Duchess. And insisted Mo was called Miranda so the Duchess didn't suss who she was. He had hardly caught any sleep last night, turmoil about what was going on eating him alive. There was something bad in the air. Really bad.

He answered, trying to brush it and the bad vibes off. 'Baby-gal said she was there having dinner with her man.'

Ruddy clucked her tongue. 'You seen any bloke with her? Because I tell you what, I never.'

'She said that he had gone to the gents.'

Ruddy twisted her lips; she had had enough of this runaround. Brother Bertie was a man who stood by the truth, except, sometimes, when it came to his granddaughter. Mentally, Ruddy shook her head in consternation. She wanted to grab him by the shoulders and shake him.

She swallowed a hearty gulp of Lord Have Mercy Rum Punch. As its fiery path lit up inside her, Ruddy put the cat squarely amongst the pigeons. 'I tell you what I think, you ole fool. Your Maureen is trying to get her sticky mitts on the Duchess' pension plan.'

'No way.' Brother Bertie's denial was a high-pitched squeal. 'Only people from a certain generation know about that pension plan.'

'What if someone from that generation passed it on to a body in the next generation? Eh?'

Ruddy drained her drink and placed the glass on the grass. The insistent tap-tapping of her finger against his arm got him to reluctantly face her. The expression he shared was riddled with worry.

'You know what I'm saying is true,' Ruddy kept up the pressure.

The denial fell away from Brother Bertie. 'I've got to stop it. I'll talk to her, set that young, intelligent brain of hers straight.'

'Nah!' Ruddy again tapped him on the arm to underscore what she was about to say. 'She might be your baby-gal, but she's also Big Mo now. She's still finding ways to prove herself, and what better way than tea-leafing what's hidden away in that club.' Her head poked forward, her eyes bright. 'Her name will be written in neon lights in East End folklore forever. The Queen of Crime who went up West and pulled off the heist of the century.' She leaned in further, voice lowering. 'As the years go on, they'll be saying she'd nabbed those gems straight out of the Duchess' knickers.'

And they would. That's how these stories went; as the years went on, the telling of them grew grander and more nonsensical. The taller the tale the more people lapped it up.

Brother Bertie was almost beside himself with distress. 'How am I going to stop her?' He thought of his daughter. 'Precious isn't here. She's gone on holiday with her friends up north. Something about a spa and sauna.'

The pressure of the pad of Rudy's finger on his arm grew. 'There's only one person who can stop her. We're going to have to go and talk —'

With raging horror, he cut her short. 'Never!' Furiously, Brother Bertie struggled out of his chair to his feet, knocking over his stick in the process. Rising tall over Ruddy, he told her straight, 'You must be losing what little sense you've got in that pickled brain of yours.'

Ruddy savagely cut the insults she knew he didn't really mean to shreds. 'You don't have a choice, Bertram. If Mo nicks the Duchess' pension plan, that's going to lead to one thing. Outright war.'

Ruddy got to her feet, her features sagging with the weariness of someone who had seen too much in her time. She stepped in front of her most trusted friend. 'We don't have a choice.'

As Brother Bertie's face filled with twin images of hatred and sorrow, she continued, 'We need to go and see Jimmy Southpaw.'

A chorus of spontaneous greetings welcomed Brother Bertie, pork pie hat at a jaunty angle closely followed by Ruddy when he walked into the bookies on Commercial Road.

'How's tricks, Brother Bertie?'

'Long time no see.'

'That rum punch still moving with the Holy Spirit?'

The punters who frequented the betting shop for a flutter on the horses all knew him. Everyone knew Brother Bertie. He was a man known for his eye-winking joshing, charm and putting a brotherly arm around a person's shoulder. He was also known for giving a friend in need the last penny in his pocket.

Keeping up the cool vibes, Brother Bertie hailed them back with a good-humoured wave of his stick. He cracked back, 'It's moving with the Spirit *and* the Holy Ghost.' That raised a rousing laugh. Only he and Ruddy knew that beneath his happy-go-lucky cheer, Brother Bertie felt sick to his very bones. The bookies was also the HQ of his sworn enemy, Jimmy 'Southpaw' Steele. Him and Jimmy had an unresolved history that went beyond sharing a granddaughter. He might loathe every step he took within these walls but he would walk through fire if it meant saving his precious granddaughter from harm.

The laughter caught the attention of Sidney who everyone called Sid, the man who stood behind the counter reading a newspaper. Mouth tensing around the Cuban cigar clamped between his teeth, he lowered the paper, eyes narrowing watching the newcomers head his way. Sid had a dog-eared appearance that gave him a homely, worn look which most initially took to mean he was a real softie, a dead pushover. Wrong! In another life he'd been one of the toughest men around. A man who'd been in much demand for his lethal knowledge of whips and canes.

His real purpose in the bookies was to keep an eagle eye on who came through the door to ensure they weren't a threat to his boss upstairs. And that's why, when he saw Brother Bertie, Sid's hand slid to the double barrel kept inside a harness tapped to the underside of the counter. He considered retrieving the shooter and waving these two off, but that would only provide a show. And the boss man wasn't partial to his business being played out in front of an audience. Nothing the East End loved more than gobbling up gossip and dining on the scandal of others.

'There's no need for that,' Brother Bertie said when they reached the counter. He had been around long enough to know when someone was reaching for a shooter. 'We just want a friendly word with the landlord.'

Very few people knew what had caused Brother Bertie and Jimmy Southpaw to become deadly enemies. Sidney was one of the ones who did. He was there when it all went down.

Calm and collected, Sid gave a fake smile, his shoulder muscles relaxing as his hand fell back from the gun. 'The gaffer ain't in.'

Ruddy pushed herself forward, snorting. 'Whose that Bentley belong to outdoors then? The Devil?'

Brother Bertie sent her a warning glance, quickly intervening. 'Five minutes, that's all we want of his time.'

Shaking his head with a sigh, Sid quietly argued, 'Coming here is only going to cause aggro. Leave it alone. Why don't you let me have a word in the gaffer's ear, then I'll get back to you.'

Brother Bertie's body stiffened from head to toe. 'What I've got to say is between him and me. And —'

The ring of the black landline on Sid's desk interrupted his words. Jimmy's man on the counter picked up, listened, nodding. Not a word left his mouth until he placed the receiver back down and told them, 'Through the back. Up the stairs. You've got three minutes to say your piece.'

They found Jimmy behind a large desk in a room that wasn't much to look at which couldn't be said of one of the most feared people in this part of London. Jimmy's large, raw presence dominated the room. He captured his visitors in his startling steel-grey eyes. He did not offer them a glass of the malt on his desk or a seat.

He gave them a smile, though, one that would make schoolkids scream. 'Well! Well! Look who the dog dragged in.' He stared them up. And down. A smirk broadened his lips. 'A ventriloquist and his dummy.'

Brother Bertie gritted his teeth, letting the insult fly over his head. Leaning on his stick, he took a step closer. Not one step more; he wanted to stay as far away from this bastard as possible. 'I want to talk about my girl, Maureen.'

Jimmy relaxed back, the pressure of his big body making the chair slightly swing. 'You've got a nerve coming here.'

The other man ignored his baiting. 'I think Mo is going to do something that will cause big-time ructions. You need to stop—'

The suddenness of Jimmy's forward move, leaning over his desk, the muscles in his powerful body straining against his shirt, robbed Brother Bertie of the words. Jimmy growled, 'You don't waltz into my manor, shouting the odds about what I've got to do or not do. I don't take fucking orders from the likes of you. Especially when it concerns my granddaughter.'

Brother Bertie could hold himself back no longer. 'I should've known that Mo would end up in deep cacka-doo-doo sooner or later with your treacherous hand guiding her.'

'Treacherous.' Flinging his chair out of the way with such force it tumbled bang onto the floor, Jimmy leapt up, frothy at the mouth. 'You've got a bloody nerve talking about traitors after what happened to my sister, Sin.'

Ears buzzing with raw rage, with a sweep of his hand, Brother Bertie unleashed the sword that was housed inside his walking stick.

He was so caught up in his fury he never heard Ruddy roar, 'No! Bertie don't.'

But Jimmy just cracked with scornful laughter. 'I ain't scared of you, old limping duffer. Bring. It. Fucking. On.'

Heavy breathing shattering the room, Brother Bertie danced a step further, sword firmly stabbing Jimmy's way. 'I should have killed you years ago for what you did.'

Emotion shook Jimmy's frame. 'You destroyed her. Ruined her life forever.'

They both knew they were no longer talking about Mo, their shared granddaughter.

Suddenly Sid appeared in the doorway, shooter lodged with lethal intent in his hand. Ruddy elbowed him across his nose. Blood spurting down his face, the gun tumbled from his hand. In a quick one-two move, she smartly kicked the gun across the room and pulled a hairpin from her beehive and held its steel pin not far from his throat. Sid froze because he knew Ruddy from back in the day; she wouldn't hesitate to stick him to protect her friend.

Shoulders sagging, Brother Bertie suddenly looked every year of his age. The memories his enemy had awakened were too much for him to bear. He picked up his stick, sheathed the weapon back it in and, head bowed, feet dragging, left. He might not have anything to say, but Ruddy had plenty.

Pointing an accusing finger at Jimmy, her body vibrating with anger and disgust, she hissed, 'Y'know what, Jimmy, you're an evil bastard.'

'Fuck off outta here, you satanic slapper.'

She wasn't done or scared. 'I'd set the C word on you,

but it's too decent for the likes of you, Jimmy Steele.' And with that, Ruddy defiantly spat on the floor.

Chest rising and falling heavily, Jimmy grimly watched the empty doorway. He was several steps ahead of those two interfering geriatric wankers. He knew exactly what they were talking about. The Duchess. But he was safe on that score because Mo had given him her word that she wasn't interested in pulling a heist at the Duchess' club.

Jimmy heard his mobile go off in his office. When he picked up, he forgot all about a robbery that was never going to happen because it was Nico with news from Spain.

Chapter Twelve

'It's him,' Nico told Jimmy Southpaw on the phone.

'Are you sure?'

Nico's rangy body was arranged on a lounger poolside at the villa in Spain. His hair was swept back, the kiss of the sun darkening his natural olive skin. Damien and his crew were out enjoying the nightlife. Actually, the lads hadn't been the nightmare he was expecting. He put that squarely down to Damien pulling them into line. Good boy!

Before Nico answered Southpaw, his mind rewound back over the last number of days. Right back to that first day.

The day Nico knew he'd found his target. The bloke had that look of a hunted man around his gills. Y'know, someone who knows that no matter how much time has passed, how many things have changed or how many players have died, he'll always have to constantly check over his shoulder. *Miguel* was right where Jimmy's message on the plane had said he would be. At a bar that he was keeping hush-hush that he owned. It was a typical Brit watering hole. Chairs and tables out front with patio umbrellas hanging overhead.

When the evening rolled in, the neon lights flashed on, its tourist trap to lull punters inside.

The guy was alone, sitting on the terrace of the bar. He had a good twenty years on Nico, wore shades and was dressed casually. And had the seasoned demeanour of someone who had seen too much of life. Where he'd chosen to sit was no accident. It was a position where he could see the road from both directions. A man who didn't like surprises. That made sense if what Southpaw claimed was true. Mind you, the bloke would know the place inside and out because he owned the bar.

Nico didn't make eye contact. In fact, he ignored him, went into the bar and ordered a coffee. Turning on the charm, Nico swapped some friendly chat with a waitress and explained he was a Cypriot businessman looking to invest in property. Then he sat on his own for around an hour before leaving. Again, he strolled past the man as if he didn't exist. As Nico got into his car, his side-eye caught the guy going into his bar.

He would bet his life that he knew what the geezer was doing: grilling the waitress about what Nico had said to her. 'Who was that man? What did he want?'

And, like a parrot, she'd feed him the exact info that Nico had fed her.

On Nico's second visit, his target was sitting in the same place, watching the road. This time Nico smiled at him as he went into the café. He got no response.

On his third visit, Nico did get a comeback. Deliberately, Nico had taken his coffee outside, sitting a few tables away from his target. Taken out a Greek newspaper. Of course,

Nico couldn't read it but he made a good job of appearing to be doing so.

'You Cypriot?' The guy's tone was more accusation than question.

With an easy-going style, Nico glanced up from his paper. 'That's right. From Famagusta.'

The owner of the bar gave Nico the once-over before stating, 'You don't sound like a Cypriot.'

Nico had the answer to that all ready to go. 'Born and bred in Enfield. When my granddad died, he left me and my bruvs some business interests back home, so we all went back. No disrespect to my dad's old man, but he did us a real favour checking out and I ain't just talking about the money either. When I think of Enfield, all I can hear is the rain drumming on the roof.'

Turning back to his paper, he casually dropped, 'You're a Londoner yourself?'

'Nah!' Nico noted the quick response. Too quick. 'You've got that wrong, mate. I'm from Manchester.'

Nico restrained himself from doing an eye-roll. Who did this cupid stunt think he was kidding? His accent was straight from The Big Smoke.

Nico gave it a bit of drama when he checked his watch. 'Blimey! Is that the time? Gotta run.' He stood. 'The name's Andreas by the way.'

It was an obvious invitation to provide his name and, somewhat to Nico's surprise, he did. 'John. My name's John. Or Miguel.'

'I'll see you around. John.' Nico paused. 'What's the

brekkie like here?' Nico had to keep up the pretence that he didn't know that the man owned the bar.

'Tasty.' That brought a smile to his target's face. It smoothed out his go-to hooded expression.

Next morning, while he tucked into his breakfast, Nico started his campaign of schmoozing John. Got him so nice 'n' relaxed he admitted to owning the bar. John's revelations didn't stop there; he spoke of having been a lawyer who'd tired of his work and retired to Spain to open a bar.

'Good money, though, the law,' Nico added.

The other man's expression became guarded again. 'Money isn't everything.'

Nico proceeded to chat footie, dog racing, pubs, in fact, any 'manly' activity that might get John to open up again. Then he clocked John's drifting gaze towards the telly where a game of cricket was on.

Nico mentally allowed himself a smug smile. 'Is there a local cricket club?' he asked.

'You? Cricket? You don't look like the type.'

Nico grabbed his chance. 'I grew up in Enfield, mate. I was a demon between the wickets, and the way I bowled a Yorker was nobody's business, stumps all over the shop. I trialled for Middlesex, actually, but it didn't work out.'

John was laughing, now displaying crooked side teeth. 'There's one or two clubs here, they have trouble finding people to play. I'll look up some numbers for you.'

'That's good of you. As long as they're not fielding any villains. I can't afford to get my bails knocked off by bank robbers or drug traffickers.'

John's good humour vanished. 'No.'

Nico didn't miss a beat. 'Then again, you were in the game yourself.'

John tensed up. 'I beg your pardon?'

'The law.' Nico tightened his net. 'You said you was a lawyer?'

The geezer had obviously forgotten his claim he was a retired brief. The twat had forgotten the golden rule of pretending to be someone else. Make up a simple cover story and stick to it.

'Oh that. Well, I was on the right side of the law, of course.'

While John was off balance, Nico struck. 'I could never do that. Watch the bad guys cleaning up while you're earning an honest living. Is that why you quit?'

A troubled and vacant John stared into the distance. 'It was something else. One of my clients was involved in a tragic and mysterious death.'

Nico was careful. 'And your superiors blamed you?'

John's voice was ghostly. 'Let's just say that someone did.'

'It's him, all right,' Nico confirmed again to Southpaw.

Jimmy clenched up. He'd had his plonker pulled too many times with false starts and trails gone cold. 'Are you one hundred and ten percent sure?'

Six years Jimmy had been waiting for this moment. Six long pain-filled years since his son had perished in a fire in a police station. And all anyone could tell him, by way of an explanation, was it was an accident. Fuck off was it! In public Jimmy towed the official line that the electrics were so old the joke was Thomas Eddison had put them in hisself which had caused the cop shop to go up in a ball of flames. But behind closed doors, Jimmy had grieved and seethed, knowing that the story was basic bullshit. Someone had murdered his boy, and Jimmy had spent years trying to find out who'd lit the match.

Now one of the scum involved had finally risen to the surface. *'If you wait by the river long enough, the bodies of your enemies will float by.'* That's what one of the old-timers had told Jimmy when he was a green lad coming up.

'As sure as I can be,' Nico tentatively replied, backtracking slightly. 'He's had a bit of work done on the face and claims to have been a lawyer before tucking away his wig and silks for good before coming here.'

'That ain't going to work for me, Nico.' Nico heard the fury but also the desperation in the other man's voice. 'I don't want to end up having a sit down with a dodgy accountant who's scarpered with the Darby & Joan's Christmas fund.'

Nico was uneasy. Of course, he couldn't be absolutely sure. 'He's got that look of a cowboy who's tired of running.'

'I'm not in a Western, Nico, I just want my guy back in England to answer a few questions. Know what I mean?'

Nico knew exactly what he meant and shuddered. Jimmy Southpaw wasn't in the habit of sitting around and asking questions. 'I've got it all in hand. I'm going to lift him soon. I know a team who run drugs from Morocco to Paris.

They've offered to do a special delivery to a service station off the M25. I'll keep you posted.'

'You bring that feckin' dirty cop, Carlson, to me.' Jimmy rang off.

Detective Robert Carlson was one of the two police officers who had arrested Robbie in mysterious circumstances the night of his death. As far as anyone was aware, he was one of the last people to see Robbie alive. After the incident, both Carlson and his partner, Phillips, had vanished off the face of the earth. Jimmy was convinced that one or both knew how and why his son had been burned alive. And they must have something to hide because only the guilty did a runner. Jimmy had hunted this bastard high and low. Then info had suggested someone matching Carlson's description was running a bar in Spain.

Nico had a problem that he didn't share with Jimmy. He'd been tailing Carlson to various places when he left his bar. But which one was his address? Nico was pretty sure it was a villa up in the mountains that the bloke drove to most evenings. But he stayed the night in other places too. And Carlson always varied his routes, including driving down dead ends to see if he was being followed. But the villa had to be the place.

God have mercy on Carlson's soul when Nico delivered him into the hands of Jimmy Southpaw.

Chapter Thirteen

The next day, Mo pressed the door buzzer and waited outside the jewellery shop that was located in a narrow side street off Hatton Garden in Holborn. The area was known for its gems and jewellery so it was no surprise that security was tight. The door made a long, whining sound and unclicked from its lock. Mo stepped inside. The place was a bling paradise. Transparent displays sparkled with tray after tray of rings, necklaces, earrings and so much more.

A man stood behind the counter. He was small, nearer Mo's height, with tuffs of untidy hair, and a face lined and faded by life. His gaze had a depth about it that suggested this man rarely missed a trick.

'What can I tempt you with, young lady?' he asked, his eyes glittering.

'Are you Sammy Sapphire?' After she'd discreetly put the word out, that's the name that came back from several sources.

He grinned broadly displaying two front teeth, each with a tiny sapphire drilled into them. *So that's where he gets his nick from.* 'Samuel Taylor is the name, the sparkling business is my game.'

Mo couldn't resist smiling back; there was something infectious about this man.

She told him, 'I hope you aren't going to keep talking in rhyme because that would properly do my head in.'

Sammy Sapphire's shoulders lifted with a snorting nasal laugh. 'What are you after? A ring? Necklace? A secret surprise for your other half?'

Other half? For a few seconds her mind turned to Eddie. He was up to his eyeballs in work, so she hadn't seen him. Mo was frustrated. And a little afraid that he was getting ready to chuck her. She loved the guy, in her own way and would do anything to keep him.

Mo caught Sammy's gaze and held it with confidence. 'I'm Maureen Watson. You may have herd of my grandfather, Jimmy 'Southpaw' Steele.'

He stiffened, his cheeriness congealing on his face, while two splashes of red warmed up his cheeks. 'You must be Big Mo, then. Good to meet you.'

He stretched out his hand. There was a brief moment of hesitation before Mo took it. His smile slapped back in place, more strained this time. 'You should've said who you were. Me and Jimmy go back years. How can I oblige Mister Southpaw's gorgeous granddaughter?'

This geezer was certainly sure of himself in the charm department. 'Did my father, Robbie, ever come to see you about something?'

Sammy suddenly leaned over the counter and whispered, 'He did. In fact, he left something with me.'

'What?' Mo's heart raced with anticipation.

Sammy patted her hand, the sapphires in his teeth winking at her. 'You wait here, dear, and I'll bring it out.'

Mo tried to play it cool, but truth was she could barely keep a lid on it. And prayed that Sammy returned with information about the blag Robbie had planned. Then again, Sammy might be pulling a fast one and about to do a runner out back. Mo had that base covered; Josh and Dell were positioned at both ends of the street in case of such an eventuality.

The other snag was Granddad Jimmy. His warning came back to her. *'Don't even think about trying to steal her gems. The Duchess is vicious and very, very dangerous.'* Mo had given him her word that she wasn't thinking about ripping the Duchess off. Mo had never lied to her grandfather. Honesty being the best policy was a reality between them. On the other hand, yesterday's events at the club meant things had changed. This wasn't just about making a few bob or seeing her dad's big job actually come to pass. This was personal now. The Duchess would live to rue the day she'd made a show of Mo in front of all those high-kickers inside her club.

Mo heard footsteps. Sammy was heading back. She braced herself. He re-entered the front of the shop…

'What the fuck?' Mo blasted.

It wasn't Sammy who stood in front of her. It was her stepmother. Kristal.

'You! What the bollocks are you doing here?' Mo demanded.

Mo sat opposite her stepmother in the upstairs sitting room in Sammy's shop. The room felt more like something out of a country cottage than a room in the hurly-burly of the city of London. It had an old-fashioned air, filled with chintz and clocks of various sizes with a log fire all ready to be lit up.

Sammy had locked up shop for an hour and gone out, giving them privacy.

Mo was seething and not frightened to show it. 'Are you following me?'

Sammy left them a pot of tea which Kristal now calmly poured into a pair of tiny porcelain cups.

Kristal sipped her tea before answering, 'I didn't need to follow you to know where you were heading. You're not the only one with eyes and ears around town too.'

The pieces were starting to fall into place. 'Sammy tipped you off that I was coming here to meet him.'

Kristal glanced over the rim of the cup. ''That he did. He's a proper gent, that man.'

Mo reined in her tongue so she could think things through. Something was going on here. The light bulb finally pinged on in her mind. 'The only way you could've figured out I was going to contact Sammy Sapphire was if you knew he was in Robbie's plans for the heist. Or at least his name was in the papers. Which means —'

Kristal triumphantly ran over her words. 'I know exactly what job Robbie was planning.'

Mo shot to her feet and furiously loomed over her stepmother. The anger coming off her was incendiary. 'I'm the head of this family, so you don't lie out of your rear-end when I ask a question. I asked you point blank if you knew —'

Kristal slammed down the fragile cup. It broke into pieces onto the table, some scattering on the floor. Matching

Mo's fury, she barked, 'I don't care if Jimmy's set you up as The Second Coming, I don't answer to you or no one. Especially when it's business that was between me and my husband.' She gulped back some of her anger. 'Now if you want to know the specifics of what I know, you'll park your arse down and shut your noise. And listen.'

Mo visibly bristled; she was used to giving the orders not the other way round. 'You wanna watch your step,' she warned. 'And remember that I've got the biggest nuts in town.'

'Balls?' Kristal tutted, shaking her head with woe. 'What you've got to learn, girl, is that we're women. We think deeper and harder than any man. We don't have bollocks between our legs, we've got something much more powerful than that.'

Kristal held her gaze. 'Brains. That's what we've got in the downstairs department.'

When she pointed at the seat Mo had vacated, her stepdaughter retook it. Mo kept it zipped, allowing Kristal to fill her in.

Kristal lengthened her neck. 'I know you're planning to do the job. And I, being a woman with a heart of gold, am prepared to tell you what I know.'

Mo began to interject, but her stepmother placed an insistent finger in the air. 'I'll tell you. On one condition.'

Typical! Nothing with Kristal was ever straightforward.

Mo stared Kristal down. 'What do you want?'

'I want in. I want a cut of the heist.'

Kristal's blatant demand shook Mo up. For once in her life she was lost for words. Team up with big-mouthed, conniving, back-stabbing, acid-tongued Kristal? Okaaay! Maybe that was unfair. She would admit that her stepmother wasn't always having a go, that she did have her good qualities. And that was the dilemma with Kristal. You never quite knew where you stood with her. One minute she was all playful, innocent Kitty-kitten, the next a raging tigress, sharp teeth and claws at the ready to scratch your eyes out and bite your head off. Kristal might be a member of the Steele family, but the reality was Mo had only ever seen her be loyal to two people – her boy, Damien, and brother, Nico.

Sensing her indecision, Kristal set her mouth in a thin smile, grabbed her brushed leather Prada handbag and got ready to leave.

'You're in,' Mo flashed out. Shit! *Am I going to live to regret this?* 'Spill the beans. And I mean *all* the beans.'

With glee, Kristal wriggled her shapely body, getting comfy. 'I know you've already sussed that Robbie was planning to raid the Sixes and Sevens Gentleman's Club. The place is owned and run by a posh bit of hoity-toity called the Duchess. In one of the rooms is a safe where the Duchess keeps the family heirlooms. Jewellery.'

A jewellery heist! Which means that under all the respectable, teasing glitter, Sammy must be a fence. Mo was ecstatic.

Mo's brain ticked away. 'Do you know what kinda bling we're talking about?'

Kristal shook her head. 'No one's quite sure, not even Sammy. Betcha they won't be your bog-standard birthstone rings and belcher chains. You're probably talking about gems. Diamonds too.' Her eyes sparkled. 'Robbie was clever that way.'

Mo squinted. 'I don't follow.'

'It's all good and well to doing a smash-and-grab of cash. There's a big snag with that, though.' Mo hung on her every word. 'Bags of cash are heavy work. Imagine doing your getaway with one of them in your hand. It's gonna slow you down. Now gems and jewellery, they don't weigh more than a newborn babe, if that. Stash them in your bra and you're on your toes in seconds.'

Mo couldn't believe she was getting an education in blagging from her stepmother of all people.

'So why didn't Robbie carry it out?' Mo's bafflement showed.

'When Jimmy got wind of what was going on he put the kybosh on it. Told Robbie to knock it off.'

'Why would he do that?'

'Dunno.' Abruptly, her features sank, her expression becoming stark and haunted. 'Then it didn't matter. Robbie was dead.'

They said nothing, sitting in the mournful silence, Kristal remembering the man she had married and Mo the father she had never known.

'He could be as lovely as pie,' Kristal broke the silence, voice faraway and soft, 'and a right shit.'

'Did you love him?'

Mo's whispered question was one she had always wanted to ask Kristal. The idea of her father living with a wife who didn't care two hoots for him had never sat well with her. In her mind's eye she'd often seen images of a swaggering Robbie coming home to a house filled with warmth, homemade food and huge cuddles; lots and lots of cuddles. Kristal might be considered a rough-around-the-edges sort, but Mo only had to think of the way she pampered Damien to know that this was a woman with plenty of love in her jaded heart.

Kristal stared at her hands in her lap. 'Love? There was a time in my life when I thought I knew what that was. Then something happened to make me realise that what I took for love was actually something very ugly.'

Mo knew that bad stuff had happened to Kristal as a child. What that was she didn't know.

Kristal jerked her head up sharply at her stepdaughter, her gaze hooded. 'I gave your father all the love I was able to give.'

Mo steered their discussion back to the heist. 'Let's get one thing straight. I'm the boss of this raid. You follow my every word.'

Kristal joked, 'Whatever you say, Nazi Mo.'

Without warning, a sour taste invaded Mo's mouth, a wave of sick flying up from her stomach. Desperately, she clamped a palm over her mouth. Seeing her dilemma, Kristal got into action and got Mo to the small toilet on the landing. Inside Mo heaved and heaved, chucking up her guts until her tummy spasmed with nothing left to give.

'You all right in there?' Kristal called.

Mo felt so weak she could barely get the response past her lips. 'Yeah. All good.'

But it wasn't. This was the third day on the trot she'd thrown up. What was happening? There was nothing for it, she was going to have to see the doctor. Whatever the issue was, she needed to deal with it quickly. God and nobody were standing in the way of her doing Robbie's heist.

Mo rejoined Kristal in the sitting room. Heavily sat down. 'Sorry about that.'

Kristal sent her a very penetrating look. In fact, Mo noted, it was a dead-on imitation of the gaze she'd sent Mo after she was ill in the coffee house in Hoxton.

Kristal said, 'I know you said I've got to heed everything you tell me.'

Gimme strength! Here we go already! She should've known Kristal would have other ideas.

Her stepmother continued. 'During the robbery you can't be doing any fighting.'

Eh? Mo was puzzled. 'Why not?'

'Because, boss-girl, you're eating for two.'

Chapter Fourteen

Twinkle picked up her stick, intending to go to the ladies when she spotted Mo stride into the club. She frowned. Mo looked like she was in a right hurry. *When isn't she on the go these days,* Twinkle cynically summed up. Hold up. Twinkle peered closer. No, Mo seemed to be in a fair ole two and eight. *What's going on?*

Her bestie marched over. Grabbed her arm and dragged her towards the exit, with no heed to her dodgy hip and leg.

Twinkle cried, 'Where are you taking me?'

Mo kept schtum, continuing to propel her mate since primary school downstairs and into her office. Mo sat Twinkle in the chair at her desk. Then she reached into her bag. Placed something on the table between them.

Twinkle stared hard at it, brows crashing into a deep scowl. 'That's not what I think it is?'

Mo nodded. 'A pregnancy testing kit.'

Twinkle gasped, struggling to control her breath. 'Fuck me, Mo! You're never in the family way?'

Twinkle rarely cursed, which went to show how shocking

she found Mo's revelation. She was a serene soul who didn't see the need to go effin', blindin' and jeffin' her way through life. Still reeling, Mo collapsed in her chair in a stunned stupor. Her mind was a total fog. When Kristal had told her she was pregnant, initially Mo had thought the other woman was chatting drivel, as per usual. Up the duff? Her? No way in heaven. Mo had been meticulous about there being no slip-ups when she was with Eddie. As much as she wanted to have a family, this wasn't the right time to put down roots. Her number one priority was carving a name for herself in the criminal underworld. Settling down Mo had put on the back burner until she was thirty.

How had this happened? *The bloody night of the Eddie's birthday celebration is how, you ninny. He tickled your fancy and had you up on the kitchen counter so fast you weren't thinking of precautions then.* It was all coming back to her. She'd taken him out for a curry in Brick Lane, back to her hers in Wapping for a bottle of fizz and, as they say, the rest is history. Or a baby. Chucking up, dizziness, sore boobs; what a premier league idiot not to have recognised the symptoms.

After leaving Kristal, Mo had instantly picked up a pregnancy testing kit. One pink line later and it was confirmed; Mo was going to be a mummy. Self-consciously, her palm lay gently towards her belly. She couldn't believe it, there was a baby in there. Another human being.

'Who's the father?'

Twinkle's question brought Mo's mind back into the room. God. Eddie! Hell, what was he going to say about this unexpected news?

Twinkle added, hurt creeping into her voice, 'I didn't know you were seeing anyone. You never told me.'

Mo felt guilty about not letting on to her bestie. Twinkle would've have kept her lips buttoned about Mo's relationship with Eddie. The reason she hadn't opened up to her best friend was because she was so paranoid about Granddad Jimmy finding out. One slip, one wrong word, that's all it would have taken for him to find out she was having it off with the enemy. Mo fortified her spine. Well, Great Granddad Jimmy was going to have to suck it up. When this heist was wrapped up, Mo made a vow to sit Granddad Jimmy down and tell him the truth. Hopefully, even bring Eddie by to meet the clan.

'His name's Edward, Eddie for short,' Mo told Twinkle. And smiled, bright and ditzy. 'Oh, Twink, he's gawg. A bundle of fun where it matters, you get me?' Oh, Twinkle got her all right. Amen to that.

'I love the guy to heaven and back. And he feels the same way about me.'

The minutes ticked away as a dreamy-eyed Mo regaled her friend with why her guy was the best this earth had ever produced.

'So, what's the problem?' Twinkle had known Mo long enough to sense something was up. Twinkle's jaw dropped south when she figured out what it must be. 'Blimey, he ain't a law-abiding Joe?'

The merriment drained out of Mo, leaving her face a sickly shade of brown. Reluctantly she admitted, 'It's worse than that.'

The other woman's brows crashed together. A deep scowl marred her forehead. 'What could be worse than that?' Her eyes widened. 'He's never a married man.'

Mo was outraged and showed it. 'Get out of here. As if!'

Never put your mitts on another gal's man was one of Mo's life-long rules. That was bang out of order in her book. If she had been that way inclined, she'd have tried her luck with Nico years ago. His wife and kids were very lucky people. The irony of her very existence being the product of a wedded man and the other woman was not lost on Mo.

'What could be worse than that?' a genuinely confused Twinkle asked.

Mo gathered courage and shared her secret. 'He's a solicitor who puts criminals away.'

'Shut up!' Twinkle was horrified. 'What were you thinking?'

'With my fanny,' Mo cracked.

They both creased up, hooting with laughter. It felt so good to lighten the mood even though Mo knew this was no laughing matter. There would be a serious accounting to be had when she confessed to Granddad Jimmy.

Quickly, Mo grabbed Twinkle's hand and clung on tight. Her friend gasped from the pressure of her grip, as Mo begged, 'Promise that you'll keep this between us.'

'You should know you don't have to ask.' Mo's bestie's hand shrank a little in her hold, and that disgruntled undertone was back in her voice.

Twinkle's heart died a little because back in the day, Mo would never have asked if she would keep a confidence. That's what they did, held on to each other's secrets. East

End Girls Forever. The distance between them widened even more. Twinkle was keeping her own certain something close to her heart. She wanted to tell Mo but this wasn't the time. That was a laugh! It was never the time these days.

Something pulled Twinkle from her turmoil. 'You have told Eddie he's going to be a father?'

A pensive Mo stood outside the lawyers' chambers where Eddie worked. It was in Holborn, funnily enough not that far from Sammy Sapphire's fencing operation. That was London for you, law and disorder going about their daily business around the corner from each other. Outwardly, Mo appeared calm and collected, inside she was spitting nails. She'd been calling Eddie all afternoon to arrange a time to give him the good news, but all she got was his bloody voicemail. Sure, he might be in court, but a sixth sense told her he wasn't.

If the mountain won't come to Mo...

'Excuse me.' The receptionist raised her head and assessed Mo with a quick once-over. She wore no slap and had the manner of a tough old bird who would fight to the death. 'I'm here to see Eddie... I mean Edward Harvey.'

The woman's head tilted, her gaze gliding over Mo. 'I'm afraid he's not —'

'Mo?'

The startled calling of her name pulled her attention away from the reception towards a side door. Eddie stood there, ashen-faced like he was about ready to lose his lunch. *Is he looking peaky because I've turned up?* A shaft of pain knifed through her. First, she'd stood outside for five minutes like some homeless because she was so nervous about going in. Now he was making her feel as welcome as a rash in a place she already felt uncomfortable in. Mo avoided coming to a law firm like the plague. She'd never forget sitting in a reception area with Granddad Jimmy at the firm that represented his interests. A woman was softly sobbing in her husband's arms. Mo later found out that their son had been stabbed to death. Mo's heart broke for them. But something happened too. It got her to thinking about the innocent lives her crimes might be hurting.

Eddie hastened over. In an ultra-professional voice, he formally addressed her. 'Miss Watson, I wasn't expecting to see you today —'

'Well, here I am.' Her apparent jaunty reply was laced with enough sweetness to give him diabetes. She was fucked off with the way he was treating her, like he didn't know her from Eve. 'Shall we go to your office?'

'No! No!' Before Mo could query his behaviour, Eddie somehow manoeuvred her towards the exit. 'Let's take this outside.'

Through the noise of Holborn traffic and commuters spilling out of the Tube station he managed steer Mo to a quiet side street.

The agitated sweep of his fingers through his hair showed he was pissed. 'What do you think you're playing at? We agreed I don't show my face at Club Class, you do the same in my place of work.' Mo tried to get a word in, but Eddie was pacing, words flying out of his mouth. 'What if someone your grandfather knows saw you there? Saw us there, *together*?'

The stark truth of what she had done laid bare before her pushed Mo to lean heavily into the wall. Eddie was right. She had nearly screwed up, big time. Nevertheless, she couldn't stop the tears of despair pricking her eyes. Mo loved this man so much and all she wanted to do was all the things other couples did. Walk hand in hand with him in the street, take him down the club and have a spin with him on the dance floor. Introduce him, arm in the crook of his, to her mum, Brother Bertie and Jimmy. Push their baby's pram in the park. *I just want what everyone else has. Is that too much to ask?* A cloud of brutal sadness pulled the tears down her cheek.

'Hey! Hey!' Noticing her tears, Eddie moved closer and his biting anger fled. He cupped her face, raising it up to his. 'Forgive me, darling.' He kissed her tears away. This man was so special to her, so loving. And now she had his young 'un growing in her body.

'I'm sorry.' Her low words thrummed against him. Then she remembered. 'When we were at the Sixes and Sevens, how did you leave the club?' In her mind she saw the torn material of lining from his jacket on the toilet catch.

He looked at her strangely. 'Via the main door, how else?'

Maybe I was wrong. Maybe it belonged to someone else's coat. Eddie doesn't have a monopoly on blue paisley lining.

Mo shook off the guesswork, arriving back at the real and urgent reason for her visit. This wasn't easy. Taking a deep breath, she launched on. 'I need to speak with you. I've got something I have to tell you.'

Eddie drew back from her, his gaze now speculative. 'I know you've been trying to call me, but I've been tangled up with back-to-back meetings today.' He searched her face. 'What do you want to tell me?'

Suddenly Mo noticed their surroundings. The dirt and dried pigeon droppings, the stains of stale rainwater on the ground. The ripe odour in the air. *This is an alleyway, for fuck's sake. Is this really where you're going to announce to the man you love he's going to become a father?*

Her fingertips lightly caressed his cheek, while she decided what to do. 'I do need to speak to you. Come over to mine later.'

Grimacing, he stepped back slightly. 'I wish I could. In fact, I won't be able to see you for the next couple of weeks or so. I've got a trial coming up that involves working with a team of lawyers in New York.' He sent her a quizzical look. 'Are you sure you don't want to tell me now?'

Mo firmly shook her head and tried to muster a smile, although it felt like her lips were merely shaking. 'Don't worry. It can wait until you're back.' *I'll introduce you to our baby then.*

Chapter Fifteen

Expertly balancing a tray of drinks, the waitress entered a room known as The Lady on the third floor of the Sixes and Sevens Gentlemen's Club. The walls of the room were bare except for the huge oil painting of a lady from the Regency era hanging on the chimney breast above the decorative marble fireplace. Her sumptuous, metallic purple dress and artificially pink cheeks shone against a background that faded from deep red into unfathomable black. Her lips were tilted into an ever-so-naughty, knowing smile. It was rumoured that she'd started life as a Covent Garden flower girl who became the mistress of the first owner of the club. Like the Duchess, her real name had long been forgotten.

Maybe that was why it was the Duchess' favourite room, which was why it was no surprise to the waitress that she'd been called to deliver refreshments to the boss lady who sat on the grand, forest-green Chesterfield sofa that dominated the room. As usual, her faithful assistant, Jane, was close by, discreetly sitting in a corner reading a book, but with one ear and eye on her boss to be ready to meet her needs. And Arthur, the Duchess' Doberman, happily snuffled and sniffled, tucking into a very tasty top-quality rump of steak.

The Duchess had company. Her grandson and his fiancée. The waitress maintained her discretion as she got their drinks ready.

The Duchess elegantly crossed her long legs, the soft velvet of her A-line dress slip higher on her toned thigh. The Duchess was always turned out to perfection. Always a lady. Never refer to her as a woman. Women were a penny a dozen, while ladies were worth a ransom in gold.

'Darling,' she preened with pride at her grandson, who sat in the two-seater opposite next to the young lady who would soon be his wife. 'A select group of fifty will be coming.'

Directing an irritated glance her way, he groaned. 'Do so many people really need to come?'

She clucked her tongue indulgently at him. Now if this was anyone else questioning her actions they would be mentally yelping in pain from the slashes and cuts of the sharp edge of her tongue. She would never do that to her grandson. The truth was she spoilt him. He was the apple of her eye. The Duchess and the Duke had taken their grandson in when he was nine-years-old after their son and his wife were tragically killed in a boating accident in the Caribbean. Three years later when the old Duke had met his maker – contrary to tittle-tattle that had nothing to do with the Duchess, of course – her grandson had become the centre of her life.

The Duchess lifted her ruby-red lips into the special heart-stopping smile she reserved for her grandson. 'I want everyone to be here. Your marriage is going to be the wedding of the year.' Slowly, she turned her full, intense attention to his fiancée. 'Don't you agree, Phillipa?'

Phillipa rapidly swallowed, nodded, her eyes blinking ten to the dozen. She was in awe of the Duchess. How a lady that old could ooze natural coolness and taste like a second skin, the ultimate in stiff-upper-lipped style, Phillipa would never know. But Phillipa was sure of one thing: she wanted a slice of it. She couldn't wait for the day when she had the ability to sweep into rooms with such sexy power and grace that every eye turned her way.

Privately, the Duchess rubbed her two hundred pounds manicured palms with glee at her grandson's choice of wife. The girl ticked every box on her wish list. Such as coming from an aristo family that could trace its roots back to a warrior who had landed with William the Conqueror. And being as dull as washing-up water and bland right down to the plain wraparound dress she wore. Most important of all, she was biddable.

The last thing the Duchess wanted was a wife who was going to be demanding and creating scandal for her grandboy. A few weeks ago, the Duchess had sat the girl down and had a chat about her job as wife, being to direct the housekeeper who would direct the help in how to properly take care of the home, be a flawless hostess and pop out an heir and a spare within the first three years.

Once the waitress had laid out all the drinks on the table, The Duchess picked up her glass of sherry, that only those in the know in the kitchen knew was really lager and black.

With a flourish, she stood. Now she didn't just have the attention of her grandson and his fiancée, but also that of her assistant and Arthur, who was lying down, belly satisfied, one eye open. Without any fuss or noise, Jane tucked her book neatly away. On her olive-green 1940s retro heels, the Duchess sashayed to stand beside the painting of The lady. Only she knew that behind it was the safe that was filled with gems. Some of those gems she was going to present to her grandson's wife the day after their wedding.

The Duchess thought back to that girl she'd caught in the room. Maureen-Miranda. There was no way the girl would have been able to lift the painting of The Lady down to get to the safe. By nature, the Duchess had a suspicious mind. Nevertheless, in this case she'd concluded that the girl had been having a sneak peek in the parts of the club she shouldn't have been. The building The Duchess had inherited from her husband was an impressive example of its period. To a girl from some slum in the East End it must have look like a palace.

Maureen or Miranda? That was the only thing that still gnawed away at her. The girl's name was either Maureen or Miranda. So the Duchess was making subtle enquiries to discover the truth.

The Duchess forgot about nobodies from the East End and raised her glass in toast to her grandson and his soon-to-be bride. 'To the glorious and happy day this Saturday.'

On her way back down to the kitchen, when she reached the second floor, the waitress tucked her tray under her arm and pulled out her mobile. 'Big Mo, it's Dell. I've found the perfect day for the heist.'

A wedding? Mo couldn't hold back her elation, a huge grin transforming her features. She listened carefully to Dell filling her in on the particulars of the wedding of the Duchess' grandson. This is what they had been waiting for. Her mind rewound back to the first planning meeting for the heist she'd convened with Kristal and Dell.

'The day we do it there has got to be a distraction,' Kristal had pointed out. 'Something so big going on every mind in that club is consumed with that one thing. They won't have any time to think on anything else. Plus, if anything out of the ordinary looks out of place they'll just put it down to whatever's happening.'

Mo came back with, 'I hear they have fifties night every Friday. People come dressed to the nines as a fave fifties character. Y'know, Elvis —'

'Screw Elvis, my girl. Keep that brain of yours focused. Eyes on the prize.'

Mo bristled. 'I ain't your daughter to be talked to like that.'

'But you could've been.'

A strange silence had ensued where neither woman had wanted to put under the magnifying glass exactly the meaning of what their terse exchange could have meant.

It was Mo who pulled them back to the heist, coming up with a possible answer. She'd called Dell to her office and sat her down.

'What we're about to tell you, don't dare breathe to another living soul, even Josh.'

When they filled her in on their plan, Dell's face darkened. 'Does Mister Southpaw know about this?'

It was Kristal who told her straight, 'Stuff ole Grandaddy Southpaw. He's too busy twiddling his golf clubs to notice a thing these days.'

Mo took over. 'We need a pair of ears on the inside of the club to find out if some big event is coming up.' Mo looked her cousin up and down. 'How good are you at serving drinks?'

They also made the decision that Kristal would be the getaway driver.

The thief woman.

The inside woman.

The wheel woman.

Everything was in place.

A strong knock at the door brought Mo back to the present. Mo kissed her teeth lightly; she did not want to be disturbed. So she didn't answer. That did not deter whoever it was because the door opened. An older woman with short grey hair and large brown-framed owl-style glasses peered in.

Mo tried to dial back on her vexation. 'I think you've got the wrong day, luv. The over-sixties dance club is on a Tuesday afternoon.'

Mo had inherited the tradition of putting on dance classes for the older members of the community when she got the club. Most would have put a halt to them, not Mo. The oldies deserved their pleasures just like everyone else. On a Tuesday afternoon it was not unheard of to find Mo grooving with them on the dance floor.

The woman inched inside, shoulders hunched, and shut

the door. Her voice was shaky and weedy. 'Are you Big Mo Watson?'

Mo knew she should make quick work of moving her along, but she was intrigued. 'Who wants to know.'

The woman smacked her lips together. 'Word is that you're planning a *Big One*.' Mo stiffened.

'All I ask is that you save a diamond for me.'

Mo was on her feet. 'How did you —?'

Suddenly the old woman bent over, clutching her belly, creasing up for all she was worth. Her eyes, dancing with wicked devilry, flicked up to Mo. 'Gotcha!'

'Kristal?' What was going on here?

Her stepmother straightened and then did a twirl. 'I'm testing out my new disguise as the getaway driver.'

Mo shook her head, finding her seat. 'Are you crazy. You look like you're channeling Mary Whitehouse.'

The other woman snatched the wig off her head. 'That's the beauty of it. No one takes any notice of the grey-haired brigade. It's the perfect disguise for me waiting in our getaway motor.'

Mo had to give it to Kristal, she had a point. Mo was pleasantly surprised to discover that working with her stepmother hadn't proved to be the shitshow she'd expected. Don't get her wrong, Kristal was still a livewire, but also a real pro.

Mo got out the Campari and lemonade. Her stepmother preened with pleasure that Mo had taken note of what her favourite tipple was.

'This heist is on.'

The women clinked glasses.

Chapter Sixteen

'Jean-Paul, are your people in place?' Nico asked, voice urgent through his ski mask.

Nico was perched, hidden, on a hillside with a pair of binoculars and a clear view of the villa where Carlson lived. Assumed he lived, if Nico was being totally honest. It was rigged with security but nothing too heavy. Carlson had played a blinder because he'd deliberately dampened down on the security, keeping everything low-key. Too much razor wire, walls that were too high, too many cameras were bound to attract attention that someone or something valuable lived inside.

Jean-Paul's deep French accent replied, 'Yes, my friend. Stop worrying. Flush your guy out and my team will take it from there. We will have him in England before you can sing your national anthem.'

Jean-Paul was the head honcho of the team who were going to package Carlson up all lovely and hunky-dory and leave him for Southpaw to pick up on a motorway. Nico was nervous, there was no getting away from it. Even Jean-Paul's attempt at humour couldn't banish the knots twisted in his gut.

Jean-Paul and his gang were in a vegetable lorry that had been converted to house a hidden purpose-built cell inside for Carlson's long journey home. They were parked in a lay-by two miles away.

What was making Nico's nerves go into overdrive was there was no sign of Carlson. Perhaps he'd sussed that 'Andreas' was bogus and skipped town. If he'd scarpered, never mind Jimmy Southpaw, Nico would hunt him to the ends of the earth. If there was one thing Nico hated it was being outwitted. He picked up his phone to call Jean-Paul again but thought better of it. He was starting to behave like a rank amateur. He fingered his pistol and toyed with his ski mask. Carlson was normally back at the villa by sundown.

Where was the bastard?

Suddenly, in the distance, Nico was alerted by a sound. Then a pair of sidelights came into view on the dirt road towards the villa. Through his binocs he saw that it was a black Mercedes. Nico frowned; Carlson didn't drive a Merc. Carlson's motor of choice was a battered hatchback that was in keeping with a guy dunking out of the limelight.

The Merc pulled up outside the gates to the villa. Two men, big, muscular, got out and scanned the surroundings. Nico ducked lower. He watched with an eagle eye. The men sauntered up to the gates, pushed it open and when they reached the main door one of them knocked. No one came. They peered through the windows. One of the men went back to the door and pounded his fist against it while the other peered up at the upper floor and shouted, 'Carlson! You there?'

Carlson. There was the confirmation that Nico had been right all along.

'He ain't here.' They were Londoners.

'Neither are the others then. This is a right plum pudding and no mistake.'

'Wrong time?'

The other guy checked his watch. 'Nah. They must have blown out. What should we do?'

'Don't know about you, bruv, but I'm heading back to the hotel. I ain't house-sitting.'

They strode back to their motor and once inside, did a three-point and drove away. The scene fell quiet. Nico couldn't believe the turn of events. How the heck was he going to nab the guy if his target wasn't indoors and, if that wasn't enough, it looked like Carlson was hosting a meeting of some kind. And what tightened the rope around Nico's neck even more was tonight the only window of opportunity Jean-Paul had this side of his own import-export drug business. Or, as he'd put it, 'Shipping coke from Morocco to Paris is a full-time job, my friend. I can do you a special. But it's a one-night-only thing.'

Nico stood, his black-clothed figure blending into the night as he hurried down the hillside. Passed the motorbike he'd arrived on resting in a hollow on the hill. Nico checked the street before picking up speed through the gates of the villa. The place was shuttered and closed like a shop during siesta. Nico didn't have a choice. He was going to go to Carlson's café and hope he was there. Alone.

Nico was about to turn, then froze. What was that noise? He listened. It sounded like the small engine of a car.

Bollocks! He couldn't be caught here. Nico bombed it out of the gates. The lights coming down the road were those of a car, but one of them was broken. Carlson's old banger had a broken light. It had to be his guy. Yet another twist in events had turned everything back to Nico's advantage. All he had to do was wait for the scumbag to get out of his car… and pounce. Nico hid behind a row of bins and took the safety catch off his shooter. And watched. And waited.

A hatchback huffed and puffed through the open gates. That's odd, Nico thought, listening to the engine. It wheezed, struggling against the weight it held. Like too many people were in it. Carlson wasn't alone. The question was, how many others were with him? They might be armed.

The front doors on the hatchback opened. Carlson got out of the driver's seat while a black woman wearing a shawl got out of the other. Her face looked familiar to Nico but he couldn't place her. Carlson pulled forward the front seat to let two more guys squeeze themselves out of the back.

They weren't happy. ''Ere Carlson, have you thought about getting yourself a better motor? You can afford it.'

Carlson was grim. 'I don't want to attract attention.'

The guy wasn't convinced. 'I thought you had attracted attention? That's why we're here, ain't it? Although personally I think you're being para.'

Carlson was angry. 'Paranoid? I know when I'm being felt up. I know when a bloke posing as a Cypriot property investor comes into my joint and he isn't all he appears.'

Nico's heart sank. He'd been rumbled. He doubted he'd been grabbing Carlson tonight.

The guy who'd been grumbling pulled a phone. 'We're here. All accounted for. Backup's coming but it's a bit delayed. We're tooled up to the max. In the meantime, we'll have a glass of sangria.'

Two more cars turned up, including the Merc he'd seen earlier. Another five men got out, all carrying shooters.

The man who'd been on the phone was obviously the one in charge of security. 'You two, man the gates and keep your mince pies peeled. The only motor we're expecting to roll up is an Audi sports. Anything else comes, blast it out of the water.' He turned to the woman. 'You OK?' A nod was his answer.

Nico wished he could remember who she was. He racked his brain. It was no use, the memory remained out of reach.

Carlson, the man and woman soon disappeared inside the villa. The two guards closed the gates and took up position, guns in hand.

This was a small army. Usually, Nico thrived on danger. He hadn't reached the heights of being one of the ranking Faces in South London by turning tail and legging it. But the odds stacked against him here were crazy. He was not looking forward to calling Southpaw later with the news. He grimaced, thinking of listening to the old man go batshit ballistic.

Nico bided his time. Waited for the inevitable boredom to set in with the guards. It didn't take long. They were already getting bored keeping their eyes peeled over the desolate and empty hillside where the gloom was full-on and the last rays of the sun coming over the top of the mountain.

Soon, they were checking their phones next. Perfecto!

Nico climbed on the bin. Grabbed the top of the wall. The stone and mortar crumbled beneath his fingertips. Nico started slipping. Clasping a handful of the rubble, he fell back and back, down and down. With a jarring thud he hit the ground. A seismic pulse of pain ricocheted from one end of his body to the next.

'Oi! What's your game?'

Nico didn't hesitate. Despite the pain, he leapt to his feet. Vaulted up on the bin and onto the top of the wall. Bullets tore through the air. Shots whizzed so close to his head it was like thunder booming past his ear. Dropping down to the other side of the wall, Nico ran up the hillside, zigzagging as he went, desperately searching for cover. More shots, chucking up the dry earth near him. He spun around to check behind him. Silhouetted against what was left of the light, one of the guys was shooting at him from on top of the wall.

Nico raised his gun and took him out. The man was blown backwards off the wall. And that's when it hit Nico with the full force of a stun grenade. He knew exactly who the black woman was.

Precious.

Mo's mother.

Chapter Seventeen

Nico couldn't move. His bombshell discovery held him in the grip of pure shock. For a few seconds he forgot he was in danger. Mo's mother? With Carlson? The man who was involved in Robbie Steele's murder? The same Robbie Steele who had fathered Precious' daughter? What the feckin' bollocks was going on here? None of it made any sense.

The sound of a shot brought Nico back to the peril he was in. He dived to the ground. Put everything else out of his mind except his survival. Began to dig a little furrow in the dirt and stones with his hands so he had some cover. The men from the villa were scattered outside firing wildly into the gloom so Nico didn't shoot back. He was safe for now. He had one advantage that the other guys didn't. The barrel of his gun had a suppressor so there was no giveaway flame to show where he was. Theirs didn't. He observed their shadows running in the twilight, but the discharge of their gunshots clearly pinpointed their exact positions.

Suddenly, they changed tack, retreating backwards to the villa.

The voice of the bossman of the security team yelled in

disgust, 'What the hell are you doing? Get back out there and find the bastard! He can't have gone far.'

'He's armed and loaded, boss,' one shot back. 'We've already got one down, we don't want any more.'

'It'll be a lot more than one dead if you don't get out there, I'll see to that. Catch him or kill him, I don't care. But bring him back.'

The men didn't argue. Crouched low, their silhouettes were large mushrooms-like shapes crossing the ground, they fanned out from the villa. Occasionally, a shot was fired, but it didn't land near Nico. He looked up the hill. His motorbike was hidden only a couple of hundred yards away. If he could get to that, he could escape. But if he tried, he was going to be spotted. There was nothing for it but to sit tight and hope they got fed up.

Nico stilled at the sound of footsteps. Two of them were approaching. Nico peeped over the top of his furrow. They were stumbling almost in a direct line to him. He looked achingly up the hill. The bike felt so close he wanted to reach out and touch it, but it was really so far away. The two men were looming towards him. Nico took aim. Two shots to the body. Both men went down.

One was obviously still alive because he screamed, 'He's here!'

Nico took off. Climbing up the steepening hill while shots of orange flashed on the hillside below. Hugging the ground and running to and fro, he could hear the men behind closing in. Nico turned and fired single shots to slow them down. Half a dozen of them were closing in on him now. He was nearly there. He jumped over a stone wall to find his baby waiting for him, all ready to go. Yanking it upright, Nico climbed into the saddle and turned the ignition. It chugged and chugged before falling silent. No fucking way! The men were getting closer. Once again the engine made noises but failed to spark into life. He wasn't going to make it. A furious fusillade of shots came over the stone wall. Nico ducked. But didn't let go of the bike.

'C'mon, baby. C'mon.'

The engine coughed. Spluttered. It was obviously dead. And so was Nico going to be shortly. He threw the bike to the ground in fury. The only thing left was to make a final stand by the stone wall. Although it wasn't going to be much of one, his gun's magazine was nearly empty. There was nothing in his plan that made provision for a shootout. It was just a case of a barrel pressed in Carlson's ear and an order to move.

Nico looked over the wall in between the occasional shot from below. They were working out who was going to lead the charge. More of them were going to die and no one wanted it to be them. He couldn't help laughing when a phone began to ring below. He wondered what the guy's reply to the caller would be:

'Not now! I'm caught up in a gunfight…'

There was a lot of movement and whispers below but no sign they were moving in for the kill. Or perhaps they were trying to outflank him on either side. Nico dropped onto his backside. It didn't matter what direction they were coming from, he was done for. If he was going down, he was taking some of them down with him.

Minutes away from believing he was going to lose his life, Nico found a moment of peace to think of his gorgeous family. His wife and kids. How they'd turned around the life of a young man heading off the rails. How his daughter and son were doing him proud at school. He wasn't one these Faces splashing the cash without a care for the future of his children. Nico had made it his business to privately educate his. Set them on a road where they didn't have to prove their worth doing battle for turf in the street. He thought of Mo…

All of a sudden Nico realised that the hillside was silent. He peered out. The gunmen were gone. They'd been called back. Down by the villa, there was lots of activity. Shouting, car doors slamming, engines starting. A convoy of vehicles emerged through the gates and began driving up the road at speed. Even the hatchback was giving it some welly. Within a few minutes, the taillights of the cars had disappeared.

It made sense. Even in a spot as remote as this, someone was going to notice the gun battle sooner or later and call the cops. They were getting away while there was still time. Now Nico needed to do the same. But how?

He climbed on the motorbike to give it one final chance. 'If you don't start, I'll shoot you and leave you in flames on this hill to die.'

The bike responded to the threat by bursting into life. Nico allowed himself a light laugh. The wind whipping up and blowing in Nico's hair, the bike bumped and swayed uneasily down the hill to where the villa stood and the track that led up to the main road. The gates and the front door to Carlson's place were open and the lights were on. Nico started up the road at increasing speed until something occurred to him. He stopped, retraced his steps and parked up in the courtyard to the now empty villa.

In the villa there was no sign of any kind of domestic life. Except for the furniture, the place had been cleared out. Open drawers and cupboards told a story of the occupants leaving in a hurry. There was no hope that Carlson would have left any clues where he'd gone. Nico had figured out that this was not a real home, but more a hideout or perhaps an HQ. But why had Carlson been paying regular visits and kipping here? Who was he meeting? Nico knew tonight's meeting was about 'Andreas', but what else was planned and plotted in this building?

And Precious Watson? Nico shook his head; what Southpaw was going to make of that was anyone's guess. And Mo? Nico shied away from the answer to that. If he wasn't a married man, Mo would've been the type of girl for him. She was brave and beautiful, loyal and a firecracker. The type of woman he could make hot love to at night and come the day, in times of danger, she would coolly defend his back. He hated to think of her in pain. And if her mum was up to her neck in this, Mo was in for a wagonload of hurt and despair.

Nico called Jean-Paul as he wandered around the villa. 'There's been a change of plan, bruv. The job's off.'

His contact was sniggering. 'You've messed up?'

'Things took an unexpected turn.'

'Mr Southpaw will be unhappy, yes?'

Nico didn't reply. He was in a bedroom. This held some signs of life; a woman's clothes were scattered around and on a bedside table were some documents.

Nico said, 'Full price will be in your account in approximately one hour.'

He rang off, his attention on the documents. Nico rifled through them. False passports, driving licences, ID cards and various paperwork from Spanish officials. He sank down onto the bed in stunned disbelief, clutching the documents, not knowing what to do or whether a bullet and slipped unseen into his head and scrambled his brains.

Nico rang Southpaw.

'Jimmy, there's been a development. I need to talk to you in person.'

'What is it, Nico? What's happened? Come on, out with it.'

'I'll get Damien and the lads all sorted so we can come back pronto.' He avoided answering. 'When I touch down I'm coming straight over to your place. There's some things you need to see.'

Nico rang off. Jimmy called him straight back. Nico switched his phone off. He went through the documents again and again, certain that there must be a simple explanation or that he'd missed something. His hands turned over and over like an automatic teller until there was no doubt left. Nico stuffed what he'd found down his trackie top before running out of the villa and climbing onto his motorbike.

As the engine started, he whispered, 'There's going to be hell to pay.'

Chapter Eighteen

'This is nuts,' Mo belatedly decided.

She faced the Duchess' club on the other side of the road. Mo wore a black tracksuit and a baseball cap pulled low to hide her face and held a kitbag over her shoulder. Mo patted her belly, a reminder that there was a baby in there. Her child. Was she really going to climb up and then go in and out of that building, lower herself down a chimney and cut open a safe? And then do the whole thing in reverse? She hadn't read her ante-natal briefing but she was pretty sure that wouldn't be on the agenda for expectant mums. Although seeing as the little one was going to be a gang boss' kid, perhaps she would have to get used it. Mo flinched at that suggestion. Should any child get used to a life of crime?

Mo turned her attention back to the building. The front of the club was decorated with garlands of white flowers in celebration of the Duchess' grandson's wedding. From the state of affairs it looked like the happy couple were already inside. The place was a hive of activity. A constant sea of flunkies running down the steps to open the doors to cars and escort various chinless wonders and their lady friends into the club. The Duchess was greeting her guests with a champagne reception before the main sit-down event got underway in a grand downstairs room that fronted the street with a pair of fancy French windows. The Duchess was so security conscious, mobiles were collected at the front desk. Everyone looked happy and caught up in the bliss of the wedding celebration.

Which, to Mo's mind, meant that the heist was going to be a piece of piss! Mo couldn't believe it; here it was, the moment she was going to earn the respect of her dead father by carrying out his final job. Mo's tummy tightened. This meant so much to her.

She stroked her tummy again. 'Don't worry, little one, I'll get you back safe and sound. I'll buy you a gold crib with the winnings.'

Time to get this party started!

The plan was simple: get in and out as quickly as possible and then hit the road to the getaway car where their wheel woman, Kristal, waited. Hunched over, Mo moved down the street in the shadows while another carload of Little Lord Fauntleroys and their braying escorts tipped out of a saloon and went into the club. She refocused. Went down the side street where she'd re-entered the club her one and only time here through the gent's window. This time she didn't look up but down. In the pavement were the twin doors for a beer drop door hatch which had once been used to bring barrels into the club. Their inside woman, Dell, was on the lunchtime shift and had unlocked them for Mo.

Mo made her way through the damp and dark basement.

Found the flight of steps used by staff that took her to the second floor. Another unlocked door. This led out onto the fire escape at the rear of the building. Mo scampered up the stairs that took her up four storeys to a small balcony on the top floor. On it rested a step ladder that Dell had placed so she could access the roof. This had been the easy part. Now things were about to get tricky.

Carefully, Mo walked up the rungs. Stepped onto the roof. The slates were old, some broken and covered in moss. And if she fell… she was dead. Her baby was dead.

'This is nuts.'

Mo shook off the warning. Carrying a heavy kitbag and the welfare of her baby made manoeuvring difficult. She took one step at a time, keeping her balance and not avoiding looking down. When she reached the ridge, she walked with a foot on each side until her hands could rest on the chimney stack. Her arrival sent a flock of frightened pigeons off into the late afternoon sky. The stack itself was a massive Victorian construction, the middle one of six with other silent chimneys. Mo wondered if it was really a ship's funnel. She unzipped her kitbag and took out her gear.

She had Kristal to thank for that. Disguised in a wig and coloured contacts and bearing a fake passport, her stepmother had flown to Switzerland and bought the climbing gear with a throwaway credit card. The two of them had studied climbing videos, but of course there'd been no way to organise a practice run. Mo was going to have to learn on the job. She pulled on a potholer's helmet with its lamp. Assembled the harnesses and ropes. Mo put an industrial face mask on to cover her mouth; the last thing she wanted was to ingest nasties that reached her baby. She climbed up on the stack and peered down the funnel. Up close, the chimney was much bigger than Mo had assumed whereas inside was narrow. The width got narrower and narrower as it went down. And boy, did it go down. It seemed to have no end. Who the hell had her father been proposing to put down there? The slimmer of the year?

Mo tied a piece of cord to the chimney stack and dropped it inside. Robbie's plan told her the exact length it needed to be to bring her level with the safe behind the chimney. A compass told her the exact angle she needed to dig the bricks from to get at the safe behind.

Mo went down the chimney. Her world turned from light into near black. Claustrophobic. She hardly needed the rope in places, the space was so narrow it supported her as she went down. It narrowed and widened before narrowing so much Mo was like a cork in a bottle. It was a good thing she didn't suffer from panic attacks. Looking down was like peering into a never-ending tunnel. The view was enough to make Mo feel dizzy.

The brickwork in places was incredibly fragile, so she'd need to take care where she placed her feet. One slip-up… There were clumps of strange black stuff that wouldn't have been out of place in space. She suspected that they were clusters of soot and other chemicals that had stuck together over the years. Mo coughed and spluttered as mortar and ancient soot was thrown up.

Suddenly a small bird's head peeped out of nowhere. The

shock of it had Mo swinging and nearly losing her grip. Panting, she managed to settle down. Fixing her legs securely in place, she checked where the bird had appeared. In a gap in between the bricks were a couple of chicks in a nest. They were frightened outta their feathers, poor things. Mo made a mental note to be triple careful on the way back. She loved animals and did not want any harm to befall those two cutie baby birds.

She tensed the cord, and the compass showed she needed the flaky brickwork at 76 degrees from the north. Behind those ancient crumbling bricks were the Duchess' jewels. Her heirlooms.

She'd made it.

Mo shone the light on her helmet on the right spot and began to pull away the bricks. Robbie's plans had been bang right again; the bricks came away easy as you please. She didn't need to use her builder's tool to scrape away any mortar. There wasn't any. Mo dropped the bricks into a bag between her legs. When the hole was big enough she peered inside. There was the metal casing of a safe except the back. The back of it was gone.

Inside the safe was empty.

A stunned Mo hung in the chimney in disbelief.

She'd been robbed. Someone had got here before her. No wonder there had been no mortar around the bricks and they had been so easy to move. Mo let the bag of bricks drop all the way down to an empty fireplace below. Temper rising, she hauled herself back up, careful to not disturb the chicks.

Mo was so mad she didn't even notice the journey back up or the trip over the roof to the fire escape because her head was spinning. Who had stolen the jewels? Who? Mo felt like a proper grade A fool. Someone had been playing a fast one on her. But who?

Focus! Focus! Focus! That's what she needed to do to get out of here. Kristal would be waiting for her in the getaway car. Mo flew down the fire escape. Mo was in a rage as she ran through the club down to the basement.

But then she was brought up short by laughter rippling through the wedding reception downstairs. And a voice. One she recognised. It too came from the wedding reception. Mo knew she should have headed back to the basement but in a trance-like state, the voice drew her downstairs.

The voice was giving a speech.

'Ladies and gentlemen, I would like you to raise your glasses. Let's begin this fine day by toasting Her Majesty the Queen.'

'Her Majesty the Queen!' the wedding party chorused.

Transfixed, Mo walked down the spectacular staircase to the huge room at the front. She stood on the outside looking in. No one noticed her presence, everyone caught up in the glamour and glitz of one of the weddings of the year. The room was a mass of ranked tables and guests. Presiding over proceedings was a long table set on a podium, where the Duchess and bride and groom had pride of place. The groom was the one on his feet toasting the Queen.

The groom who was the Duchess' grandson. The groom who was also Mo's lover, Eddie.

Chapter Nineteen

On the verge of falling apart, Mo staggered out of the club. Short, sharp pants of air sliced and lacerated the inside of her throat. And her chest where her heart lay … Lord have mercy! The pain there was horrendous. Crushing and squeezing until Mo thought she was going to pass out. Heartbreak crippled her very being. Suddenly her tummy turned upside down and she knew it had nothing to do with the baby. Mo only just made it around a corner before heaving up the contents of her insides.

Trembling, legs shaking so much Mo had no idea how she remained standing. Resting her palm against the wall, she steadied herself. Fat tears blurred her vision and crawled scalding down her skin. Distraught, she moved her other hand and cupped her belly where her baby lay. Eddie's baby. Eddie who had claimed to love her. Eddie who was another woman's husband. *Another woman's husband. Another woman's husband.* Over and over the shameful words drilled a hole deep in her very soul. It was those very words that finally shook Mo up.

And something red-hot and choking consumed her. Dashing the tears of heartache away, she marched to where Kristal waited in the getaway car.

Instead of going to the passenger door, Mo yanked opened the driver's door.

Kristal half-jumped, startled. She wore her old lady disguise complete with wig. 'What the fuck?'

Mo demanded, voice biting and remote, 'Move over into the passenger's seat.'

Kristal peered hard up at her stepdaughter. Something was wrong. Terribly wrong. Her appearance shocked Kristal to the core. The girl looked like she'd just crossed paths with the Grim Reaper. Mo was scaring the life out of Kristal. That's when Kristal sussed that Mo didn't seem to be in possession of any stolen jewellery.

'Where's the loot?'

Voice distant and robotic, Mo told her, 'The safe was empty.'

Kristal dialled up the volume of her voice. 'You what? How can that be?'

'We'll dissect the wherefores and whatnots later.'

Mo barged into the driver's side so fast Kristal had no alternative but to scramble over to the passenger seat in a move so quick her grey wig went skewwhiff.

Kristal's gaze dropped meaningfully to Mo's waist. ''Ere! Be careful of the little one that you're carrying.'

Mo paid her no mind. In fact, it seemed like she hadn't heard Kristal, locked in her own world, unable to hear or respond to anything or anyone. Eyes glassy with retribution, mouth compressed into an ugly, frightening line, Mo turned the ignition key.

The guests at the wedding gasped at the Duchess' dress when she stood to toast the bride and groom. Some of them wondered, wasn't there a rule where no one was meant to outshine the bride? Well, that memo hadn't reached the groom's grandmother. Her dress was nothing short of spec-tac-u-lar. Feathered and figure-hugging, it swept to the floor, comprised of sequins in every shade of golden that shone like jewels, dancing and dazzling in the sunlight coming through the French doors. The Duchess stood tall, spine erect. And proud. She overflowed with pride that her darling Eddie had cemented that next step in his successful life. This was her only grandchild's nuptials, and she was going to celebrate it to the hilt. If that meant putting the bride in the shade then so be it.

Furtively, the Duchess spared a disdainful glance for her grandson's new wife. God above! The girl was turned out like Little Orphan Annie in a white dress that the Sally Army would refuse. That was all down to the girl's idiot mum, twittering away about an exclusive designer she was acquainted with who knew how to dress to impress. The guy should never be allowed near a sewing machine was the Duchess' cutting opinion. Still...no matter. There would be time enough to take Eddie's bride in hand when they got back from their exclusive honeymoon on a private island in the Caribbean owned by a long-time friend of the Duchess'.

She graced the assembled with her attention in the grandest

room in the club with its floor-to-ceiling windows, arched French windows and trio of eighteen-piece chandeliers. Holding her champagne flute aloft, she declared, 'Thank you all for joining us today to celebrate the perfect union of my dearly loved grandson, Edward, and his new wife, Phillipa. And…'

A car smashed through the French windows with an almighty crash. Shards of glass glinted in the sunlight, splintering everywhere. The table displaying the wedding cake was in the car's direct path. On contact it collapsed to the floor, sending the wedding cake somersaulting in the air. It crash-landed with a messy noisy splat on a nearby table, showering the occupants with sponge and icing. Stunned, people dived for cover, some screaming. Eddie hauled his new wife protectively to his chest. Only two people didn't move. The Duchess and her dowdy assistant, Jane.

Mo emerged from the car, leaving a speechless Kristal cringing, arms crisscrossed defensively over her face in the passenger seat. Mo ignored everyone, her boiling stare reserved and zeroing in on one person. Eddie.

Strutting towards him, Mo stabbed an avenging finger his way. 'You look like you're about ready to do it in your pants.' And he did. His face was a mask of incredulity, 'You dirty, filthy, two-timing man-whore. All this time you're screwing me into next week knowing full well that some other girl is wearing your engagement ring. And now she's your wife.'

The guests gasped at the accusations. Mo almost

staggered back with the force of what she saw on his deceitful face. It told her exactly what her status had been in his life. She was just his side piece, his East End tramp that he fucked on the quiet. He'd screwed her over big time. Literally! The realisation that she'd been royally taken for a ride nearly shattered her into a million pieces. *What a fool I've been.*

Her cheating lover's new wife jerked from the protection of his arms. 'Edward, what's she talking about? Who is this… this… woman.' Withering scorn dripped like the vilest poison off each word.

It wasn't her fault, mind. He'd played them both for idiots. In such matters it was easy to want to scratch the other woman's eyes out. It was the man who was at fault. Mo would never, *never* lower her dignity to fight over a man. If he didn't see what a jewel he had in her, he could do one thing. Fuck right off.

Mo's denouncing finger swivelled towards the woman, who, as far as Mo was concerned, possessed enough ice to freeze Jamaica. 'I'm the *woman* who's about to tell you some home truths. You've tied the knot with a rat and you want to be careful you don't end up strangled by his double-dealing.'

The Duchess had heard enough and marched around the table to confront Mo, closely followed by her assistant, Jane. 'I told you never to show your common face in here again.' Voice clearly playing to the audience, she sneeringly added, 'Now, if you've been letting all-comers have a bit of a jolly between those bargain basement thighs of yours, you can't blame a red-blooded man like my grandson for what's on offer.'

Before Mo could give it to this haughty highborn piece with two barrels, another voice joined the fray. Brother Bertie. 'Maureen? Maureen, what the raas are you doing here?' He tottered to his feet, a bit worse for wear from the fizz he'd been downing every chance he got. Suddenly his faced filled with thunder, turning his gaze to the Duchess. 'Did you just call my granddaughter a slapper?'

Ruddy, close behind him, backed him up. 'Yeah! You wanna mind your manners.'

The Duchess bared her teeth at them. 'So, she's your granddaughter, is she. Bertram, you need to get this girl out of my sight before I do something.' Her voice dropped to a threatening pitch. 'And you know what I'm capable of doing.'

Brother Bertie and Ruddy shook under her gaze.

Mo stood her ground. 'I ain't going nowhere until I've had my say.'

The Duchess transformed from grandmother of the groom into a pit bull in a designer dress. 'Open the ears, close the mouth,' the Duchess warned between gritted back teeth. 'Get. Out. Of. My. Club.'

Mo didn't budge. The Duchess lunged for her, which Mo easily side-stepped.

Dell, in her guise as a member of the waiting staff, seeing Mo in danger knew exactly what she had to do. It was her job to protect Mo at all costs. Locating her rucksack, which she'd hidden under a table, she flung it on her back, unzipped it and produced her machetes. Roaring like a banshee, she leapt forward. Raised one of her lethal blades… Cried out with pain when a whip lashed around her wrist.

The large blade dropped from her hand, clattering to the floor. WTF! Barely able to believe her eyes, Dell wildly looked up. Her jaw went south with disbelief. Handling the whip was the Duchess' assistant, Jane. The woman's usual drabness had disappeared, replaced by the attitude and stance of a fighter. Her lip curled, eyes gleaming with fire. Off balance, Dell hoisted the other knife aloft… Another whip cracked around that wrist too, the fate of the machete gone the same way as the other.

Face emotionless, Jane loosened one of her whips from Dell's wrist. She cracked it against the floor, whirled it in the air, and with a snake-like flurry it came for Dell again. Mo's minder tried to move… Too late. The whip coiled around her neck. With a tug and a flick, Jane hauled Dell to the floor.

The guests couldn't believe what they were seeing. A waiter with machetes? The Duchess' prim and quiet assistant cracking whips? All hell broke loose then. People ran for the doors and any other exit they could find to make their escape. Others remained concealed by tables, watching the showdown that escalated into all-out war between the Duchess, Jane and Mo, Dell, Brother Bertie and Ruddy.

And Kristal. It had taken her a while to cotton on to what was going on. When she had, Kristal kept a grim eye on Eddie as she emerged from the car. He still had his arms protectively wrapped about his new wife like he was a modern-day Sir Galahad. This was the father of Mo's child. What a rotten, cheating toerag. Kristal was steaming with outrage.

Kristal got up close and friendly. 'You the Romeo rat who's been interfering with my stepdaughter?'

He gave her a scornful, contemptuous glance, replying in his most haughty lawyer's voice, 'Madam, I haven't got the faintest clue what you're talking about.'

'You're lucky I don't have time to drag your nuts over your face. But I do have time for this.' Without hesitation, she grabbed his front and wrenched him forward, dislodging his protesting wife. She head-butted him on the bridge of his nose. Robbie had taught her how to do that. Strike high and hard.

His bride screamed blue murder as he toppled backwards. Kristal stared down at him with grim satisfaction. The Duchess came after her, but Kristal stayed her with a hand, a warning. 'Strutt your muff somewhere else, granny. You don't want to mix it with me.'

The Duchess screamed, 'Get out. All of you.'

Kristal smartly clapped, catching the attention of their thief woman and their inside woman. 'Time to clear out, ladies. We don't want to outstay our welcome if the plod show their face.' The meaningful arch of her brow reminded them that what their original reason for being here was to rob the Duchess.

The women bundled into the getaway car, which, surprisingly, was still roadworthy. Kristal drove them hell for leather out of there. Mo had no idea that it was the start of one of the longest, darkest day and night of her life.

Chapter Twenty

'You nicked those jewels before I got there,' Mo accused Kristal. She raised the small hammer in her hand and smashed the driver's window of the getaway car.

The industrial park where they were was deserted. It was located in an out-of-the-way spot on the outskirts of London. They had driven straight here after leaving the botched heist job and the mayhem and revelations at the Duchess' grandson's wedding reception. Dell was in another locale ensuring all evidence remained gone for good.

Mo stepped back, allowing Kristal to pour lighter fluid inside the car. Mo's accusation instantly got Kristal's back up as it was meant to. Kristal sent her stepdaughter a look so sharp it could cut throats. And cautioned, 'You don't wanna go down that road, babes. There's only one thing waiting for you at the end – a car crash. Me at the wheel and you under them.'

Mo knew she should probably reel it back. Consider what she was saying. In fact, wait until she got inside the four walls of her home to logically work it out. But she couldn't get rid of the words marching through her head.

Someone betrayed me! Someone betrayed me!

Mo wouldn't let up, her voice turning bitter. 'Who else would it have been? Apart from Dell, you're the only other person who knew about the job —'

'So let me get this straight. Just in case I'm a right thicko and don't get it.' Kristal threw the fluid can in the car and twisted to face Mo, levelling her with a look of glacial disdain. 'I tea-leafed the sparklies in that safe all on my tod. I somehow climbed up that building, stuffed my graceful rounded hips into that chimney and had the lot away.'

Breathing through clenched teeth, Mo stalked over, handing the other woman a firework. 'You've hated me since the day you found out that Robbie was my dad.'

Kristal snatched it, her face burning red. 'I'll tell you what I thought when I heard it: Ole Wandering Wanker Willy Robbie has been at it again. What surprised me was there weren't more of his bastards taking up air out there.'

Mo was furious. 'You want to watch your bloody mouth before I do something about it.'

'Oh yeah!' Kristal volleyed back, pitch-perfect. 'Move out of the way, you dozy bint.'

Kristal lit the firecracker and chucked it inside the car. Both women ran back as the flames spread and lit up the vehicle. They took refuge in another car and watched, the tension between them at boiling point. The flames were soon licking through the car and then with an almighty roar it burst into a ball of fire.

The job of torching their getaway vehicle done, Kristal turned to the young woman, an irate finger pointed in her face. 'You keep blowing it outta your rear-end about me resenting you. But do you know what? The truth is it's the other way around. You resent me.'

Mo cast her a deep dirty look. 'That Botox you keep stiffening yourself up like a corpse with must be leaking into your brain. Resent you? You're having a laugh.'

Kristal's bitch buttons had been well and truly pressed. 'You couldn't hack the fact that your father already had a family. A family that you weren't part of. That it was *my* house he came back to every day. *My* bed he slept in at night. *My* face he saw every morning at brekkie...'

Her harsh words went on and on until Mo thought her mind was going to go the same way as the car, explode. A sudden wave of choking emotion squeezed and rushed up her body. She tried to control it but couldn't.

'You're a friggin' liar.' She raised her fist like she was about to pummel Kristal to a pulp. But her hand stalled, wavering in the air. Abruptly she collapsed against her stepmother, crying wretched tears against her shoulder.

Kristal's mothering instincts kicked in. Fiercely, she hugged Mo. 'Cry it out, babes! Let that poison go!'

''Ere, have a slug of this. That will put the stuffing back into you.' Kristal handed Mo a small glass of Hennessy.

Kristal sat beside Mo in a lounger by the indoor pool in her large mock-Tudor six-bed, twin-garage house in Hertfordshire. Along with her son, this house was her pride and joy. Stuff those who called it naff – behind her back, of course! – with its chunky Italian-style furniture, huge framed photos of her and Robbie and Damien, leopard-print wallpaper and bubble-gum-pink sofa. As far as Kristal was concerned, in this life you should go for what *you* wanted not what others said you should. Besides which they were all rank jealous.

Kristal asked, 'Are you going to keep the baby?' She didn't hold back. 'After Lord Whore-Whore had had his fun I wasn't sure you'd want any reminders of him around.'

Mo bit her lips, horrified by what Kristal had put out there, plain and simple. Scrape her baby out of her womb? Was Kristal going cray-cray? No how! No way! It wasn't her baby's fault she had a cheating dipshit for a biological father. A child should never, ever be blamed for the behaviour of its parents. A child is an innocent soul looking for and giving love. Mo heard her mother's words on the day of Robbie's memorial: *'I cherished you from the first day I knew you were growing in my belly.'*

That's how Mo felt about her baby. She would love and cherish it with every fibre of her being. Mo's chest trembled with a shattering breath. 'I'm going to bring my child up to be good and strong.' She pressed her hand possessively to her belly. 'It's not the little ones fault it's got a bloody cheating lying toerag for her a father.'

Kristal breathed a sigh of relief that Mo was going to keep that baby. Not that she would diss her if she didn't – her body, her choice – but in Kristal's book a kid should never pay for the sins of their parents.

Mo sat back and swallowed her drink. 'Y'know what hurts me most of all? That I've ended up a carbon copy of my mum, having a baby with a married man whose kicked me to the kerb.' Her gaze gleamed. 'I swore that wasn't going to happen to me. That I'd have the oh-so-perfect family. The best guy on my arm. The most gorgeous kids. All living happily ever after.'

Kristal eased back too, considering the right words to say. She remembered what it was like being a young girl, gushing with big dreams. The problems with dreams were you walked around with your head so far in the clouds you didn't see the pitfalls and traps up ahead. Especially girls, there were so many deep holes waiting for them to fall through.

'That baby is your family,' was what she eventually said; this was not the right time to be telling Robbie's daughter what an A-plus cake she'd been. 'Together you will work it out and find your happy ever after.' She paused before softly adding, 'So where did you meet the Duchess' grandson?'

The whole story poured out of Mo. Then, 'Not that long ago he took me to his grandmother's club. Of course I never knew they were blood family. The geezer was behaving so weirdly I should've sussed something was fishy. But I was stuck, starry-eyed in La-La-Love Land where Eddie could do no wrong.'

'What are you going to do about him?'

Mo knew exactly what Kristal referred to. Revenge? Break the bastard's legs? Sort his willy out so it could do no more wrong ever again? Make him disappear?

'I am not going to touch a hair on his deceitful head,' Mo finally answered. 'Y'know why? I don't want to give numbnuts the satisfaction of thinking I cared about him.

That he wrecked my heart.' Her next words were spoken with fiery conviction. 'But I tell you this: that bellend ain't coming anywhere near my kid.'

Mo knocked back the last of her drink and said, 'If you weren't the betrayer,' Kristal lifted her brows at that, 'then who was?'

'Dell.' Kristal didn't hesitate. 'She was our inside woman. Being in the club twenty-four-seven gave her the opportunity to get her mitts on the loot. Plus, she was the only other person in on the plans.'

Mo shook her head with conviction. 'Dell would never, *never* double-cross me. Loyalty is her middle name.'

Kristal picked up the brandy bottle and poured herself another. 'Who else could it have been? No one else knew.'

Mo stood and slowly strolled to the edge of the pool. Staring at her watery and wavering reflection, her mind went a mile a minute trying to figure this puzzle out. Who else knew about Robbie's plan? Of course!

Pivoting on her heels, Mo faced Kristal again. 'There are two other people who may know. Benjamin Birdwhistle, that light-fingered ponce of a solicitor. And Sammy Sapphire.'

'Sammy?' Kristal wailed. 'You sure? That doesn't sound like his style.'

Urgently, Mo sat back down. 'But check it out. We asked if he'd be interested in fencing the gear for us, and his answer was he's walking the straight path these days. So it's a no thank you very much from him.'

'Hold up a minute!' Eyes widening excitedly, Kristal

scrambled out of the lounger and bunded into the house. She finally reappeared, clutching a photo in her hand. She shared it with Mo. It was a snap of Robbie, Sammy Sapphire and Benjamin Birdwhistle.

Kristal filled in the blanks. 'It's all coming back to me. Robbie told me that he had the same solicitor as Sammy Sapphire.'

A terse glance passed between the women. Mo said what they were both thinking. 'Birdwhistle and Sapphire have been playing us from the get-go. They've had the loot away under our noses.'

Mo took out Robbie's gun. 'We'll see about that.'

Chapter Twenty-one

'You've been screwing your wife's younger twin sisters,' Solicitor Benjamin Birdwhistle delivered the killer blow with smug relish to the man he spoke to on the phone as he sat in his office.

'You're speaking nonsense.' Ben rolled his eyes at that answer. Of course the double-dipping dick would say that.

Time to put this idiot straight. Benjamin opened the document on the desk in front of him. 'Two years ago you fathered a child of one of your sisters-in-law and paid her hush-hush money to ensure your name didn't turn up on the birth certificate.'

'What do you want?'

Victory achieved, Benjamin smugly smiled. 'It's simple. I give you the documents in exchange for a one-off fee of fifty grand.'

'How do I know you won't keep any copies.'

'You'll just have to trust me.' Trust Benjamin Whistle? You might as well trust your head inside a lion's mouth. He was keeping copies in case any of his *clients* tried any funny business.

'Bastard.'

'No! I think that's the baby you got on your sister-in-law who calls you Uncle Charlie. Good day to you, sir.'

The solicitor slammed the phone down and triumphantly rested back in his chair. Benjamin was as sober as a judge. Up until a few weeks ago, most days he was as pissed as a fart. That had all changed with the very violent visit from that pint-sized punk, Big Mo or whatever her name was. She would never know how she'd done him an all-time favour. The roughing up he'd received at the hands of her goons had shaken him out of the perpetual stupor he'd sunk into feeling sorry for himself.

He realised that he was going about his get-rich-quick venture all wrong.

Sourly, he recalled how it had all kicked off with him being booted out of the law firm for so-called dodgy expenses. Puhleeze! Everyone and the feckin' cleaning lady there were up to their necks in *creative* accounting. He'd been made an example of, possibly because he'd shoved his tongue down the boss' unwilling daughter's throat at the Christmas party. He received a knee in the family jewels and his marching orders. But he didn't leave the firm alone. He left with a number of very interesting documents. Dynamite that certain people would not want to see explode in the light of day.

He started to sell documents on the dark market to the highest bidder. That soon proved a problem. For starters, selling was bloody hard work. Like trying to sell jackets in the leather market in Petticoat Lane to a bunch of vegans. Mo Watson had pounded the other problem into him.

Documents pertaining to well-known criminal types could earn him a massive kicking. Blackmail was now the name of the game. The juicy stuff relating to people portraying themselves as simple, salt-of-the-earth family men and women. It was always the ordinary ones who got up to the most filth. And Benjamin was going to milk them dry.

There had been one tiny balls-up in his brilliant scheme. One of clients hadn't taken too well to finding out her secret of having been a prostitute years before meeting her MP husband was now his secret too. Yesterday word reached him she'd been found hanging in her family's garage. Nasty business. Still, brush it under the rug and move on.

Suddenly, Benjamin looked towards the door of his shabby premises. Was that a noise?

'Is that you, Linda?' He finished with a loud tut, thinking it was his receptionist who had come back because she'd forgotten something. She was doing that a lot lately. When the dosh started rolling in it would be time to put the old bag out to pasture and get a tasty dolly bird in her place.

Benjamin stiffened. There was definitely something out there. Hell! Not those rats again. All the building work being done in Stratford was upsetting nests of the nasty creatures. The handle of the door to his office began turning. It must be Linda.

But it wasn't. The person who stood in his doorway was out of his nightmares.

Petrified with fear, the solicitor froze in his chair. 'What… What…?' His jaw worked; no words came out.

The person calmly closed the door with their gloved hands. 'Been doing a spot of blackmailing, ole Benjy-boy?'

'Me?' he squeaked. 'I swear on the soul of my dead mother I would never do such a thing.'

Benjamin nearly wet himself when his uninvited guest reared large on the other side of the desk. The person glared at him in disgust as if inspecting an insect.

'From what I hear you have no idea whether your ole girl is dead or alive because she skipped out on the family when you were a little nipper.'

Benjamin tried to save himself. 'I know what you want —'

'I don't think you do, Benjy-boy.'

The person advanced towards him. Benjamin shrank in his seat. 'Please…' He held his hand up as if trying to ward off evil.

The person looked put out. 'There's no need for that. We're ole mates, me and you.' They pulled out a bottle of whisky. 'I hear you're partial to a slug of the hard stuff.'

Benjamin knew better than to refuse. Three weeks ago, the booze would've been down his neck in no time at all. But that was the old Benjamin. Gingerly, he placed the opening at his mouth and sipped.

The other person roared with laughter. 'You ain't drinking up at the Queen's tea party.' The laughter dried up, replaced by a harden voice. 'Knock it back. That's it. Down your throat just like that woman whose neck snapped after she hung herself because of the dirt you had on her.'

His visitor moved to stand behind him.

The lairy group of lads who thought they were all that and a bag of chips were prancing and preening for all they were worth at the bottom of the stairs that led to Birdwhistle & Son's Solicitor's. Mo's back teeth ground together. She was so not in the mood for any argy-bargy. She was dead on her feet, sheer will and rage keeping her upright. She was here in Stratford to knock Benjamin Birdwhistle's block off if he'd betrayed her. Had he been plotting all this time behind her back with Sammy Sapphire?

One of the boys was holding forth about charges he was facing. 'So I says to my solicitor, how can it be assault when I was acting in self-defence? Right? And he says to me, you chased the bloke down the street with a length of lead pipe. That ain't self-defence, bruv, that's assault. So I says, yeah, and if the bloke don't pull the charges, I'll be chasing him again and I'll do a better job next time.'

They all creased up.

Mo kept it nice 'n' polite. 'Excuse me.'

Motormouth turned from his friends. 'What's up, shorty?'

Mo didn't blame the boy for giving it the big I am in front of his friends. He was only young. 'You're in the way. I'd like to go up the stairs.'

The youth shrugged. 'I was here first so you'll have to wait. These boys are my legal team and we're having a consultation.'

There were sniggers and snickers. Mo knew she'd have to pull rank but she gave him once last chance. 'Well, move it down the road a bit.'

The youth leaned menacingly forward. Jabbed his grubby finger in Mo's face. 'Are you deaf? Go and play with the other six dwarves and come back later.'

Her gramps, Brother Bertie, had a saying: *If you can't hear you must feel.* Mo walked a few yards down the pavement and picked up a street bin. The boy didn't see her walk up from behind. Mo turned the bin upside down over his head before pushing him into the gutter. She glared at his friends who all backed off. The dazed boy, covered in fag ends, used tissues, the dregs of tin cans and other unsavouries struggled to his feet.

Mo pushed him over again. 'Size isn't everything, cowboy. You're lucky I'm in a good mood. But if I see you again, I might not be. Remember that.'

Mo stopped up short when she found the door of the solicitor's open. No lights were on inside. A heavy chill walked up and down her spine. Mo quieted her quickening breathing. If someone was inside, other than birdbrain Birdwhistle, the last thing she needed was to be heard. Soundlessly, she pulled on her gloves, took out Robbie's gun and pushed back the door. Raising her shooter to eye level, she stepped inside. Settled into her shooter's stance, knees always flexible, ready to shift positions fast. Mo used her gun to check every corner of the reception office.

The place had been turned over. Furniture was upended, the desk lay on its side, papers strewn everywhere. Mugs were smashed on the floor alongside the kettle. A robbery would explain the open door. Cautiously, Mo proceeded forward, one silent step at a time towards Birdwhistle's private office. Deep breath. Then she slowly opened the door. She peered into the dark and relaxed.

There was that twat Birdwhistle sitting pretty in his chair. He had his back to her so she couldn't see his face. Her nose wrinkled at the stink. Whisky fumes permeated the air. The empty bottle lay discarded on his desk. *Probably pissed out of his nut.* Was that going to deter her? *Hell to the no!* If she had to dunk this teef's head under water for five minutes straight to sober him up, so be it. Mo hadn't come all this way for no answers.

Shooter put away, she marched purposefully around the desk. As she flipped the chair to face her, she told him how it was going to be. 'All right, sunshine, it's time for some — '

Robbed of breath, Mo stumbled back so quickly she nearly tipped over. Birdwhistle's head was cocked at an unnatural angle. A vicious red line cut a circle into his throat. His eyes were open. Flat. Dead. Staring at nothing. The shock of it forced the air to leave Mo's body in short, harsh spurts. Self-consciously touching her tummy. It scared her that her baby would be present at such a gruesome scene.

She whispered, 'Close our eyes, little one. Close your eyes.'

It was in that instant, standing not far from where a man had been strangled, that Mo questioned herself about having a child in the criminal world.

What terrible things will they see? Will they witness you hurting people? People hurting you? You bloody and dying in front of their eyes?

Mo crushed each question. She didn't have time for that

now. *Don't forget your ambition is to be the Queen of Crime.* Mo collected herself. Searched the room. It had been turned over like the reception room. Was that what happened here? Birdwhistle was murdered during an attempted robbery? But what was there to rob? More importantly, that was worth a man's life?

She walked over to the table and looked down at the whisky bottle. It was an expensive brand that was well out of Birdwhistle's price range.

This was no simple robbery gone wrong. But was it connected to the heist?

Chapter Twenty-two

Jimmy Southpaw calmly stood on the street watching the light on in his office on Commercial Road. Someone was in his HQ. No one went into his place without his say-so. And that's why Jimmy was calm. Whoever his evening visitor was wasn't scared of him. In fact, this person would have cleverly used the many eyes and ears Jimmy had stationed on his manor to ensure that word reached him that someone had come a-calling. There was no motor outside to indicate who it might be. No matter. Jimmy was tooled up if this was an ambush. Sidney wasn't far, waiting in the car if Jimmy needed him.

Jimmy walked across the road. Opened up and went inside. Trouble. That's the smell that smacked him in the face. The air was ripe with it. His days boxing in the gym as a young lad had given him a seventh sense about trouble. He cast his eyes into the dark gloom, searching for anything out of the ordinary, anyone concealed in the shadows waiting to pounce. Nothing. Which could only mean trouble waited upstairs. Upstairs, Jimmy didn't miss a beat opening the door of his office. And who he found inside was an old foe he'd never wanted to clap eyes on again.

Callous. Cruel. Cold-hearted. Ice-cold beautiful. Each one fit the woman sitting behind his desk, predictably in his chair, to a T. The Duchess. Queen of West London's Underworld. Her team of minders were two toughs with significant muscle.

'Well, well, well, if it isn't my old friend, Her Ladyship.' Jimmy's words were sarky to the hilt accompanied by a mock bow. 'I see you left your pitchfork outside. I hope someone is minding shop down there in Hades while you're away? Take a seat – oh, I see you already have.'

The metallic, red catsuit the Duchess wore fit every curve and crevice in her body so well it looked like liquid scarlet had been poured over her. Her braless nipples pebbled against the front. She made a big show of crossing her long elegant legs and removing a tendril of hair from her eyes.

Her plummy voice dripped with contempt. 'Same old Jimmy Southpaw, I see. No manners. No class.' Her gaze did a disdainful sweep of the room. 'Honestly, Jimmy, I've got heels with higher standards than you. And you can be sure if I ruled Hades, there'd be no misbehaviour of any sort, in the same way that I rule London and there's no misbehaviour of any sort on my patch. I'm sure we can agree on that?'

Jimmy came right back. 'Misbehaving, like killing your ole man?'

She just smiled at that one. The rumours were she'd put the Duke in his grave early. By her own hand.

He continued in a more conciliatory manner, 'We might disagree on who's the top banana in the London underworld, but since we have an understanding about our respective *patches*, I see no need for any disputes about *misbehaviour.*' When he got no answer but a cold stare, Jimmy's anxiety added, 'Is there?'

The Duchess tilted her head back slightly, pushing her boobs more fully against the catsuit. 'There's been a theft at my club. A set of family heirlooms were stolen from a safe.'

Immediately, Jimmy thought back to Robbie's robbery plan, the one he'd forbidden. Jimmy was a prize fighter but even he knew better than to take on an undefeated heavyweight champion, especially one who could punch below the belt like the Duchess.

'I'm sorry to hear that. Still, I've no doubt you're a friend of the Chief Commissioner and the boys in blue are already belting around town with their blues and twos flashing. I'm sure the poor bollocks will be in the slammer soon before you can say diamond ring. If that's it, why don't you flap those bitch wings of yours and Pan Am it back across the river.'

The Duchess said nothing. She was the mistress of the ominous silence. She looked around the room and then back at Jimmy. 'I don't need any help from the constabulary. I fight my own battles, as well you know.'

Oh, he knew her, all right. Long before she had become some snooty-snob with a title. The Duchess had started life as Rita Evans from Stepney. The seventh child in a family of ten kids living in the basement rooms of a ramshackle, damp Victorian terrace that either the council should have done up or been condemned years ago. The family had been known as the Wild Bunch. Always up to one thing or another. Their mother had done her best to enforce some order and discipline but when it became clear she was losing the battle she took refuge in a bottle of Mother's Ruin and never resurfaced.

The only one who'd escaped the moniker, the Wild Bunch, was Rita. She was a stunner, always careful with how she was turned out. Her and Jimmy had stepped out for a time, attracted by both the sex and the crime. What a buzz they'd got from stealing and running rings around authority. Until she dumped him. Jimmy was to learn the hard way that Rita Evans was only loyal to one person – herself. Her looks were her meal ticket out of the East End. Soon she was parading around the West End. A companion was what she called it, more like a paid-up member of the flesh trade others had sworn blind behind their hands. So what if she had to lie on her back to earn a keep. Better to be doing it with guys plump in the pocket than giving it away for free to lads without a shilling to their name.

A born brawler, she had elbowed and kicked anything and anyone in her way. Rita was ruthless with a capital R. When the word went round that she'd nabbed one of her clients, a real-life duke worth a mint, no one was surprised. She might have gone up in the world, but she used her newfound wealth to create an empire that was way more lucrative than the Steele's. Prostitution, gambling, including racecourses and a West London property portfolio that was valued at more zeros than most people would see in their lifetime. She had crafted and slipped into the role of the Duchess so well, most couldn't even remember her real name. And those that did knew to keep it to themselves. Except for Jimmy.

The Duchess shifted forward. 'I know who took my precious gems.'

'Oh, yeah.' Jimmy played it casual, but he clenched up with fear.

'Your granddaughter. Goes by the street name of 'Big Mo'. I've caught her twice at my club 'casing the joint' as you oiks like to say.'

Jimmy was horrified. He tried to brush it off but he couldn't manage it. 'My Mo? You're having a buzz, luv. She wouldn't do that.'

Suddenly the Duchess peered at him, the picture of concern. 'There's something, right there, just at the corner of your mouth.'

'What?' Instinctively, he rubbed a finger at his mouth.

'Bullshit,' she spat. 'I'm not going to waste words on you. I'm only going to give you fair warning. If I don't get my gear back, you can forget about inviting Big Mo to your Christmas party this year because she won't be available.' Another ominous silence. 'Or for any future ones.'

Jimmy stormed over to the table and leaned on it. The veins in his forearm popped and corded with fury. The Duchess' protection rushed forward. Her raised hand held them back.

Jimmy gritted out, 'You should know better than to threaten me, Rita.'

'Should I?' Her gaze insolently cruised his face. 'Remember the last time I threatened you? I bested you then,

Southpaw, and I'll beat you and your dim-bat grandkid now.'

Jimmy's face flamed just thinking back on it. The last thing he wanted was those uncomfortable memories invading his head. Him and the Duchess had an agreement, and now Mo had unwittingly broken that.

Jimmy stepped back. The Duchess stood to her considerable height and prowled around the table towards him. She sent him a tight, dark smile. And allowed her accent to slip, speaking the lingo of her East End youth. 'Been on the ole Viagra, Jimmy? Because you're a bigger cock than you were in the past.'

'You didn't have a problem with my manhood when we were young.'

She scoffed. 'Manhood? More like senilehood these days.'

Then she surprised him by pushing him into the wall and covering his lips in a long, lingering and deep kiss. She rubbed an expert hand over his crotch. Jimmy suffered through it. She nibbled his neck for a time.

Cockney to the core, she admitted, 'I always had the hots for your neck, Jimmy Steele. Couldn't get enough of it.' Huskily, she blew into his ear. 'I'd frig myself silly at night, creaming and dreaming about sinking my gnashes into your flesh.'

She pulled back from him, slipping back into the Duchess, grinding Rita into the dirt. 'Big Mo has got until nine tomorrow, bright and breezy, to bring back my heirlooms. Tick-tock! Tick-tock!'

The Duchess sashayed towards the door. Before she opened it, she tuned back and said, 'I nearly forgot. This might be a little incentive for Big Mo to move proceedings along.' She took something from one of her men that Jimmy hadn't noticed. She threw it at him.

He caught it, one-handed. Shit! Shit! Shit! Jimmy cursed a blue streak. For him this meant nothing. But for Mo... She was going to lose her mind.

On the heels of the Duchess' departure, Sidney appeared. 'Had a visit from the ghost from the past, I see. Everything above board?'

Jimmy filled him in, finishing on, 'I need to find Mo and get her out of harm's way.'

Sidney looked puzzled. 'But you just said the Duchess gave you a deadline.'

Jimmy's features were grim. 'You and me both know Rita from old. Giving me a deadline isn't going to stop her from hunting Mo down like a dog in the street.' Panting, he added, 'No one fucks the Duchess over and lives.'

Chapter Twenty-Three

1971

If Jimmy Southpaw wasn't yet heading towards the top ranks of London's underworld, then his latest caper meant it was only a matter of time. He and his team had just brought a truck load of Morocco's finest wacky baccy through the port of Dover without getting nicked, and his distribution network was moving it across the city. His main rival in the East End had thrown his hand in and left the country at Jimmy's suggestion. The other big players in town were all treading on each other's toes, talking business with the Southpaw and were now drawing up peace agreements on favourable terms.

And he had his own club these days where he was holding court with his key people celebrating that first big shipment. But he was keeping the bookies he'd formally used as an HQ. He liked it. Kept him connected to the East End.

Jimmy sat around a big table that groaned under the weight of drinks, cigars and ashtrays. All his key people along with some hangers-on and wannabes surrounded him and were trying to make an impression. Everyone knew this was the coming man.

'Drinks are on the house, lads! You all done a good job. London's now safe for aging hippies to smoke stuff at very reasonable rates while listening to their Grateful Dead records. They salute you! So do I! Onwards and upwards! We're going to the top!'

There was laughter, cheers and the clinking of glasses, so much so that at first Jimmy didn't hear a woman shouting, 'Oi! Southpaw! I wanna a word with you!'

When he finally did, it was to find a slim, tall, glamazonian pushing aside two heavies and getting right into his face. Jimmy went a little red. This was his big night. This wasn't in the script at all.

'Wotcha, Rita. Don't remember inviting you? But no matter, why don't you calm down and get yourself a drink? It's a party night and Jimmy Southpaw's meeting the tab. But if you're here touting for work, forget it. There's loads of women out there these days who'll do the business with my lads for nothing. And no disrespect, Reet, but they're in better shape than you are.'

The last was a blatant put-down. Rita Evans was one of the genuine stunners around.

He went to give her a friendly pinch on her cheek, but she smacked his hand away and yelled, 'Were you rude to my friend, Bel, when she needed some help? Did you call her a mangy old tart and push her out of the way in that pub?'

Had he? It was the sort of thing he might have done? 'Dunno. Does it matter?'

'It matters, all right.'

Rita appeared to be vibrating with anger, but Jimmy was too high on his success to take it seriously. 'All right then, when I see her again I'll say I'm sorry. Happy now?'

'No, I ain't. I want you to go over to her place and say sorry now.'

That was too much for Jimmy who rose to his full height. 'Look, luv, you're starting to get on my tits. Who the fuck do you think you are to come in here, my club, and start mixing it on my big night out? Now piss off before I have you chucked in the gutter.'

Jimmy was a successful boxer. He knew all the moves and dirty tricks, legit or not. But he didn't react when Rita threw a right-hander at him because it came so fast, a momentary blur, before her fist hit his face. The onlookers winced as the blow hit home. They could feel it in their own bones how much it hurt.

Jimmy stumbled backwards but stayed on his feet. He spoke but his dazed words came out all wrong. 'Listen…but… to me.'

Another one, this time a flying left that hit his nose so hard it bent inwards. She was like quicksilver, impossible to guard against. You couldn't tell where the thump was coming from. Jimmy went down like a sack of spuds. Rita loomed over him, but his shattered eyesight told him she was hovering above him a dead ringer for a banshee screaming at top volume.

'Come on! Get up and fight like an East Ender!' She goaded.

Nothing would have delighted Jimmy more. But his legs and arms had stopped working and he wasn't quite sure where or who he was.

The image above disappeared with a shout. 'Let that be a lesson to you. Mind your manners in the future.' And a sneering put-down: 'Some gangster you are…'

Two guys helped Jimmy to his feet. He was in a bad way, but even in that state, he knew some urgent damage control was required.

'Help me onto the table, boys.' Jimmy drew breath and did his best as he addressed the revellers. 'Right, people, as you know it's against my principles to hit women, so I let… my lady friend there have her little bit of fun. But it's not against my principles to hit men. And if any man should suggest that incy wincy ruck was anything other than me sticking to my principles or whispering that she duffed me up, they will be getting a visit from me in person to show them what it's like. You've been warned.'

Everybody stayed warned from that day on. Rita might be a different matter.

A week on, Jimmy Southpaw found himself at a brothel. He didn't like going to brass houses. If word got about he had to pay for it then that wasn't good for business. Not that he'd ever do that to his Mini waiting indoors for him. Best lady a man could want. Popular opinion was of the view that only sad sacks who couldn't catch a break with the girls became johns. Obviously Jimmy couldn't allow that perception to get around town; image was as important as shooters in his line of work. But when he got a tip-off that Rita plied her trade at a discreet and deluxe knocking shop in Mayfair, he felt he had no choice but to go along. It was obviously popular with wealthy and well-connected sad sacks. He gave a false name at reception and asked to speak to the madam.

When she appeared, she sat him down on a plush sofa in reception. 'Mr Albert Johns? Welcome to my humble establishment, Mr Johns. Perhaps I can get you a drink and we can discuss what type of company that would refresh and please you for this evening?'

'I'll skip the drink, doll, I'm in a hurry. I'm looking for a woman.'

She did her best to try not to appear confused. 'You've come to the right place. We're well supplied with those.'

'A particular woman. Goes by the name of Rita. I understand she works here?'

The madam's face turned down. 'Rita? I don't believe we have a Rita on our roster.'

She was using a false name, of course. 'Rita' sounded like a charlady rather than a courtesan. 'Perhaps you know her as something else?'

'Describe her for me, if you can.'

Jimmy resented having to admit, through gritted teeth of course, that Rita was rather stunning, leggy, buxom and all the other features that had earned her a gig at a plush outfit like this. Although he couldn't resist adding that she was a bit of a 'mean bird.'

'It sounds as if you mean Sasha, but I wouldn't describe

her as a 'mean bird'. She's a pussy cat.'

'Yeah, I bet she is,' Jimmy muttered to himself.

The madam stood. 'Let me see if Sasha is available.' A seasoned, shrewd expression tightened her features. 'She's very popular so I'm afraid we have a charge… a little extra.'

The madam disappeared to speak with the receptionist. She came back beaming. 'You're in luck, Mr Johns. One of Sasha's companions has had to cancel. He's got to vote in the House of Lords. If you'd like to go up to the first floor, Sasha will be waiting for you in the Pompadour Suite.'

Jimmy took the stairs and knocked on the door of the Pompadour Suite. A sultry, husky, come-hither voice on the other side answered. 'Is that a cheeky boy outside? If it is, he can push open my entrance anytime. As hard as he likes.'

Jimmy rolled his eyes. Talk about tacky! When he went in, it was to find Rita disporting herself on a bright-pink ottoman sofa in expensive silk lingerie. She wore a very tasty jade necklace. The sultry voice didn't last long. ''Ere! What are you doing here? If you think you're getting a shag out of me, you can piss right off. This is a respectable establishment not a joint for plastic hardmen who take beatings from women. Now naff off before I call security.'

Jimmy shook his head. He looked at her not with lust but with disbelief that this slim if well-covered woman could have punched him out. 'I'm here on business but not your kind of business. I've got a proposition for you.'

Rita stood and shook her hair back. She chucked on a very mini dressing gown and lit a Players No.6. 'I don't need any deals from the likes of you, Jimmy. My plans are all ready to rock 'n' roll. Rita Evans is going to the top. A small-timer like you doesn't even figure into it.'

Jimmy examined her perfumes and pomades on a dressing table. 'I can believe it. And I can probably guess what your plan is. No doubt some dopey politician, judge or other worthy is going to come along and offer to take you away from all this by making you his wife? High society beckons, am I right?'

She sucked hard on her fag. 'A girl's gotta do what a girl's gotta do.'

Jimmy nodded. 'True enough. But if a gossipmonger was to spread the word that Lady Fauntleroy used to be a street corner tom, that wouldn't be good, would it? Almost as bad as if an East End gangster was rumoured to have been slapped around by a street corner tom.'

'Now if you were to spread around that the licks you gave me were just a previously arranged act that I went along with. Chuck into the mix I put the frighteners on anyone who mentions your previous employment when you join the smart set, we'd have ourselves a deal.'

Rita burst out laughing with derision. 'Is that what you've been telling people? That the beating you took at my hands was an act?'

Jimmy struggled to control his temper. 'Well, it was an act, you caught me cold.'

'Don't get the nark, mate. You ain't the first bloke I've decked and you won't be the last.' Rita mashed out her smoke and nodded. 'Okey-dokes, that works for me. You've got yourself a deal.' Her hazel eyes glassed over like frozen ice. 'As long as you remember never to cross me in future. I've got the nuts on you, mate.'

Jimmy let out a sigh of relief. They shook hands.

As he left, Jimmy Southpaw checked he had all his fingers after shaking hands with her. The woman gave him the willies. He made a mental note never to cross this woman. She was too unpredictable. Too dangerous.

Chapter Twenty-Four

Hands trembling like crazy, Sammy Sapphire slammed the lid of his bulging suitcase shut. Fear running like a river through him, he was upstairs in the sitting room that his mum had done up and adored. Since she'd passed over to live with the angels two years ago now, he missed her something chronic. However, he might miss her but certainly didn't want to join her, and that's exactly what would happen if he didn't get his arse into gear and get away from here pronto.

His eyes closed with relief when he heard the car engine outside. The cab had arrived. Heaving the case in his hand, he quickly made his way downstairs. The front of the shop was empty. He'd placed all his precious jewellery for safekeeping in a safe deposit box he'd had for many years. His heart beat with sadness. Each and every piece of his jewels was like a friend to him. He loved them with all his heart until he could find the right home for them. The right home being, of course, the person who had the most money to spend. Sammy had always had a love of money. Since the day he'd gone to school with no underclothes and shared two pairs of trousers with his brother, his biggest dream had been to have as much money in the world as possible. You could never have enough of the stuff. Some called him a right greedy bastard, but then again, they'd never had to share a pair of trousers with a brother who was five inches smaller than him.

Dismissing the past, Sammy locked up, went out around the back and made his way up the side street to the cab waiting up front. There was no greeting for the driver, he merely got in the back and instructed, 'The airport, sharpish if you please.'

'In a hurry are you, sir?' came the chatty reply.

Gimme strength! Sammy thought, his features scrunching up in displeasure. *Don't ya just hate a cabbie who can't keep it shut!* Some of them could talk for England. Besides which, Sammy was a secretive sod who didn't like many getting wind of his business. You mind yours and I'll mind mine, was what his mum had bred into him.

The cabbie had different ideas because their motormouth wouldn't give it a rest. 'Where are you flying off to, sir?'

'Timbuktu,' Sammy smartly snapped. 'Which is where you'll end up if you don't keep your eyes on the road and that mouth of yours shut.'

'There's no need to be like that, sir. All you've got to do is tell me you don't fancy a chat.'

Letting out a long-suffering sigh, Sammy didn't answer. Instead, he slumped back, eyes closed, relief washing over him that he had managed to dodge yet another bullet. In five hours' time he would be nicely tucked up in his holiday pad in Portugal, hopefully with that very yummy young man who he'd had a thing with six months ago... He must've drifted off because twenty minutes on he woke with a start. Shifting to sit straight, he quickly glanced outside. And kept looking, squinting in the dark.

Outside didn't look familiar, so he asked, 'What route are you taking to the airport?'

'Are you talking to me, sir?' the cabbie enquired. 'Thought you didn't want me to say anything.'

Sammy's chest puffed up with fury. 'Don't get sarky with me, sonny. Where are we?'

'Never you mind yourself about where we're off to, Mister Sapphire.'

How did the cabbie know his name? Horror crept through Sammy. He jerked forward. 'Who the hell are you?'

'You just relax yourself back and enjoy the scenery.'

Sammy lunged for the door handle. It wouldn't budge. He wrestled with it until the sweat on his palm meant his hand slip away. His body started overheating, his clothes sticking to him.

Terrified, he twisted to the driver. 'Ring the Duchess now and tell her I don't know nuthin'.'

He got no answer. Sammy collapsed back. When the Duchess got her claws on him, he was done for.

Around half an hour later, Sammy was hauled out of the back seat and frogmarched by the driver to the entrance of a back door in an alley. They entered to the sweet, serenading beat of Gnarls Barley's 'Crazy' playing somewhere in the building before it receded as Sammy was heaved down a set of stairs to a dark basement corridor.

'Please,' he pleaded. 'I don't know sod all. And if I did, I wouldn't tell a living soul.'

He wrenched out of the hold and made a run for it. A baton whacked him in the crease of his knees, sending him tumbling onto his face. The driver grabbed his collar and dragged a sobbing Sammy down the corridor, closer to what he knew was his doom. He'd been around long enough to have heard all about the Duchess' basement pleasures, as those in the know called it. His captor reached a door, threw it open and flung Sammy to the floor inside.

Quickly, he raised his head to the Duchess. 'I'm telling you…' His words dried up when he realised it wasn't the Duchess.

'You!'

'You've got the nerve of Beelzebub hisself, to drag me here like I'm fodder for the underworld,' Sammy accused between sips of the glass of fine brandy in his hands.

Big Mo stared at him without compassion. He sat facing her on the other side of her desk. It was Dell who had pretended to be his cab to the airport. Now he'd been taxied to Mo.

Not cushioning the blow, she informed him, 'Benjamin Birdwhistle is dead.'

His hands shook; his gaze skidded away from hers. 'Benny who? The only whistle I know was an antique police whistle that a client commissioned me to hang from a gorgeous, eighteen-carat-gold chain.' A gleam shone in his eyes. 'Now, I could do you one of those up a treat.'

Trying to butter me up like you do your clients! No chance, buster! Mo put the frighteners on him. 'Whoever killed ole Benjy, you know who they'll be hunting next. You!'

Sammy's trembling hand slammed the glass down. 'On my life, Big Mo, I haven't got a clue what any of this is about.'

Mo eased forward. Casually crossed her legs. 'I beg to differ. I know you were connected to my dad and Birdwhistle. This is what I think happened. My dad's out of the picture, so you and the solicitor decided to do the heist. You probably got a pro in to do it. It had to be an outsider; someone no one would know. Probably from Eastern Europe where I hear there are plenty advertising their services for hire.'

'Are you crazy?' He looked genuinely alarmed. 'Steal from the Duchess. I'd rather cut off my arm that's wanting to sin, because let me tell you this for free, she'd be slashing off more than my arm if I ever thought about ripping her off.'

Beneath the table, Mo self-consciously touched her belly as something hit. The Duchess would be her child's great-grandmother. Crikey! The thought of that woman's blood running in her baby's veins made her sick to her very stomach.

Mo pressed on. 'You knew I was going to do a smash-and-grab by way of me and Kristal asking if you'd be our fence. So you and Benjy decided to get there before us. Where did you stash the loot?'

His voice rose. 'Good Golly, Miss Mo, ain't you hearing a word I'm saying? I'd have to have a death wish to cross the Duchess' path.'

'You're in the gems trade and a well-known fence. You'd be the perfect person to hawk those jewels on the never-never market.'

A sour expression curdled his face. He did not like being reminded that he had his hands under the table dealing in stolen goods. 'Hawk?' With a sniff of superiorly he straightened his collar. 'I think you're mixing me up with someone with a stall in Roman Road Market. What I provide is a quality service —'

'If you've got nuthin' to hide, why were you running away with your arse hanging out of your trousers?'

'You see the word 'fool' tattooed here?' He swiped a finger over his forehead. 'Word reached me that some Herbert had turned the Duchess' place over. You and Kristal turned up at my place with my name on Robbie's papers. I put two and two together and was gone.'

Mo asked, 'Is the Duchess that scary?'

'Scary?' His eyes snapped with disbelief. 'Even the Devil does a runner when he sees her coming down the street.' Urgently, he leaned forward, voice low. 'The story goes that she was the one that offed her ole fella, the Duke.'

'She murdered him?' Mo's voice rose; she found it hard to grasp what she was being told.

'Shhh!' Sammy's face was reddening with alarm. He looked plain scared. 'Not so loud. He was a couple of decades older than her. Nevertheless, I heard he still had plenty of vim and vigour in him. Plenty of life. One day he's walking around, bright-eyed and bushy-tailed, the next as dead as a doornail.'

'Was she after his money?'

'And the rest.' He paused dramatically. 'Including, some say, those family heirlooms of his. The tales told about the Duchess are enough to fill a library. Here's another: Years back, when her old fella the Duke was still of this earth, the story goes that two chancers fleeced him for a good wad of cash. They were last seen going into the Duchess' club. The scam merchants were never seen again. Some folk have gone into that club and never come out.'

He carried on. 'Everyone quakes in their shoes when she passes. Even Southpaw knows to give her a wide berth —'

'Granddad Jimmy knows her?' Mo couldn't keep the surprise from her voice. 'But he's not frightened of anyone, so why would he be of her?'

'That's not my story to tell.' Sammy stubbornly clamped his mouth shut.

Mo thought on all that the fence had told her. Did she believe him? That he hadn't betrayed her? She wasn't sure. But if it hadn't been him, why would someone murder Birdwhistle? If everyone and their dog was scared stiff of the Duchess, who would have the nuts to raid her club?

The ring of her mobile cut through her thoughts. 'Hello.'

Before she could hear who it was, her phone cut out. She really needed to get a new one, it had been playing up more or less since day one. Plus, it needed some juice. She'd picked up her jacket, off to Kristal who would want the lowdown on what Sammy Sapphire had to say for himself. Mo looked at the clock, very conscious of the Duchess deadline getting closer.

Chapter Twenty-Five

'Mister Sidney, what can you tell me about whips?' Dell asked at the counter inside the bookies that was also Jimmy Southpaw's HQ.

Her luck was in because she thought that the place would be shut up for the night. Sid squinted, mouth tightening around his cigar at her question. She was lucky to catch him at this hour. He was holding on here in case the Duchess put in a repeat performance. If she did, Sid would tell her to sling her hook. He didn't have good word or memory for that woman. Pure poison, that's what she was.

Delilah and Sid had always got on like a house on fire. She enjoyed the company of the older folks and the stories they told, which she suspected went back to her grandmother having a hand in helping to grow her up in Jamaica. Sid was very secretive about his ethnic origin; the shade of his skin could place him from Morocco to Brazil. Dell suspected his heritage was partly Caribbean because every now and again he kissed his teeth when annoyed.

Back in the day, Sid had once been in demand among the London criminal fraternity due to his knowledge of whips and canes, a speciality of his being that he delivered an eye-watering caning to the soles of the feet.

Apart from a small favour to Mo five years ago, he'd left that world behind, which explained his closed expression.

Dell remained tight-lipped for a few seconds. Then, 'I'm sure you heard what happened at the Duchess' club —'

'That was a bad business what Big Mo did, going against Jimmy like that.' He kissed his teeth lightly. 'He told her to leave it alone and now there's going to be hell and righteous damnation to pay.'

'I figure you've still got connections in that world you were once in. Do you know anything about the Duchess' assistant who is also a bit whip-happy?'

Sid mashed out his cigar in the glass ashtray beside him. Then he instructed Dell to follow him. He took her down into the bowels of the building to a cellar that had been turned into a small office. 'This is my place,' he informed her proudly. 'Where I shut off the noise of the outside world.'

He strode over to a cupboard and when he opened it, Dell gasped. It was filled with whips, chains, and canes. Each was neatly mounted in place.

He winked at her. 'Always like to keep the tools of my former trade handy. You never know when you might need them.'

Transfixed by the deadly contents of the cupboard, Dell inched closer to stand in front of them. A particularly vicious-looking one caught her eye with its braided black leather handle and whip that must have been long because it was coiled many times.

'That's called a bullwhip. The crack of that against the ground and the vibration that ripples up the whip is one of the sweetest sounds on this earth,' Sid explained to her, although as far as Dell was concerned there was nothing sweet about the sound of a whip. 'All people see is something vicious rather than a thing of beauty.'

She snapped out of her trance and pointed to a smaller black whip. 'That's the one she used against me.'

'It's a snake whip.' Before Dell could protest, Sid held her wrist, exploring the circular mark left from the lash of Jane's whip. 'Very clean and precise. The Duchess' girl knows what she's doing.'

Letting her hand fall, he continued, 'The way I hear it is that the Duchess brought back a ten-year-old girl from an orphanage from abroad. Brought her up to be her personal assistant, including having the Duchess' back.' He pulled in a heavy breath. 'Don't know how the girl ended up in that orphanage, but the word was she already had a feel for the whip before the Duchess got her.'

'How do you figure that then?'

Sid's voice hardened. 'I suspect that was no orphanage she grew up in. More likely to be a gang training discarded kids in certain dark arts and then selling the kids off to the highest bidder. Those children have it knocked into them to obey. To never challenge an order they're given.'

His laboured breathing filled the air, and Dell suspected that this was Sid's own story. She didn't press him on that score; everyone was entitled to their secrets.

He carried on. 'The Duchess keeps that girl under her

thumb, total control. She can't draw air or go anywhere without that evil woman's say-so.'

Dell turned from the whips and canes, giving him her full attention. The real reason she had come was Dell was still smarting over the lashing she'd taken from the Duchess' hench girl at the wedding reception. Dell did not take kindly to public humiliation. Or being defeated. Jane, the Duchess' goon-girl assistant, was now a marked woman in her book. When they met in the duelling field again, Dell was determined to be the victor.

She told Sid, 'I want you to train me so that me and my knives can defend ourselves against a whip.'

Nodding, Sid grinned. He took down a medium-sized whip. As he cracked it against the floor, Dell pulled out her machetes.

Get a load of how the other half lives, Dell mentally dissed. She and her familiar rucksack were crouched in the dark behind a parked car, spying on the Duchess' home in Knightsbridge. Located behind Harrods, it was more mansion than house, white with black railed balconies and pretty flowers outside. In order to defeat the Duchess' whip-gal when they next met, Dell wanted to find out as much as she could about her. Night was the best time to find out what made a person tick. In the dark people let their guard down, revealing all manner of things. Dell was rewarded for her patience when the back door opened and Jane appeared. Her glasses were gone, so was the dowdy clothes look, replaced by black trainers, trousers and hoodie top. The classic clothing of someone up to badness and mischief in the night.

Jane flicked her hood up, concealing her face, and set off. Dell followed at a discreet distance. Dell hesitated a few beats when the other woman turned off and went down a cobbled set of stairs that in Dell's opinion could only lead to the sewer. This was getting weird! The stairs were made of old cobbled stones and looked, to Dell at least, like a throwback to Medieval times. Dell hung back. Peered down in time to see Jane knocking on a large door that was tucked away, far back in the shadows. The door opened and she was admitted inside.

Curiosity replaced caution. Dell had to find out what was beyond that door. She stood in front of it. It was broad, arched, dramatically decorated with carved snakes. Curious, she leaned and realised they weren't snakes. They were whips of all different sizes. *What kind of place is this?* Dell pressed the buzzer and waited.

The intercom buzzed on. 'You're not known here.'

Dell took a chance, answering, 'Big Mo and Southpaw send me down. No drama, though. Just getting a feel for the place, you get me?'

That got her in. No one greeted her so she wandered in. And then Dell didn't know where to put her face. Lord have mercy! People were walking around with full S&M gear on. Rubber, harnesses, whips, crops. Dell wasn't ignorant. Nor was she laughing at any of these people; after all, this was their world not hers. She was the intruder here. Plus, each to their consenting-adult own. The thing was, despite being

Mo's muscles and going around with machetes, the truth of the matter was when it came to sexual matters, Dell was very conservative. She had grown up in Jamaica in a household that praised the Lord at an evangelical church on a Saturday. Sex was pretty straightforward. You took you clothes off and did the ting and hopefully had a cracking time. This was outside Dell's comfort zone. Was this why the Duchess' whip-gal came here? To dress up and get her rocks off?

Dell was about to find out when the lights went completely off. The whole place went dark. A hush fell. A figure dressed in black, hoodie concealing their face, walked out on to the stage. Dell just knew it was Jane. She held her breath, wondering what was going on. Techno music started playing, and Jane pulled out two medium-sized whips. Dell had never seen this type of whip before. They were fibre optic, made up of many strands of glowing LED lights. One glowed a startling turquoise blue, the other an electric lilac against the black background. Jane started dancing, rocking her body, dipping high and low, looping and lacing the whips in extraordinary ways around her body: her arms, through her fingers, around her neck, waist, knees. The whips flowed liked liquid colour. Jane's dark clothing blended her into the background, leaving the illusion that the whips were dancing in the air on their own. The crowd looked on, stunned, mesmerised by the display. Dell was hypnotised too. It was simply beautiful. The whips flicking, swirling, swaying, changing colour to red, greens, yellows, until they both resembled rainbow-coloured mysterious creatures of the night.

Dell was astonished. No way in hell had she been expecting this. This woman creating such incredible art was a million miles away from the one who had flayed her wrists and neck with a vicious snake whip. The performance came to an end, and Dell joined in the wild applause. With a quick movement of her hands, Jane stored her whips in her pockets, jumped off the stage and, walking through the clapping crowd, head bowed, walked briskly towards the door.

Dell was on her tail, following until the other woman reached the Duchess' Knightsbridge home. Dell hid from view. She watched as Jane stumbled back when she opened the door, the reason being the Duchess stood in doorway.

Dell shoved her head down but heard what happened next.

'Jane, where have you been? You know you don't go anywhere without my permission.'

Then Dell heard a strange, barely there flicking sound in the air. Dell knew she shouldn't… She raised her head and bit back a cry at what she saw. The Duchess held a crop with which she rained blow after harsh blow down on her assistant. Jane cowered on the floor. What twisted Dell's guts was Jane didn't raise her hands or arms to protect herself. She just allowed the Duchess to beat her into submission.

'Those children have it knocked into them to obey. To never challenge an order they're given.' Sid's theory about the type of place Jane may have come from as child came back to her. It was happening right before her in living colour. Dell felt like storming over there, snatching the weapon and giving

the Duchess what for. See how she liked it. But, of course, she didn't.

The Duchess ground out, 'Don't do it again, Jane. You won't like what I do to you next time.' She chucked the crop on top of Jane and left.

Then jane slowly turned her head and caught Dell's gaze. Startled, Dell froze. The other woman had probably known she had followed her and was here all the time. A strange, electric bond held their gazes. Then Jane broke the connection when she stood. Quietly, she closed the door. Dell remained there for a time. She couldn't get the expression that she'd seen in Jane's eyes out of her head. It was that of a trapped animal who had lost hope of ever being free.

Chapter Twenty-Six

Mo threw her phone at Kristal, who neatly caught it. 'Charge that up. The battery is nearly as dead as a dodo. The phone's been playing up something chronic.'

Kristal countered, 'More like nearly as dead as Benjamin Birdwhistle.'

They were inside the main room of Kristal's flat that she kept in town. It was in Wapping, on the High Street, which was where Mo also lived in a riverfront duplex. The sound of the Thames lapped and surged in the background. The river was rough tonight, matching the mood of both women.

After following her stepdaughter's instruction, Kristal made Mo a strong cuppa with plenty of sugar. Mo looked down into it. 'You got something stronger? I need my battery recharging as well.'

Kristal sat opposite on the zebra-print chaise lounge that had pride of place in the room. She held a glass of her favourite tipple, Campari and soda. Crossing her legs, she cast an arched glance Mo's way. 'None of the rough stuff for you, my girl.' Her gaze dropped pointedly at Mo's tummy. 'You've got a little 'un in there who needs proper nourishment. You don't want her first words to be 'boozer'.'

Kristal swivelled her drink in the bottom of her glass before taking a sip. 'You don't think Sammy Sapphire killed Birdwhistle.'

Mo rested back, her mind switching gear. 'I don't know the geezer, but I got the impression he was telling the truth —'

'Truth?' Kristal squealed contemptuously. 'Take the word of a bloke who's got sapphires drilled in his pearly whites? Not on your life. I wouldn't believe the garbage coming outta his gob in a million years.'

'You've changed your tune about him from earlier.'

'Yeah, well, I've had my thinking cap on since then.'

Mo shook her head. 'You didn't see the sheer terror when he talked about this Duchess bird. You didn't see the fear of God change the colour of his eyes. Looked about ready to have a coronary.'

Forehead furrowing, Mo tagged on, 'I feel like I'm missing something.'

Some sensation, feeling, *something* had been plaguing her. Something was up here. Didn't feel right. Mo couldn't put her finger on what it was. Each time she reached to catch it, it vanished.

Kristal's voice pulled her back into the room. 'It's not going take that ole aristo boiler long to figure out that the woman making noise at her grandson's wedding is the same one who stuck her snout in her safe.'

'But it was gone. I never took nuthin,' Mo exclaimed. 'Some light-fingered chancer already had the back of the safe off and waltzed off with the goodies.'

Kristal set her glass carefully on the side table. 'I believe you. She won't. So here's the deal. I reckon the Duchess didn't know someone had had her crown jewels away. Now she does, she's going to point the finger at you. First off, she caught you having a snoop in the room where she keeps the safe. Second, one of her likely lad staff are bound to swear on their life they saw you in the vicinity of the roof.'

Mo tensed up. 'You saying —'

'She's coming after you.'

All of a sudden, Kristal went rigid, her body on high alert. She placed the pad of her finger against her lip, indicating that Mo should stay schtum. Her stepdaughter scowled back, confused. Kristal pointed her thumb in the direction of the hallway. Mo still didn't... Then she heard it. The lock of the front door turning. Mo reached for her shooter, but Kristal's flat palm in the air communicated to her to stop. Instead, it was Kristal who took out her EDC – Everyday Carry – gun from her bag. A 9mm semi with fifteen lethal rounds.

Kristal kicked off her heels. She made her way to the closed doorway of the room they were in on feet that silently sank into the deep, soft carpet. The creak of the front door reached them. The intruder was inside. Kristal made it the left side of the wall flush with the main room's door. Mo didn't need her to be told what to do. Equally as quiet, she flattened her body against the wall on the other side of the door. Strange noises came from the hallway. Grunts and smacking sounds.

Mo leaned over. Wrapped her hand around the handle.

One. Two. Three. She flung the door back, and Kristal jumped out, shooter at the ready. And shouted at two figures in the hall, 'Hit the floor or your head will be Jackson Pollocked all over the fucking walls.'

The two figures seemed to be entwined against a wall. One screamed, while the other leapt back and turned.

'Mum?'

Kristal and Mo breathed a hefty sigh of collective relief. Damien. And he had company. A very tall, leggy brunette with enough slap on to do out the counters in Selfridges.

His mum stalked up to him. 'What are you doing here? You're meant to be in Spain.'

He explained, 'Uncle Nico had to come back pretty lively.'

'Why?' That was Mo.

Damien shrugged. 'Dunno.' A silly smile took over his lips. He turned to the woman with him. 'Then again, I wouldn't have met Wanda at the airport on the way back.'

Wanda giggled and flicked back her hair. 'Instant love, weren't it, Dam.'

Instant love, is it? Kristal rolled her eyes. Mo gently manoeuvred Damien into the main room while his mum got her bag. And slipped her son's new lady friend a bundle, which was snatched with a satisfied smile. Kristal showed her the door with a 'Now, instant love off.'

'What did you go and do that for?' Damien moaned inside the lounge. 'Me and Wanda were having a fun time.'

Kristal thinned her lips. 'Wanda is probably called Wendy and works freelance in the airport lounge.' She came over to him and playfully pinched his cheek. 'My boy deserves true love.'

Mo looked on. Her stepmother was a hard nut except when it came to her boy. She overindulged him and wouldn't hear a cross word about him. She might not have changed but her son had. Damien stepped back from his mum and flexed his shoulders. Since his Uncle Nico had come into his life he had started cutting his apron strings from his mum. Manning up. *Is that going to be me with my child?* Mo wistfully wondered.

After Damien had gone up the spiral stairs to his room upstairs, Mo gulped down her tea and told Kristal, 'I've still got to find out who stole the Duchess' stash. Who betrayed me. Or found out about the heist.'

As Mo unplugged her charged phone, it pinged. Voicemail. Granddad Jimmy.

'Get to the shop now. Don't stop for anyone or anything.'

The shop was his HQ on the Commercial Road. Granddad Jimmy sounded concerned and like he was about to flip his lid. It put Mo back on edge.

On the street, the manic screech of car wheels jerked Mo out of her preoccupied thoughts. Her eyes widened at the sight she saw. Right there, on Wapping High Street, a shrieking white van without number plates was heading straight at her. A woman walking with her dog screamed a warning. The shock of it held Mo immobile. The car was getting closer, getting bigger. It's headlights swallowing her in its glare, almost blinding her.

Move! Move!

Mo didn't. Then she remembered. It wasn't only her safety she had to think of anymore. She had her unborn baby. The car mounted the pavement the exact time Mo's body curved into a dive roll. This was her favourite gym move because it operated as three fluid movements. Over she went, legs in the air, upside down on the palms of her hands. The muscles of her arms absorbed the force of movement. Then she went head over heels. Lastly, she rolled into a fluid motion that propelled her to her feet.

Then Mo ran. And ran. The fast sound of chasing feet behind soon joined her here. Mo ducked and dived into the side streets of the area she knew so well. This was her manor, so she knew that Wapping was a maze of cobbled side streets, some cast in deep shadow that hadn't much altered since the Victoria era. All she had to do was get to Granddad Jimmy's HQ in the betting shop on the Commercial Road.

There were two ways of doing that. By foot or by train. The preferred and quickest option was train. Wapping Tube station to Whitechapel via the East London Line. However, if she went underground her pursuers could have her trapped down there. And the platform in Wapping was too narrow to run along. She'd probably end up going overboard and getting electrocuted on the tracks.

So the road it was. Her goal was to reach Wapping Gardens. Get over The Highway into Shadwell. Blast through Watney Street to reach Commercial Road. Mo kept going until she reached The Highway and that's when she felt someone gaining on her. Getting closer. Their heated breath frosted against the back of her neck. Large fingers clawed into her shoulder and dragged her down. Her attacker's face looked like it was made of lumps of stone, his expression dark and dangerous, ready to do her harm.

Mo kicked him in the goolies. Street fighting was all about motion and movement and never stopping. Even when someone held you tight you kept kicking and punching, fighting with everything you had for your very life. As Mo scrambled away she let out a loud groan of pain as something scraped along her arm. Whatever it was she didn't have time to deal with it. Her mind beat to the rhythm of a single phrase.

Get to Granddad Jimmy's. Get to Granddad Jimmy's.

Gasping, legs almost cramping, Mo flipped her hoodie up. Finally made it to the betting shop on Commercial Road. The lights were on in Jimmy Southpaw's office upstairs. Mo used her key to get in. Inside she leaned heavily against the door, drawing in air. Smile quivering on her mouth, she warmed her hand over her stomach. 'We made it. We're safe now.'

Mo pushed off the door and headed for the stairs. Shrouded in the dark, she took the first step. And stopped. Something cold touched her head. Just below her ear. The barrel of a gun.

Chapter Twenty-Seven

Mo froze at the cold press of metal of the shooter against her skin.

The gunman growled, 'State your business or I'm going to blast you to kingdom come.'

Mo carefully replied, 'Granddad Jimmy?'

A hand yanked the hoodie from her head and spun her around. It was him. Mo had never been so pleased to see her grandfather in her life. But the feeling wasn't reciprocated; he didn't look pleased to see her one bit.

He leaned down into her, breath seething and hot. 'What the crap have you been playing at?'

'Dunno what you're going on about.'

He'd drummed into her one of the basic rules of the criminal life was to admit nothing. Let those pointing the accusing finger show you their hand.

'The bloody blag,' he roared. 'You promised me that you would leave it alone. You lied to me.'

Mo knew there was no denying it. 'I had to do it.'

Jimmy waved his finger and huffed, struggling to hold the full force of his temper back. His rage was a frightening sight to behold. Veins bunched and corded in his neck, muscles ticking in his cheek and those famous arm muscles of his bulging to breaking point.

'You know what impressed me the most about you, doll?' he roughly told her. 'You were a listening, just like Robbie. When they were growing up, Harry was always kicking off, impulsive, doing shit before thinking, usually leading to all sorts of ructions.'

A gentle smile tugged his lips. 'Robbie was so different. He'd sit at my knee and really listen. Always had so many questions he'd drive me doolally sometimes with them.' He caught her gaze. 'I understand that you've got to carve out your own path, go your own way, do your own thing, but when I give you a choice piece of advice there's a reason for it.'

'I had to do it. For him,' Mo practically shouted.

Confusion marred Jimmy's brow. 'Who?'

'Robbie.' Her father's name drove out of her with a shrieking strength. How could a man have so much power over her from the grave? 'When I sussed what he'd been planning to do I realised that I could do it. Carry out his last big job.'

Suddenly the real truth struck her. 'When I was young, I was always dreaming about what my dad looked like. What his name was, where he lived. Did he have a family? Another little girl like me? Then when I found out that my dad was Robbie he had a name, a face, a family. The trouble was, I still hadn't seen him in the flesh. Held his hand. Kissed his cheek. Got to know the ins and outs of his face. Hear his laugh. Carrying out his last big job was something special that I could do for him. I want Dad to feel proud of me.'

Jimmy clenched up. He watched the shadow and play of different emotions cross her face. He felt for her. But he gave his granddaughter another truth. 'Trying to live up to the expectations of a parent when they're living is hard enough. Doing it when they're dead is a losing battle. Y'know why? They will never be able to pat you on the back because they're dead. And gone.' He touched her shoulder. 'My Robbie would be so proud of you. He'd have loved you from here to Mile End Road —'

'Only Mile End?' Mo cheekily chipped in, a twinkle in her eye. 'That's only down the road.'

After a chuckle, Jimmy got back on with business. 'The Duchess has paid me a visit. You've got until nine tomorrow morning to deliver her jewels back to her.'

The pieces started to fit into place. Kristal had been right. The Duchess was coming after her. So the toughs who had been lying in wait in Wapping had been courtesy of the that feckin' woman.

Mo told her grandfather, 'I admit to doing the heist… All the way to the empty safe.'

The storm stirred back up into her granddad's eyes. 'Are you making a mug out of me?'

Mo wasn't having that. Not even from one of the men she most revered in this world. 'I broke a promise to you once, and I put my hands up about it. I've explained once I didn't nick those jewels. And I don't expect to have to say it again.'

Jimmy nodded his approval. The baton of head of the family empire had well and truly passed to Mo. And he'd better not forget it.

'You're the only mugshot in the Duchess' book. She's coming after her jewels which means she's coming after you.'

Mo swayed slightly. 'I'm going to have to hit the streets and find out who has got the loot and where they've stashed it. All before the morning.' As her head came back up a wave of dizziness assailed her. The walls around started to move. Somehow Mo didn't think this had anything to do with the baby.

'Mo,' her grandad warned as she swayed.

Somehow, she gripped the railing and sank heavily onto a step, panting. Her head fell forward.

'What's that blood on your arm?' Jimmy urgently asked.

'What blood?' Her head was foggy.

Her grandfather hunched down near her. The sleeve of her trackie top was dark and sticky. Gingerly he rolled the material back. He sucked in his breath.

'You've been stabbed.'

'Will you put me down,' Mo insisted firmly. She rolled her eyes.

But her Granddad Jimmy wouldn't hear of it. His mouth stubbornly tightened as he continued carrying her up the stairs to his office. When they got there, Mo was shocked to find someone else inside. Nico.

'What are you doing here?'

'Bloody damn! What happened?'

Their questions came out at the same time. Nico was on his feet in a flash, the colour draining from his face. With the greatest care, Jimmy eased her down to his chair and placed her arm on the table.

He asked, 'This was a hello from the Duchess, I take it?' Mo's curt nod confirmed his suspicions. 'There's a doctor I've got on retainer —'

'No time.' Mo waved his suggestion away. 'It's not that deep. We're operating against the clock here. We need to find the Duchess' stash or whoever took it before her deadline. Granddad, get the first-aid kit.'

Grimly, Jimmy left the room. Nico was next to Mo in an instant. Tenderly, he held her hand in the warmth of his. Mo so wished that Nico was her man. Then she'd be able to rest her head against his chest now.

He teased, 'Dell took you for a target, did she?' His trademark humour was one of the things she adored about him. Tone serious, he said, 'You should've steered clear of that headcase, the Duchess. King Ted told me two things about her. Never walk on the same side of the street as her. And never look her in the eye.'

The day's events started catching up with Mo, the emotion washing over her. 'I messed up. Big time.' Her voice quivered.

'You can sort the Duchess out with one hand tied behind your back.'

Mo forlornly shook her head. 'I'm sure you heard me talking to Granddad Jimmy downstairs, so you will know that I stupidly tried to rip the Duchess off.'

His brief nod confirmed that he had. 'But that's not what you're trying to tell me now. What else is going on?'

'I got tangled up with the Duchess' grandson. Turns out to be Rat Number One.' Despite the huge breath she took her voice came out so small she didn't even recognise it. 'I'm going to have a baby.'

For the first time that day the full enormity of all that had happened struck Mo with the devastating impact of an express train. The tears fell and lashed her face. He leaned over and kissed her on the cheek, the touch of his flesh providing the warmth she needed.

Mo desperately cried, 'Why did he make me open my heart to him? Why do people do that? Eh? Cast a spell over you and then wander off leaving you holding a thing called love that's not warm and heady no more but gooey and nasty.'

'Forget the scumbag.' His command was super gentle. 'He's trash. He don't deserve a queen like you.' He kissed her other cheek. 'And do you know something else? You're going to be the best mummy in the world.'

Jimmy's reappearance cut short their intimate discussion. Taking the first-aid box, Nico carefully cleaned her wound. Then took out a small tube of special glue which he used to stick the ragged edges of her wound together. His finger passed over her wound like a caress.

As Nico worked, Jimmy casually asked, 'How's your mum these days?'

That provoked a sharp look from Nico to Jimmy. Mo was bemused. Her mother hated Granddad Jimmy with a passion, and he was indifferent to her. She answered his odd question. 'She's up north with some mates for a couple of weeks, chilling and pampering.'

That funny look travelled between the men again. Mo dismissed it and knocked back a couple of painkillers.

Her Granddad Jimmy laid something on the table. 'Along with her deadline, the Duchess left this with me. In her words, she wants it to get you to hurry along proceedings.'

Mo cried out with dismay. It was Brother Bertie's walking stick. He never went anywhere without it. Mo lovingly caressed it. The last place she had seen him was at the wedding. This could only mean one thing – the Duchess was holding Gramps. *She's got Gramps. Got Gramps.* In a frenzy, Mo tried to stand, but her other grandparent wouldn't have it. He placed an insistent hold on her shoulder, pushing her back down.

'Rest up, doll. That West End bitch can wait. Get some kip for an hour. When you wake up we'll figure this all out.'

Mo closed her eyes until they left the room, then punched them back open. Teeth gritted, she tested the flexibility in her arm. Not too bad. More sore than pain. She headed for the door and was surprised to hear Nico and Granddad Jimmy speaking. Quick, low whispered words. She caught snatches of their conversation. *Spain… Villa…. Shootout… Documents to show you… Precious.* What? Did she just hear her mum's name? Mo listened more intently. Nah! She must've heard wrong. Then again, hadn't Granddad Jimmy just asked after her mum? Mo couldn't work it out. That strange feeling that something else was going on here nipped at her heels again. What was it? Mo thrust it off.

Besides which she didn't have time to hang around to find out. She suspected that Jimmy was going to stop her from doing anything. She'd made an almighty mess of things. There was only one place where she could figure it all out. Quietly, she walked across the room. Pulled up the window. Then shimmered down the building. Mo disappeared into the night.

Chapter Twenty-Eight

The Duchess' emerald-green stilettos clicked-clacked against the grainy stone stairs, moving with the briskness of someone with business to attend to. Bad business. At the end of the lead in her hand was a disgruntled and sleepy-eyed Arthur. Jane followed meekly behind as usual. Duchess reached the bowels of the building. Not many people ever saw this part of the Sixes and Sevens Gentleman's Club. Here the gloss and glitz were nowhere to be seen.

The Duchess stopped outside the large cellar door. She hesitated before going inside, instead casually turning to her assistant. 'I want to thank you for what you did earlier at the wedding reception.'

Jane dipped her gaze. The rule was she never looked the Duchess in the eye. 'I am pleased that you approve, Duchess.'

The younger woman nearly jumped when the Duchess placed a slender finger under her chin. Her nail dug into the younger woman's skin. Voice as icy as the North Sea, she said, 'What I don't understand is why you didn't lash the bitch to a bloody mess in front of everyone.'

Jane swallowed. 'I didn't... You would...' When the Duchess made her this nervous, Jane's command of English sometimes fled. She sucked in a thin funnel of air and started again. 'Your grandson's wedding was so perfect I did not want to spoil it with blood.'

The Duchess swiftly slapped her face so hard it viciously snapped to the side. There were no tears in Jane's eyes. She'd long ago learned not to cry. Jane bowed her head. Arthur let out a high whine.

The older woman told her, 'The spilling of blood is sometimes the most beautiful thing.'

'Yes, Duchess.'

Dismissing Jane, the Duchess turned her attention back to the door. 'Now, for my guests.'

The cellar they entered was cavernous and dingy with bare brick walls that were stained white from years of damp. The unpleasant odour of mildew lay thick in the air. There were a few items of battered-looking furniture including a table shoved up against the large disused fireplace.

Her *guests* were Brother Bertie and Ruddy. Each sat in a chair, with one of the Duchess' goons standing behind them. How his pork pie hat still remained on his head Brother Bertie would never know. The same went for Ruddy's beehive which was barely hanging on. They were both still in a state of shock at the drastic turn of events. The crashing appearance of Mo and her connection to the Duchess' grandson had stunned them. They had tried to leave, but the Duchess had sweetly said that they hadn't had their wedding cake yet. They should have known that was a bogus bit of bullshit to keep them there. Neither Brother Bertie nor Ruddy had gone quietly when her bullyboys forced them downstairs. Brother Bertie had received a slap or two for his troubles, the removal of his stick while Ruddy was slung over a shoulder. They had been held captive for hours.

'Rita, girl, what kinda foolishness is this?' Brother Bertie demanded, his bloodshot eyes wide with outrage.

Ruddy was right on his tail. 'Whatcha think you're playing at?'

The Duchess pointed to the door. 'You can leave through *that* anytime you like.' Neither asked if there was a catch; there always was with her. 'All you have got to do is answer a question.'

'Don't leave it stuck between your teeth,' Ruddy bristled. 'Spit it out.'

'Which one of you told her? Put her up to it?'

Confusion marring his voice, Brother Bertie answered, 'Put *who* up to *what*?' His expression became angry. 'I turn up here, in my good clothes and best aftershave for your boy's wedding, and now I'm trussed up like some raas Christmas turkey waiting to be stuffed.'

Thoroughly annoyed, Ruddy added, 'Her? Up? It? What the rat's toosh you going on about, darlin'?'

The Duchess didn't lose her rag. She rarely did. The Duke, bless his departed, rich heart, had taught her all about remaining cool and prolonging other's agonies.

She turned the full intensity of her gaze onto Brother Bertie. 'Your granddaughter. Big Mo Watson. Also the grandkid of Jimmy Southpaw.' She lifted a cynical brow.

'Fancy that, Bertie, sharing a grandchild with the man you hate most in the world.'

Brother Bertie lost the remainder of colour in his face. There was a slight tremor to his shoulders. 'Leave my baby-gal out of this.' His lip curled with contempt. 'If I had my stick, I'd bus' up that boy's head. Give that grandson of yours a caning he wouldn't forget after the way he treated my Maureen.'

The Duchess scoffed. 'Eddie could've fucked her sideways, backwards and front for all I care. That's what red-blooded men do.'

Incensed, Brother Bertie growled, 'Bring his cheating skin in here now. This minute. I'll show him how a red-blooded man deals with a pussy-raas like him.'

Brother Bertie was in full flow, his Jamaican accent strong, his cursing ripe. After the shock of seeing Mo drive a car through a window into the reception, and the penny dropping about what had gone on between her and Eddie, he'd been ready to lick down the younger man. Only Ruddy holding him back had stopped him.

He tried to spring at the Duchess. One of her men grabbed his shoulders and slammed him so hard back in the chair an audible cry of pain punched out of him.

'You all right, Bert,' Ruddy called out in distress. Furious, she switched her anger to the other woman. 'Whatever you've got to say, say it now. Stop dicking around.'

The Duchess told her, accent going downmarket. 'Only three people knew about the jewels in my safe. Me and you two fuckwits. During the wedding, your tea-leafing grandkid stole my gems.'

'What?' Brother Bertie looked aghast, desperately trying to catch his breath. 'My Maureen would never teef up you tings.'

The Duchess ignored his pleas. 'What I wanna know is which one of you two piss-poor, interfering gobshites blabbed to that girl about my stash and where to get her grubby hands on it?'

'We never told Mo a thing,' Brother Bertie vehemently insisted. 'You must be losing whatever sense you were born with.'

Ruddy jumped in, giving the Duchess what for. 'You off your rocker or what? We've kept it schtum all these years. Ain't told a soul. Cross my heart.' Ruddy followed up with the gesture.

Their ardent denials didn't go down well with the Duchess. 'You must think I'm the idiot of the century.' She shrugged. 'You can't say I didn't ask.'

She nodded to one of her men, who dragged Ruddy in the chair to a new position where she faced Brother Bertie a certain distance away.

Ruddy made noise and protested all the way. 'You should be ashamed of yourself, young man, mishandling a defenceless, disabled, confused old lady this way. I don't even know what day of the week it is.'

Ruddy stared straight into Brother Bertie's eyes, and her expression silently communicated that they were in trouble. Big trouble. They had been in many scraps over the years and managed to see their way through. The Duchess, however, was in a league of her own. And if it was true that

Mo had had the Duchess' pension plan away, they might not make it out of here alive.

The Duchess gestured at her assistant. Jane hunched down on her knees near Ruddy's bare legs. She placed a pretty small piece of cloth with delicate care on the floor. From her pocket she took out what looked like lengths of black string.

Fear gripped Brother Bertie's heart. 'What are you doing?'

Jane held on to one string which she tied around Ruddy's lower leg.

''Ere, get your bleeding sticky mitts off me,' Ruddy belted out, trying every which way to wriggle her leg free. But it was no use, Jane managed to finish her task, leaving a piece of the string loose at the end.

Brother Bertie might not be able to figure out what the Duchess was doing, but he knew it was some kinda evil. Pure evil. A look passed between the Duchess and Jane. A lighter appeared in Jane's hand. No!!! Brother Bertie growled deep and long like a caged animal. He attempted to bolt forward, but one of the thugs was on him in two seconds flat, wrestling him back down. The man raised his hand to cuff him.

'No!' the Duchess instructed. 'I don't want him dizzy. I want him to be able to see this in twenty-twenty vision.'

'Don't do this,' he begged. 'Please. Put me in the chair instead.'

'I'm all right, Bertie.' Despite her reassurance, Ruddy couldn't hide the fright in her voice. 'A V2 bomb dropped on my pram when I was a baby. If the Nazis couldn't take me out, the Queen of feckin' Sheba here stands no chance.'

Jane pressed the lighter on. She touched the flame to the loose piece of string at the end. And that's when it became apparent that it was no string. It was a firecracker fuse. A sizzling hissing sound joined by a sparking flame travelled the circuit of the fuse, burning into Ruddy's flesh. The room filled with her agonising scream.

Brother Bertie thought he was going to lose his mind. 'Stop. It.'

When it reached the bone in the front of Ruddy's leg, the flame sparked with fury, growing larger, the ferocity of the burning turning Ruddy's screams hoarse. Finally, it moved on, sparking, hissing and eventually dying at the end. Ruddy slumped forward, head hanging low. But her spirit wasn't broken because she managed to mumble, 'Y'know what, Bertie? She wants to check up that skirt of hers cos that fake-up accent must be sending her drawers into a right ole twist up her bum.'

Brother Bertie wanted to laugh but he couldn't. How could he when his companion of over forty years was hurting. Tears clouded his rheumy eyes.

The Duchess smirked at his discomfort. 'Jane, explain to this fool why this is so painful for his dumb friend.'

Jane kept her head low. Her voice was expressionless. 'The fire will burn into the skin, of course. But the tibia bone in the leg has hardly any fat or muscle in front of it. That's why I put more explosive in the fuse at that point because it will hurt the most.'

The Duchess jumped in with relish. 'Can you imagine that Bertie? The pure, hot, excruciating pain Ruddy must be going through? The suffering? The torture?' Her voice softened like she was trying to comfort a baby. 'All you've got to do is tell me what I want to know. Which one of you told Big Mo about my heirlooms?'

He shouted back, 'We never opened our bone boxes to no one. We would never do that.'

'How the effing fuck did she find out, then? Only us three knew about it.'

With difficulty, Ruddy lifted her head, spit dripping down the side of her mouth. 'We would never…' She fought for breath, air visibly trembling in her body, pushing her chest unnaturally high. 'Betray you.'

The Duchess snarled back, 'You pair of dipshits must think I was last year's Christmas tree fairy.'

She waved her hand at Jane who switched legs and lit another fuse. Ruddy's body convulsed; her scream this time was choking, choked with tears.

Brother Bertie was so charged with hate. If he got his hands on the Duchess he would put them around her throat and not stop. 'You were a bitch then and you're a triple bitch now.'

'A triple *rich* bitch, thank you very much. Very rich indeed.' She stepped back. 'It looks like I'm going to have to ask Big Mo herself —'

'You touch one hair, *one hair*, on my baby-gal's head and I'll —'

'You'll what?' she sneered, neck thrusting forward.

'Attack me? With that bum leg of yours?' Ugly, humourless laughter snaked out of her mouth as she poured acid on her insults. 'You're nothing but a cripple, Bertie.'

Her vicious jibe hurt. But he needed to focus on Ruddy. 'I'm warning you!'

'If my precious jewels aren't back in my loving embrace by nine tomorrow morning, Big Mo is dead. And you two has-beens will be has-gones right alongside her.'

Seconds later the corridor outside echoed with Ruddy's piercing scream.

Chapter Twenty-Nine

'Oh, stone the crows! Not her again.' Eileen Dripsey looked heavenward, rolling her eyes.

She'd been in her boudoir when she heard the squeal of a Merc outside her drum. A quick peep behind the curtains of her prefab confirmed that it was none other than Kristal Steele, flashing her pins as she got out of her flash set of wheels. There was no doubt the world of fortune telling and other works of the supernatural had been good to Eileen. Nor was there any doubt that Kristal was a client who didn't mind paying well over the odds. But there had to be a limit to even Eileen's patience, and Kristal had reached it. Perhaps it was Kristal's recent enquiry about hair. Apparently, Kristal's son Damien was worried about losing his and she was hoping Eileen could get in touch with her boy's dead ancestors to find out if there was any baldness in the family. It seemed a shame to turn the money down, but Eileen felt she had to say no.

Now the woman was back.

Eileen took refuge behind a wardrobe while the knocker knocked and the ringer rang. Then the front door fell silent.

She checked behind the curtain to see if Kristal had gone. Unfortunately, she did so just as Kristal remained at the gate, scanning the windows for any sign of life. Their eyes met. Eileen's heart sank. A delighted Kristal waved her hands, beckoning her to come and answer the door.

Viewing her reflection in the mirror, Eileen dishevelled her hair and fixed a tragic face. When she reached the front door she said, in her best seance voice, 'Is that a spirit calling from the beyond the grave at my door at the Devil's own hour?'

'You what?' came the abrupt response. 'It's Kristal Steele. I know it's late but it's imperative I have a word.'

Eileen opened her front door. 'I'm sorry, Mrs Steele, but you have to understand that I'm taking a sabbatical at the moment.'

'A sabbatical? I didn't know you were a churchgoer?' Her lips pursed. 'You and Monty thinking of getting joined in Holy matrisnoggy?'

Eileen's face fell, her cheeks staining red. 'Monty is no longer of this address. The witch who ran the fruit and veg stall put a spell on him with her ripe bananas.'

Kristal was dismayed on her behalf. 'His loss, luv. Although, it's strange you couldn't have put a hex on him to stay here for all eternity.'

Still smarting from Monty's defection, Eileen bit her tongue. 'I'm taking a break from my work. You see, I'm dealing with powerful forces that are beyond the ken of the average man. It's a dangerous business and if one pushes too far, it can mean burnout, breakdown or worse. For the time being I'm withdrawing from public life and taking care of my own spiritual wellbeing. I'm sure you'll appreciate that.'

She attempted to close the door, but Kristal was too fast. Her kitten heel was in the gap in a nanosecond. 'I totally get it, babes. Believe me, I could write the book on burnout. The number of times I've had to check into a spa is nobody's business. But this is an emergency.' Kristal patted her red handbag. 'I've got five grand in here says you can help me. You're the only person who can.'

Eileen was in shock. It wasn't the money that caught her eye but the bag. A Hermes Birkin. It must've cost a cool ten grand plus. Not able to help herself, Eileen leaned over and petted it with her pinkie.

Taking Eileen's gesture to mean she was well into the five large, Kristal coaxed, 'There's more where that came from if you come up trumps. We're not doing exorcisms, curses or hair loss here, babes, we're talking big league.'

Eileen forgot she was supposed to be suffering from burnout. All she could see was herself waltzing up to that fruit and veg stall and showing off her bag to that bitch as she dipped into it to pay for a pound of pears. *You keep Monty, I'll keep the bag!* Feeling mightily cheered up, she asked, 'Do you mind if I ask in what connection?'

'Look, babes, I'm not talking business on the doorstep, now am I? Are you going to let me in or are you going to let a big payoff go walkies?'

She didn't wait for an answer but pushed the door and barged past Eileen into her front room. The fortune teller followed; her curiosity aroused as much as her eye for the Birkin plus five big ones.

'What are you doing?' Eileen asked when Kristal began checking behind clocks, handling cushions and feeling the wallpaper.

'This place ain't bugged, is it?' Eileen shook her head. 'Are you sure? Only walls have ears in my line of work, know what I mean?' Kristal was suddenly alarmed. 'What about the spirit world? They won't grass me up, will they?'

Eileen was struggling to keep up. 'Spirit world? Grass you up?'

'You ain't going to share my business with Houdini or Henry the Eighth. Then they go off and whisper in the ear of some medium who then tells some crafty bastard my secrets at a séance, who's on the case before I am?'

Eileen was beginning to wonder if Birkin was going to cover this sort of trouble. 'Anything you say to me is in the strictest confidence. Those of us in the spiritual business have very strict rules about that. We're like doctors.'

Despite the late hour, Eileen drew the curtains and lit the black candles. 'Now, Kristal, take a seat and tell me what exactly it is you're hoping I can help with.'

Kristal's eyes searched the now darkened room. 'This is top secret, hush-hush and for your lugholes only.' She leaned forward and whispered, 'The thing is this. Myself and my family have recently come into an inheritance in the form of some jewellery and other family heirlooms.' She added quickly and with bite, 'It's our property. It belonged to my grandmother who inherited it from her grandmother who made a fortune out of the cattle trade.'

Kristal's voice fell so low that Eileen had to strain to hear.

'The thing is some tea-leafing bastard has had it away and we want it back.'

Eileen sat back. 'I see. Surely this is a matter for the police?'

'Old Bill? You must be joking, babes? The plod are probably on the tea leaf's payroll. No, we need the sort of specialist service only you can provide.'

'In what respect?'

'You know that thing you do where you dress up in the robes, light a few joss sticks, ring some bells and then you have a vision. We want you to muster up a vision where you see where our stuff has been hidden.'

Eileen was alarmed. She didn't mind Kristal bringing her son Damien to be exorcised or requesting curses on her enemies. But this was a bit specific. But then her client patted *that* handbag.

'The problem is that visions are highly unpredictable work and there's no guarantee of success. Sometimes the key lines become confused or a malevolent spirit intervenes with a false vision as a badness. We're in the lap of forces we don't understand here.'

'Let me just add this.' Kristal continued her persuasion charm offensive. 'If we get our gear back after you've had a vision, you're on a percentage. We're a bit like insurance companies in that respect. And we ain't talking dole money here, babes.'

The temptation was too much for Eileen. 'The five thousand is non-refundable?'

'No problem, bird.'

'And the bag?'

Kristal's lip curled. 'Trying your luck a bit there, aren't you, girl?' After a few seconds she nodded.

Ecstatic, Eileen hurried off to her props room, changed into a white gown with sun and moon motifs, grabbed a cymbal and some incense before rushing back. At the entrance to the door she stopped and moved into the room with the grace of a high priestess. She blew out a couple of candles, leaving a single one burning. The room was plunged into semi-dark.

'I want you to concentrate, Kristal.'

Incense was burned and Eileen tapped out a rhythm on her cymbal while adopting various poses. She put on a good performance. Kristal sat goggle-eyed as she wafted round the room, humming and chanting. Finally, Eileen dropped into a chair, exhausted. She commanded, 'Close your eyes and focus. Focus like you've never focused before.'

Kristal did as asked but it was obvious, she had one still open so she could have a butcher's at what was going on. Eileen placed her fingertips on her temples and shut her own eyes.

'Yes… the mist is clearing… I see something… green, lots of green… and brown… and sky, blue sky.'

'Where are we?'

Eileen snapped. 'Be quiet or the vision will be lost.' She resumed visualising. 'Green… I see trees and a man with… a spade. He's digging. He looks over his shoulder. He's digging again and placing bag in a hole…'

There was a long silence before Eileen opened her eyes.

'There's your answer. Your inheritance is buried in a forest by a man with a spade.'

Kristal wasn't happy. 'Is that it? For the Birkin?'

'Yes.' Eileen let out the word slowly.

'Buried in a forest? I was hoping for something a little bit more specific than that. I mean, which forest? Epping? New Forest? The Amazon rainforest? And what did this geezer look like?'

The supernaturalist's gaze darted anxiously at her client's handbag. 'I could hear a lot of traffic in the background. I should have added that. So we're probably talking the M25. I'm guessing Epping Forest?'

Kristal stood. She appeared unsure in the half light. 'Epping? That makes sense. Are you sure you didn't see a sign or something? Any clues? X marks the spot?' When she got a slow shake of the head by way of reply, Kristal said, 'I suppose that's something to work with.

She opened up the handbag, pulled out her personals and chucked it and the money at Eileen. The fortune teller patted the Birkin before placing in upright on the sofa as if it were a guest.

Eileen accompanied Kristal to the door. Her client was already pulling her phone from her pocket. As she walked down the garden path, her voice was clear. 'Mo? Listen up. I know where the swag is hidden. Some geezer buried it in Epping Forest. For real… Whatcha mean, how do I know? I've just paid serious money, plus one of my fave bags to someone for a vision… No, I'm not taking the piss.'

Eileen closed the door and examined her Hermes and

winnings. She decided to bank the cash as fast as possible before 'Mo' came round to demand Kristal's money and bag back.

Chapter Thirty

Exhausted, panting breath freezing in the air, Mo collapsed to her knees into the icy-cold earth in front of her father's memorial. And begged, 'Dad, I need help. Please tell me what to do. *Please!*'

Anguish had driven her to the place of the dead. And gut-clawing guilt. The graveyard had been closed so she'd picked the padlock to gain entry. A half-moon shone above. It should be pitch-black but the place had a strange light about it. Creepy and blue-black, the moonlight adding a hazy edge, turning the cemetery into something that belonged in another world. The tombstones stretched tall and erect like they were about ready to rise. The many statues of the Virgin Mary and cherubs, their stone eyes seemed about ready to snap open, back alive again in full colour. Branches of the trees were dark fingers reaching into the eerie, soulless night. Mo was a woman who didn't do scared. But she'd have to have no blood in her veins not to feel fear here.

The Duchess has got Gramps. Mo was still reeling from the twisted turn of events. If that crazy woman hurt Brother Bertie, touched a hair on his head – Mo gulped – if he died,

Mo wouldn't be able to live with herself. The guilt would eat her away for the rest of her days. If only she could rewind the clock; she would never do any of this.

As soon as she'd hightailed it away from Granddad Jimmy's she'd got on the blower to Ruddy. No answer. That meant only one thing; the Duchess had Ruddy as well. The thought of her precious Gramps and his closest friend at the mercy of that evil woman had Mo wanting to go up the Sixes and Sevens to tear the place apart until she found them. *And say you did that and it turned out they weren't being held there. Turns out the Duchess has got them stashed someplace else. To get her own back she kills Gramps and Ruddy. You'll have blood on your hands then. Blood on your hands.*

This was Mo's darkest hour. With a stare as bleak as the night, Mo stared up at her father's memorial. The angels at the statue's side seemed ready to flap their wings and take him up to Heaven. Mo's mind rewound back to the day Granddad Jimmy had sat her and Damien down to put forward his idea of a memorial commemorating the life of their father. What he wanted to discuss was what the memorial should be. *Of course, as expected, she and her half-brother had very different ideas.*

'Arsenal,' Damien had stated without hesitation. 'It's a no-brainer. A statue of Dad in an Arsenal shirt. Holding a football. Turn the top of his grave into a footie pitch.'

Mo had kissed her teeth, seeing it very different. 'Dad's in Heaven now. He's at peace. It should be something traditional like a statue of him with angels bearing him up to his place in Heaven like the hero he was.'

They'd argued back and forth until Granddad Jimmy had put a stop to it. And this was what he'd come up with in the end, a compromise between what both Robbie's children had wanted. Robbie being raised to Heaven by angels who wore Arsenal shorts.

'I've got myself into a right ole pickle, Dad,' Mo spoke, coming back to the present. 'I don't know what to do. If I could wind the clock back I'd do it in a heartbeat. When I got your property back from Birdwhistle I should've done one thing. Burned the lot.'

Mo pulled in a ragged breath, voice wretched. 'I only did it because I wanted to get close to you. And look what's happened. My selfishness, only thinking of my own needs has put those I cherish the most in danger. I —'

Mo violently spun around, pulling her gun out at the same time. Sixth sense alerted her something wasn't right. Then she knew what it was. Someone was watching her. She could feel their hot eyes, shrouded in the dark, observing her every move. Mo scrambled to her feet, nearly slipping on the cold earth.

'Whoever you are, step out of the dark and show yourself.' She fought to control the air pumping in and out of her.

Nothing. No movement. Mo wasn't in the habit of asking twice. Gun level with her eyeline, she advanced into the graveyard. The frost-bitten wind tightened around her. Had someone followed her here? Or were they here all the time? Why would someone already be here at Dad's grave? That prickly, unnerved sensation she'd told Kristal about earlier was back. There was some kinda shit going on here that she couldn't figure out.

Although it was cold enough to freeze Hell over, sweat beaded along her hair. A drop fell down the centre of Mo's back. Gun raised high, Mo did a slow three hundred and sixty, searching every inch of ground she could see. What the fuck was that? A flicker of movement? Mo increased her pace forward. Kept going. A shadowy figure started running. Mo went after them, hell for fucking leather. Was it the Duchess' people here to finish her off? If that were so, why were they running away instead of towards her?

Savage revenge thrummed volcanic-hot in her blood; whoever it was would rue the day they'd ever set eyes on her. The watcher was much bigger than her which gave her an advantage. Being small meant Mo could dodge, duck and dive more quickly. Gun by her side she picked up speed, jumping over a low-level tombstone. Snaking between graves, Mo was making up ground. She raised her gun and took a shot. The bullet slammed into a tree. Bastard. Her opponent was a pro because they started running in a zigzag formation which made it much harder for her gun to target them. The night air swallowed her up. Twisted around her. Mo panted faster and faster. Gaining. Getting closer. Closer.

Suddenly her foot tangled in the large exposed root of a tree and she tumbled over, her gun accidentally discharging into the air. Mo didn't give herself time to lie there. She sprang into her feet and was back in action. But when she cast her gaze around he was nowhere to be seen.

'Fuck! Fuck! Fuck!' Mo stamped a foot in disbelieving

fury. 'I fucking had the bastard!'

Then again, her opponent might be laying low somewhere. For the next fifteen minutes, Mo took her time combing through the graveyard. She found nothing. She knew he was long gone.

Dead on her feet, feeling the need to smash her fist into something, Mo briskly walked back to her dad's memorial and grave. Just as she saw it coming up into view, deafening boom erupted. An almighty force propelled Mo backwards. It lifted her off her feet, tossing her like a rag doll high into the air. She landed on her side on the grave of a girl who'd passed from this life to live with the angels at the age of five. Winded, Mo lay there. My baby! Urgently, she placed her palm on her tummy. A crazy buzzing filled her ears. Other than that there was no pain.

What the fuck just happened?

Struggling to breathe, Mo carefully rolled to her back and sat up. There was debris everywhere, mainly earth and shattered remnants of statues. Dazed, Mo's fingers dug into the wet, soft earth for support to help her stand. When she got to her feet, shivers rocked through her body with the grip of a fever. Trepidation at what she would find marked every step she took towards her father's grave. The closer she got the greater the destruction. Mo looked over to the resting place of her father. But it wasn't there. Mo stared listlessly into the darkness. Stunned, her brain couldn't comprehend what had happened. She couldn't utter a word, her tongue heavy and as leaden as a corpse. Then Mo figured it out.

The Duchess had blown up Robbie's grave.

Slowly, Mo inspected the damage that had been done. Robbie's beautiful statue had been shattered to smithereens, its white plaster and dust strewn across the neighbouring area. The hole where Robbie's coffin was laid to rest was now a huge crater. It resembled something from a war zone. The coffin had been blown to bits. What did lie inside the hole was the head of Robbie's memorial statue. The strangest thing was it was totally intact, the eyes staring back up at Mo. It was obscene and macabre.

Mo scrambled down in what had once been her father's grave and picked the head up. She held it with love to her chest. Head bowed, Maureen 'Big Mo' Watson, legendary hardgirl of the East End, broke down and bawled like a baby. In her mind, the bomb had murdered the father she had been desperate to know all over again.

Trembling with fury and hate, Mo tipped her head towards the sky and howled, 'Duchess, I'm coming to get you. This is war.'

Chapter Thirty-One

The private jet touched down in the Ghost Airport. It was located on the outskirts of London. This was no ordinary airport. It couldn't be found in an A to Z or via GPS. It was a huge stretch of land belonging on an estate with a magnificent eighteenth century mansion house. Only those in The Know knew of its existence. And those with the necessary readies to shell out the exorbitant fee for its use. It was part of that deep, dark underbelly of the criminal world that had been expressly created to provide discreet services to those who wished to remain outside the glare of the authorities. Banks, documents, hotels, transport, homes, you name it, it had the works. All the services anyone would need to travel through life unseen and uninterrupted.

The Ghost Airport had no passport control, no immigration checks, nor specialist machines to inspect luggage and bodies, no sniffer dogs. That's why the solitary figure who emerged from the jet had chosen it. No one would know that they were going to be in London. Despite the dark they wore sunglasses to conceal their face. Their clothing was black to blend into the night.

A shadowy figure greeted them at the bottom of the airstairs. Names were not exchanged. 'I hope that you found your flight satisfactory.'

'Very. Thank you,' was the clipped, curt answer. Their voice was muffled as if fearing it would betray them, leaving them vulnerable to being recognised.

They were escorted on to the next stage of their journey, a helicopter waiting for them in another part of the grounds. They flew over London, the multi-coloured lights breathtaking beneath them, brimming bright, resembling a crazy video game.

They didn't look out of the window. Didn't capture the moment the River Thames came into view meandering through the city. Instead, their jittery gaze stared down at their fingers starkly knotted together in their lap. They swallowed convulsively, showing their nerves. Shoulders hunched as if trying to curl in on themselves. They didn't speak. Except in their own mind. *Stop worrying. This is all going to be over soon.*

In a whirl of noise and vibrating air, the copter landed on top of a building. Its lone passenger disembarked and took the car that was waiting for them at the back entrance downstairs and finally reached the hotel.

The hotel belonged to one of the big chains. It had been deliberately chosen owing to the fact it was big, impersonal, chock-a-block with guests, the perfect place where faces blended into the sea of the crowd. Plus, despite advertising itself as all the whistles and bells, its security was shit. Many of the security cams did not work, and the guys on the door were older, only working to top up their pensions.

The person reached the fourth floor. Room 402. Inside someone else waited for them. When they saw each other they wanted to embrace but didn't. They had too much work to do. The person already in the room had earlier carried out a thorough security sweep. Every precaution needed to be taken including checking that uninvited ears weren't listening. In the world they'd lived in, deceit, danger and murderous deaths were everyday facts of life.

Satisfied all was in order, the one who had just arrived proceeded to unpack while the other got down to business on the phone. The first person they called didn't have the info they needed, so that call was cut short. The same occurred to the second, third and fourth. Number five was different.

'Hey, bruv, it's John. How's tricks?' He kept his voice upbeat.

'John?' The guy on the other end of the line greeted him.

He knew that it was inevitable that his name would be used. Still, it left him feeling very uncomfortable.

'I didn't know you were back in the ole Smoke.' The guy on the other line was an associate of his.

'I'm not. Still chilling in the sun.' The phone he used would not betray him; its signal didn't situate it as being in London. 'I hear there's been some drama going on.'

The other man scoffed, 'There's always something going on. It wouldn't be London otherwise, now would it. So that shit that went down with Petey Marsh reached ya. Ain't surprised. Talk is that they found him in six pieces, in six different locations. Should've learned to keep that gob of his shut.' He made a nasty noise as if on the verge of spitting. 'Feckin' grass.'

The man in the hotel room cut in, 'Yeah! Yeah! Heard that.' His voice lowered. 'Something else reached my ears. Trouble at the Duchess'.'

'Fuck me!' The guy got boisterous. 'The whole of London will be waking up to that news. Story goes that someone ripped her off. Not only did they clean her out, they left her looking like a rank amateur.'

'How's that then?'

'Took her to the cleaners while her grandboy is downstairs holding his wedding reception. The old girl took her eyes off the ball. Careless.'

'The Duchess won't be taking that lying down.' He heard the faint fear in his words.

'Lying down?' the other guy practically shouted. 'You having a buzz, bruv? The way I hear it she's got this city already under lockdown. Got her people digging into every crevice and corner and stone the scum who shook her down might have crawled into or under.'

A choking sensation tightened the muscles in John's throat. Finding it hard to breathe, he drew in sharp punches of air.

The guy on the other line said, 'You all right, John?'

'Yeah. 'Course.' But he wasn't. He caught the worried gaze of his companion who held on to the doorframe of the bathroom, fingers tight with tension.

Slowly, he asked, 'Any mention of who done the deed?'

The man on the other end of the line thought for a bit. Then, 'A number of names in the mix —'

'Such as?'

'Tell you the truth, John, I think people are blowing it out of their rear-end with names.' He paused. Voice dipped. 'One name that's shook one 'n' all up is Southpaw.'

The man sucked in a sharp shard of air. 'Jimmy Southpaw. You've gotta be kidding me.'

'I know. Tell me about it. That's what I said. Southpaw ain't no nutcase to dabble with the Duchess. Besides which, him and Her Ladyship have had an agreement for years. Why would he break it after all this time? Plus, the geezer's holstered his shooter for good and retired. Mind you, that little whippersnapper that's now running his outfit...'

'Are you talking about Big Mo?'

'I ain't talking about no one.' Suddenly the guy was guarded. The fear in his voice blatant. 'In fact, you heard dick from me. When you're back in town, hit me up for a drink.'

Call over. John's hand crushed around the phone.

'What did they say?' the other person asked.

He ran his tongue over his dry lips and raised his head. 'It's worse than we thought.'

John's companion let out a cry of alarm, rocking back on their heels. He strode over and placed a gentling palm on their shoulder, looking them in the eye. 'We knew it was going to be bad.' He shook his head with frustration. Wanted to smash something, *anything*, hard until his knuckles came up bleeding.

The other person sensed the turmoil he was going through, and it was their turn to lay a comforting hand on his arm. 'There's only one way to find out what's gone on here.'

They were right. John knew this. Squaring his shoulders and softly sighing, in one fluid motion he got back on the phone. Punched in another number. No answer. Tried it again. The same thing happened. He tried five times, each time his hope withering and dying more.

The other person placed their hand over his. 'Stop. Calling over and over won't make her magically appear on the phone. She's obviously not there. What are we going to do?' The panic in their voice was apparent.

'I don't have a choice.' He got to his feet. 'If she's not answering her phone, that means something has happened. I need to find her.'

Suddenly the other person's breathing became erratic. 'You don't think she's —'

'I do. Unfortunately, I think I know where she is.'

The other person caught their breath as he determinedly added, 'I am going to have to go out and find Ruddy.'

Chapter Thirty-Two

'Remember that time we drank so much Lord Have Mercy Rum Punch, we missed our stop and ended up in South End.'

Inside the Duchess' basement, Brother Bertie spoke quickly as he tried his best to tend Ruddy's wounds. He made a half-hearted effort to bind them by tearing off strips from his shirt. Despite the solitary yellow bulb only throwing a half-light, that was enough to show the circular burns on Ruddy's legs. The burns were vicious.

Ruddy was putting on a brave face, biting hard on her lip to stop from wincing in pain. Brother Bertie was doing his best to keep her mind off her suffering by telling stories.

'That's right,' Ruddy said, her body shivering. 'And we never had no money. Not a penny to rub between us.'

'If it weren't for that man with the caravan taking us in we'd have had to spend the night sleeping on the beach. That would've frozen my unmentionables off.'

'Stop, Bertie!' Ruddy commanded weakly. 'Pack it in! No need for you to minster to me. My wounds just need a bit of cream on, that's all.'

'Cream? You should be down A&E.' Anguish and raw anger knotted his stomach. Seeing his friend in so much pain was killing him inside. If that raas woman was here, he'd damage her for real.

'A bit of cream,' Ruddy repeated. 'Although I can't see our jailer providing us with any. Rita's mean like that.'

Brother Bertie held on to Ruddy's chair to stand. That bitch had taken his stick. Taking each step slowly, he made his way to the heavy door. For the umpteenth time he tried to get it open, straining against it with his hands.

'You're wasting your time, darlin'.' Ruddy wearily informed him of what he already knew. 'There are two things everyone knows about Rita. She's a cold-hearted, vicious bitch on the one side. She never makes mistakes on the other. We ain't getting out of here, not with a pulse anyway. Rita will see to that.'

Ruddy watched Bertie fiddling with the lock. He was a trier, no doubt about it. After ten minutes, though, he gave that up and sank down next to Ruddy, his back against the wall, legs stretched out in front of him. 'We're screwed.'

Ruddy squinted shrewdly. 'The only hope we've got is to get them before they get us. Look! There's a wooden table propped up by the fireplace. Let's have the legs off that. When they come back, we'll cosh them good 'n' proper.' East End steel entered her voice. 'I ain't going down without a fight. I never have and I never will.'

Bertie struggled to his feet. He took the measure of the table before starting on it. It was crumbling, eaten away by woodworm which meant it would be easier to break off the legs. Using the ancient grate to help him, Brother Bertie broke off two legs.

'Do the other two as well. One for each hand, like drumsticks. Whack! Whack!' Ruddy meant business

With two wobbly cudgels each, the two prisoners came up with a plan.

'We'll park ourselves either side of the door,' Ruddy insisted with tough determination. 'Backs flat against the wall. The door opens. Bob's your uncle, we bish-bash-bosh 'em. No messing, one blow each side of the head.'

They stared at each other. Together went, 'Bang! Bang!'

Abruptly, Ruddy raised a finger. 'Hold up! There's shuffling upstairs. They're coming.'

Bertie helped Ruddy to her feet. Cheeks depressed and hollow, Ruddy winced, her irregular breathing showing how she fought hard against the pain slicing in her legs. But she refused to give in. She'd be in her grave before she allowed Rita 'a quid a time' Evans to best her.

They took up position either side of the door. Waited. And waited. It never opened. Instead, a cloud of brick dust and soot billowed out of the fireplace. Ruddy and Brother Bertie shared an anxious glance. Then the basement was quiet again. Ruddy went to investigate. Her nose wrinkled in disgust. She peered up the chimney. There was scratching and scuffing above. 'Probably a rat, no doubt a close relative of Rita's.'

Ruddy managed to step back when more dust and remains of ancient fires began to spread across the basement floor. A trainer attached to a leg appeared.

Ruddy and Brother Bertie rushed back in alarm. 'Bloody hell.'

Then the other trainer and leg. The torso of a figure wriggled and struggled their way down into the fireplace. A figure, attached to a safety harness appeared. He was dressed in black wearing a ski mask and appeared in the cloud of dust as if Satan had been summoned.

Ruddy was the first to get over the shock. 'Fuck me! Santa Claus has gone over to the dark side!'

Brother Bertie's hurried whisper of, 'Who the hell are you?' was ignored. The figure held his finger to his lips and tapped them several times to indicate the need for quiet. The guy was fiddling with his safety harness.

Speaking for their ears only, he told Ruddy, 'I'm going back up. I'll lower the harness back down. Fasten it around yourself. Tug it when you're ready. The chimney's narrow but you're skinny enough. I'll pull; if you get stuck, tug it three times.'

After Ruddy's sharp nod, he continued. 'Once I've got you up I'll lower the harness again and we'll bring the old boy up.'

Brother Bertie stretched his lips with extreme displeasure. 'Old boy? Who you calling an old boy? You young people wanna watch your manners.'

'Stop with your nonsense,' Ruddy admonished.

The mystery man went back the way he came using his hands and feet and pulling on his rope. Within moments he was gone. Ruddy's and Brother Bertie's mystified gazes bounced between each other.

'Who the hell was that?'

'How did he know we were here?'

'Who carries climbing gear around with them?'

'Who'd know the Victorian chimneys in this building were wide enough for someone to come up and down them?'

The answer slowly dawned on Ruddy. She knew who it was, all right. She kept her knowledge hush-hush, not confiding in Brother Bertie. Focus, that's what they needed to be doing now.

The harness appeared. Ruddy fastened up. She tugged on the rope and disappeared up the chimney. Bashing and bumping against the walls, she yelped and bit her tongue as the wounds on her leg were scraped. Once or twice she became twisted on the rope and pulled it three times to let her rescuer know she was stuck. When she was untangled, Ruddy tugged again to let him know she was free. She caught a whiff of fresh air and a black sky speckled with stars. Her rescuer's sturdy arms helped her out of the chimney. She rolled slightly, feeling light-headed in the chilled night breeze. He steadied her and then got her sat down on the roof to recover. *Strange-looking chimney*, Ruddy thought. *It's a dead ringer for a ship's funnel.*

As the harness was lowered to Brother Bertie, Ruddy distinctly overheard the man mumble to himself, 'I'm getting a bit old for this game.'

Minutes later, the guy grabbed Bertie under his arms and hoisted him out of the chimney. While they both gathered their breath, their rescuer revealed the next part of the escape plane. 'We go one at a time again. Ruddy first. You need to tie the rope around yourself. Walk over the roof down there. Below that is a fire escape. That'll take us down to the second floor. Then it's over the edge we go with the ropes down to the street level. Quick, mind; we can't afford to bump into the Duchess. We don't want ole Rita to set the dogs on us.'

While the man in the ski mask held firmly to the end of the rope, Ruddy and Bertie, in turn, made their escape across the roof and down onto the fire escape. Then their unknown rescuer joined them there. They rushed down the steps as quick as Brother Bertie's and Ruddy's legs allowed.

'Here comes Spider-Man,' Brother Bertie muttered with surprising glee before sailing over onto the street below.

They hurried behind the black-clad figure across the neighbouring streets until they reached a car parked on a double yellow line.

The man in black took a look at one of the wheels. 'What the hell is this?'

Ruddy explained. 'You've been clamped, mate.'

He produced a shooter from inside his tracksuit. Pointed it at the clamp's lock and emptied the magazine into it. The sound of gunfire echoed off the neighbouring buildings like thunder. 'No wonder this country's going to the dogs.' The lock fell off. 'Get in.'

The car took off at speed, expertly driven by the guy. Ruddy studied him in the rear-view mirror. 'You should take your ski mask off. If the cops see we'll be pulled over.'

The man reached for his ski mask but then thought better of it. He drove until they reached the Island, near Brother Bertie's blocks of flats.

'Thank you very much indeed, young man, whoever you are,' Brother Bertie said, although he became preoccupied by a light in his home. He could swear he never left the lights on.

Ruddy was grim-faced. 'He's not a young man anymore. He was when he died.'

The man tore off his ski mask.

Ruddy said, 'Welcome back, Robbie.'

Chapter Thirty-Three

Jimmy picked up the passport, the shade of his skin a sickly white. He'd been through these passports multiple times since Nico had showed them to him after Mo had done a bunk through the window. He was at his desk, the dim lamplight casting his shadow gigantic and dark against the wall. He wasn't alone. Nico Sinclair sat opposite with the tension of a coiled spring emitting from his body.

Stuart Long. That was the name in the passport. Jimmy placed that passport to the side. He appeared calm enough but those who knew the big man could spot the signs that he was gagging on his fury. There were five other passports before him. He picked up another one. Jonathan Briggs was the ID in this one. John McFly the ID in the one after that. Jimmy stared and stared at the name. Suddenly he threw his head back, roaring with laughter so hard the chair groaned under the strain of his body. The laughter was one of the most menacing sounds Nico had ever heard.

The older man glanced at Nico, his grey eyes belonging to someone close to losing it big time. Between fits and starts of giggles he said, 'John McFly. That was the name of this cop on this TV show me and Robbie used to watch when he was a nipper.' His laughter grew wilder. More manic. 'Get this, when he caught a suspect, this John McFly would go.' Jimmy changed his voice to an imitation of the character which bordered on sounding like a chipmunk. "Oi! The judge is gonna throw the book at ya."

Nico said nothing. He knew better than to speak. But he was worried that the great Jimmy Southpaw was about to fall part.

Jimmy gazed again at the passports. This time at the photos. One had dyed black hair, another a moustache and goatee, another glasses that were reminiscent of ones the NHS gave out for free years ago. He placed the passports back into their envelope and shoved them into his pocket. He didn't need to see the photos that all appeared to be of different people. It was the same face. A face that Jimmy knew so well.

Robbie. His son. His boy. His firstborn.

Nico's mind shot back to being inside the villa in Spain. The documents that he had discovered had stunned were false passports and other false documents. For Robbie Steele and Precious Watson. He hadn't believed it at first. He must've had too much Spanish sun. He'd gone through them over and over, trying to convince himself that it wasn't true. Then he'd pulled himself straight, allowing the reality and the truth to set in.

Robbie Steele was alive. And from the looks of things, he and his former lover, Mo's mum, Precious, were getting ready to disappear into new identities for good. Kristal and Damien. What about his precious sister and nephew? That's what made him sick to his very stomach. Robbie Steele had cut out on them. Why? Why would he do something like that? It horrified him. A man should honour and take care of his family. Blood was everything. When Nico had got back to the villa he'd run right into Damien.

'You all right, Uncle Nic?' Damien had asked. He'd found his nephew alone by the pool.

All Nico could think was how innocent and young his nephew was. Damien might play the big I am, but underneath all that cocksure swag was just a kid. A boy who had struggled for years to match his father's reputation and deal with his death. His death. What a fucking joke!

Nico had given the lad a reassuring smile, playfully ruffling his hair. 'What you still doing up? I'm surprised none of the others are with you.'

Damien shrugged. 'They're out getting bladdered. I just fancied a bit of me-time. Y'know, reflecting on life sitting under the stars.'

Nico gazed on with proud approval. Damien had come such a long way from the young man silently grieving the loss of his father, half-deaf to the world. 'Reflecting?' Nico scoffed, a twinkle in his eye. His voice became serious. 'That's an important skill to have in the business we're in. It marks you out from the hotheads. Enables you to see things from all angles to ensure you make the right decision.'

Damien's face had fallen slightly, so Nico asked, 'What's going on, son?'

His nephew's head remained bowed. 'Can I speak some truth? Just between me and you?'

''Course. I told you from the off if you need an ear to whisper in, mine is always available. And it stays between us.'

Damien had slowly raised his head, his expression a mashup of troubled and unsure. 'The business we're in…' A shiver ran through his body. 'I'm not sure it's the business I wanna be in. See this,' a sweep of his hand indicated the pool area, 'this is what I want. Peace. Quiet. Maybe a wife and kids when the time is right.'

The look he'd settled on his uncle had made Nico clench up. The expression in Damien's eyes, Nico hadn't seen for years. Hope. Elation. Contentment. The hard knocks of the criminal world bashed that stuff out of you pretty quickly.

Next, Damien said something that would stay with Nico for the rest of his life. 'I loved my dad. Always will. But I don't wanna end up dead like him.'

'How can my Robbie be alive?' Jimmy's bewildered flat words dragged Nico back to the betting shop. Jimmy stared down at his open, raised palms, with a mystified expression which suggested he had no idea how they had got there. 'See these hands? I buried my son with them.' The volume of his voice dialled towards ten. 'How the fuck can he still be among the living?'

'Jimmy, you never actually clapped eyes on his body,' Nico calmly reminded him. 'They told you all that was left of Robbie was burning embers and charred bones'

Jimmy's voice was faint as if speaking from a distance. His countenance haunted. 'They asked for my permission to do forensic tests to confirm it was my Robbie. I says to them, if they touched what remained of my son I was coming down there with a sawn-off and blasting the lot of 'em.' He bellowed. 'What a soddin' fool! If I'd given my consent they would've found out it wasn't him.'

Jimmy held his head in his hands for a long time. Nico's natural instinct was to go over to offer some type of comfort like a steadfast hand on his shoulder. The problem was he didn't know how Jimmy would react to that. Some geezers took the solace offered by others as a sign of weakness. Then again, space was what some needed, so Nico gave him that.

'Why would he do it?' His head shot up, his bloodshot eyes filled with bafflement and a terrible agony. 'I gave that boy everything he could've ever wanted. I cherished him. Loved him. I —'

With no warning, Jimmy grabbed the table and turned it over. Standing, he roared and roared out his rage. Body trembling, he shook his fists to the heavens. It was a terrifying sight to behold. Despite the show of strength, Jimmy Southpaw looked like a man who had aged fifty years in the last hour. His sagging face carved and folded with lines of hopelessness and exhaustion. Fine blue veins stretched along the skin of his temples. And those grey eyes of his, the ones that held a fierceness that usually brought the world to its knees. Their usual flinty steel glare was gone. Now they mirrored liquid pools of anguish. And they revealed something that Jimmy would hate others to know. That Jimmy Southpaw, legendary gangster, with a left hook that had helped secure his name, was vulnerable. He hurt. Felt pain. Under all that hardman exterior he was as human as everybody else.

Nico shot to his feet, extremely concerned about Jimmy's state of mind now. He'd got to know Jimmy over the years via the big man being Kristal's father-in-law and Damien being his grandson. Jimmy shoved his emotions deep which made it hard to get to know him, really know him. Jimmy never shied away from one thing, though – sharing his love for his son, Robbie. The other son, Harry, who operated across the pond in New York, the bonds with him didn't seem as tight. Jimmy's eyes lit up like a fairground ride when he spoke about Robbie. The stories he loved to tell about him. Nico prayed that he would never have to tell stories about his son, Victor, while his boy lay in his grave.

Nico spoke quietly, trying to keep things easy. 'Let's sit down and talk about this. Think it through.' An idea came to him. 'What about if I get Sid back over?'

The big man wasn't listening. The stare he levelled on Nico was paralysing. It pierced right through the younger man. 'At his graveside.' Jimmy didn't need to explain whose grave he talked about. 'I took the shovel off one of the gravediggers. I plunged that shovel into the wet soil. The earth that was going to keep my son warm. I started digging and throwing. Digging and throwing dust on the coffin of my firstborn.'

Jimmy was so divorced from reality, he had no idea he was miming the actions with his body and hands. Digging and throwing, digging and throwing.

'That's what a father should do,' he continued. 'Bury his son with his own loving hands.'

Jimmy pulled out his gun. 'Now, I'm going to have to do

that all over again. This time it will be me putting Robbie into the ground at my own hand after I've finished killing him.'

The door thrust open. A breathless Mo stood braced in the doorway. Both men were taken by surprise by her appearance. Mo opened her mouth to speak... Then faltered at the mayhem in the room.

Cautiously entering, she asked, 'What the hell happened here?'

Granddad Jimmy's prized desk was tipped over. He treasured that desk because it was one of the first things he'd bought when he'd started his business. He'd acquired it in West London's Portobello Road Market from a dealer who specialised in selling the furniture of the upper crust who had fallen on hard times. Her confused gaze scanned the floor. Were those passports?

Then it hit her. Mo drew in a harsh breath. 'Oh my God! Has the Duchess been here again? Did she do this?'

No one answered. No one spoke. A terrible, electric silence shrouded and closed in on the room. Mo looked over at her grandfather and what she saw struck her with dread. Never had she observed her Granddad Jimmy with sunken cheeks and bleak shadows beneath his eyes. Even at the memorial he had, somehow, kept his expression guarded. Stayed in the role of the patriarch of the family, keeping his back broad, his spine tall to communicate the strength of the Steele family. Now he looked like a hunched old man.

And why did he have a gun in his hand?

Mo moved across to him. 'Granddad? Why have you got

your shooter? Is it that West End no-mark, the Duchess?'

Strangely, he looked over her head towards Nico. Mo was even more puzzled.

Mo's chest rose high with the knowledge of what she had to tell Granddad Jimmy next. He was going to be devastated. 'Granddad, she bombed Robbie's grave. I saw it with my own eyes.' Mo searched his face, waiting for his explosive reaction.

She watched as his chest and shoulders started shaking. Poor Granddad. He was on the verge of crying. But she was wrong. Jimmy Southpaw bent double, laughing himself silly. He couldn't stop. 'Bombed his grave.' His laughter grew worst. Deranged. 'Fuck me! The Duchess has bombed his grave.'

Shocked and concerned, Mo touched his arm with gentle care. 'Granddad Jimmy? Are you OK?' *He can't be,* Mo mentally answered her own question. He would never, in a trillion years, laugh at someone blowing to smithereens the resting place of his beloved son. Something was badly wrong here. Badly wrong.

She twisted to Nico and mouthed, 'What's going on?'

Nico told her a lie; the truth was not his to tell. 'Seeing the Duchess got into his head a bit —'

Jimmy snapped over him, laughter gone so abruptly it was like it had never existed. 'I want you two to take care of the Duchess. Put that crone back in her box.' He raised his gun. 'I've got other business to take care of.'

Nico strode to the door and stood in Jimmy's way. 'You can't do this.'

Jimmy bared his teeth. 'Get outta my way, young pup.'

'Jimmy —'

With an almighty grunt and heave, Jimmy threw Nico to the floor. Mo's breath hissed between her teeth at what her grandfather had dared to do. He'd put his hands on one of South London's Premier League Faces. No one did that to Nico Sinclair. Put him down on his arse? You might as well dig your own grave. This could be the start of major aggro between South London and East. And if that wasn't enough, Mo had already provoked conflict between the East End and West. She had to stop this.

Mo raced forward, but Nico waved her back. He kept his intense gaze on Jimmy. 'Go in peace, my friend.'

Jimmy looked towards Mo. With a shake of his head, Nico reassured him he would remain schtum about Robbie's resurrection.

Suddenly Jimmy's face changed as he stared at his granddaughter. A hesitant smile warmed his face. Calmly, he walked over to her, his big body vibrating raw strength. When he reached her, his finger gently caressed her cheek. As quiet as a breeze on a summer's day, he told her, 'You're the one great thing Robbie ever gave to me. And for that I thank him.'

Then Jimmy Southpaw left. Gun in hand, he went in search of the son he had to put back in his grave.

Chapter Thirty-four

Mo paced from one end of her office inside Club Class. The *bang-bang* of her heartbeat reverberated through her arms that were wrapped with barb-wired tension around her middle. She was waiting for a prized piece of information to come her way. Info that she prayed would be the ultimate retaliation against the Duchess. Somehow Mo needed to get the Duchess to release Gramps and Ruddy. It would've been easy for Mo to hit the Duchess mob-handed, tooled up to the max. But that would only lead to open war, the streets of London bathed in the blood of others.

Mo considered herself to be a new breed of underworld boss. New school not old. One who thought with her brain not a bullet. A person who had the ability to step back and see things from all angles. Someone who could outwit their foes with the minimum of violence. So Mo had got her smarts into gear and had figured out the killer way to deal with the bitch from Mayfair. Sometimes the most effective way of taking an opponent down was to discover their weakness. What secret was it they would do anything for others not to find out about? An indiscretion they had committed when young? A betrayal against someone close to them? A frowned-upon sexual fetish they got their rocks off to? An affair with someone from the enemy camp? Who was the one person they loved enough to do anything for?

It was this last one that would bring the Duchess to her knees. The person she loved most in the world. Her grandson. That cheating slimeball, Eddie. From all accounts, the old girl doted on the bastard. Mo had witnessed that first-hand at the wedding. All Mo had to do was get her hands on him. Dell was making enquires to find out where that knobhead and his bride were honeymooning. Mo didn't care if it was Lapland, she would hunt Eddie down to the ends of the earth and drag him back here. The only spoke in the wheel of Mo's plan was the Duchess' deadline. There was no way she'd have time to get Eddie back here before the time was up. She was still trying to figure that part out. One step at a time. Still, she needed that info in her hand, like *now*.

'Are you sure you haven't got other ulterior motives for nabbing the Duchess' grandson?'

Mo jerked out of her head and stared at Nico. He was on the sofa, casually sitting back. In his hand he loosely held a brandy that he'd rustled up from her private bar.

At his veiled remark heat climbed up her neck and face. She didn't appreciate him doing it. 'Eddie Harvey is merely a tool to use against his batshit-mad grandmother.'

Nico had pissed her right off. Creating some distance from him, Mo parked herself behind her desk. Granddad Jimmy had taught her that desks were not simply places to work or where you hid shooters. Desks created a barrier between you and others. Drew an invisible line where you sat on your throne and asserted your power.

Nico leaned forward, resting the glass on his thigh. 'You planning to tell him about the little one you're carrying?'

Mo huffed with irritation. She was so not in the mood for this. 'Father Nico, I didn't realise you were hearing confessions today.'

As soon as the lippy comment was out, Mo wished she could reel it back. 'Don't answer that,' she told him. Closing her eyes, she took some much-needed time out for herself. 'What's it like being a dad?'

'Hard work. Full of joy. Gut-wrenching. So much love. Terrifying. The absolute best thing I will ever do with my life.'

'Easy then?'

They both chuckled at that.

Then Mo said, 'I've always wanted to be a mum. A child of my own. Someone to kiss and cuddle in the morning and at night.' Her chest rose high with the immenseness of what she was talking about. 'But I'm shitting it that I'll make a right royal muck-up of it. That I'll end up like one of them women balling her head off in her child's face on the street.'

Nico swivelled the amber liquid at the bottom of his glass. 'Now that won't happen, not with Uncle Nico around.'

Her eyes flashed open. Straightening, she glanced at him. 'What an honour for my kid to be able to call you uncle.'

Suddenly they both averted their gazes. That old tension

between them seeped into the room. The sex-love-whatever it was thang that they chose to ignore. And would continue to do so while Nico remained a married man. That wasn't a line that Mo was ever going to cross. That brought that imbecile, Eddie, to her mind. Him with his arms around his wife at their wedding, while Mo stood there in the role of the other woman looking like a proper well-gnawed plum in front of a group of strangers. The oddest thing, though, was his betrayal seemed to intensify her secret feelings for Nico.

'What's going on with Granddad?' Mo suddenly changed tack.

She watched Nico stiffen. So she was right, something else was going on. He answered, 'Like I said before, this thing with the Duchess —'

'Don't BS me, Nico.' Her voice became strained. 'He looked hurt. Devastated. I'm worried about him…'

The door thrust open, announcing Dell's arrival. 'The information has arrived. The Duchess' grandson is on honeymoon with his bride on a private island in the Caribbean.'

Mo said, 'A private island is going to be a problem.'

Nico's phone rang. While he took the call, Mo witnessed her cousin's expression shift. She knew a 'but' was coming.

'You're going to tell me something I'm not going to like.'

Dell lifted her shoulders in an apologetic fashion. 'Being on a private island isn't the problem. The biggie is the groom and the bride are still in the air flying there. The Devil himself couldn't reach them at that altitude.'

Mo crunched her fists up in frustration. 'Which means the Duchess' clock is going to be finished ticking by the time they land. So much for outthinking her.'

Nico finished his call and looked over at them. 'Forget about the poxy grandson.'

On full-alert Mo stood. 'Why?'

'Word just reached me about Brother Bertie and Ruddy.'

Mo's heart all but fell through the floor. Her fingers gripped the edge of the desk. She could barely get the words out. 'Are they dead? Did that she-devil murder them?'

Nico shook his head. Smiled. 'They've managed to escape.'

Dell stiffened, sensing danger as soon as she walked out of the club with Mo and Nico. Rain was pounding down. In a swift elegant motion, she offered the protection of her body to her boss. Instinctively, Nico drew his semi. Dell could feel the difference in the air around them. Something or someone was out there.

'What's up?' Mo urgently asked.

Dell's neck stretched, searching into the dark. 'Something's not right here.'

Nico's gaze darted, trying to penetrate the dark. 'I don't see anything.'

Dell didn't have time to explain to him how she had a unique sense in her gut when it came to danger. She had an intuition for knowing when it lurked nearby. She'd developed it at the age of eight when her new stepfather started knocking her mother around and she had taken a machete to him, almost severing the hand he'd beat her mother with. After that, her mother quickly bundled her off to live with family in Croydon. Mo had worked with her long enough to know that her instincts were usually spot on.

Alert gaze still searching, Dell told Mo, 'You and Mister Nico get out of here. I'll take care of it. I'll give you a bell when it's all sorted.'

Worry lines marring her forehead, Mo gently touched her cousin's arm. 'Be careful. Please use the muscle in the club if you have to.'

Josh would have usually been around, but he was in Portugal enjoying a well-deserved sun-kissed break. Dell waited until Mo and Nico had driven away in his car when she acted. She couldn't see anything in front of her, anyone in the buildings nearby or anyone above. The sensation of danger vibrating in the air grew stronger.

Unzipping her rucksack, Dell took out the machetes that she sharpened every Sunday. Carefully, quietly, she inched towards the alley that ran down the side of the building, the one she had recently dragged a pleading Sammy Sapphire along. Dell looked fearsome, machetes held high, one forward, one back, ready to leap up at any time and let who ever dared, *dared* encroach on Mo's turf have it with the cutting intensity they deserved.

Abruptly, Dell pulled up short. In the distance stood a figure shrouded in the night. A shiver passed down her spine. If she wasn't holding her machetes Dell would clutch the bracelet she never took off. The one with the turquoise third eye to ward off evil.

'Who are you?' she called out.

No answer. Stretching her leg muscles, Dell moved closer and closer. Her jaw dropped when the figure came fully into view. Jane, the Duchess' whiplash girl. Normally, Dell would've attacked. However, two things held her back. First off, Jane didn't have her usual go-to lethal whips in her hands. Secondly, her face was achingly pale as if her life was about to end, her body shivering in the rain.

Both women stared at each other. Dell felt that same electric current of connection that she had when Jane had glanced over at her after the Duchess had beaten her. The bond was something that went beyond the violence they were a breath away from unleashing when called upon.

Without warning, Jane's knees gave way and she collapsed to the wet ground. Head bowed, her shoulders convulsed and shook with silent tears and freezing cold. In quick one-two succession, Dell dropped her knives and knelt by Jane. It went against Dell's nature to see a woman beaten down by life. Every time she did she saw her mother.

Gingerly but gently, she touched her shoulder. 'What's happened?'

Jane raised a face that ran and shone with rain mixed with falling tears. 'Help me. I don't have any friends, she made sure of that. I only have you. I need to get away from her. Will you help me?'

Then it occurred to Dell. Was this a trap?

Chapter Thirty-five

'Cor blimey! I needed that,' Ruddy exclaimed, thoroughly licking her lips after knocking back a glass of Lord Have Mercy Rum Punch. The stuff was like jet fuel ready to make her head blast off. 'Young Robbie, have a jar of that, mate. You'll feel born again.'

Born again. Oops! Ruddy realised that was the wrong thing to say. It set off all the tension again in Brother Bertie's sitting room. He lived in a maisonette on the Island facing the river. Brother Bertie, Precious and Robbie Steele were the other occupants of the room.

Brother kissed his teeth. 'I'm vex,' he declared. He had been biding his time while a kind nurse in the block, who would keep things quiet, had tended to Ruddy's burns. Now she was gone, Brother Bertie vented his upset.

His flashing eyes burned with laser intensity into his daughter. 'Precious, how could you lie to your father so?' Her presence had explained the lights on in their home. Disappointment shook his voice. 'All this time, you've known he was alive. You've been seeing him.'

He pointedly ignored Robbie. Wouldn't use *that man's*

son's name. He had never approved of his daughter's relationship with him. Jimmy Southpaw's son and his girl… Brother Bertie almost wept just thinking about it.

His anger rounded on his closest friend. 'You see you! What kinda person doesn't tell her closet friend, her companion, that you knew the young fella was alive.' Suddenly his face fell with despair. 'What's Mo going to think when she finds out? My baby-gal gwan lose her mind.'

Guilt and so much more was written on Precious' and Robbie's faces.

Right! Ruddy decided to step in before things got out of hand. 'Precious, take Robbie for a little kip upstairs. No longer than an hour, mind, because we need to put our heads together still to figure out how we're going to put Lady Muckety-Muck of Mayfair out for the count before she hurts Little Mo. Also gives me time to tell Bertie my tale.'

Brother Bertie looked even more confused, his brows pleated together. 'What do you mean *your* tale? How are you involved with Robbie's resurrection?'

As Robbie and Precious slipped out of the room, Ruddy started. 'You recall how we gave Rita a lift back in seventy-one…'

1971

'Rita! I know you're in there! I wanna a word with you!'

Ruddy was hammering on the door so hard that when her friend opened it, she nearly fell inside. 'Oh, hello,

Ruddy. What's with all the racket, I've got neighbours, you know.'

Ruddy was left on the front mat while Rita went back to her bedroom where she was putting on her makeup.

Ruddy marched in. 'I want it back!'

Rita was doing her mascara. 'What, the hairdryer I borrowed? It's on the side there.'

'Hairdryer? You know damn well what I'm talking about. My friend the Colonel's family heirlooms. You had them away! And to think me and Brother Bertie gave you a lift after you half-inched the Colonel! You want shooting!'

Rita pursed her lips. 'The Colonel? Remind me.'

'The fella I clean for who I asked you to give a freebie.'

Rita admired her look in the mirror. 'Oh, him. He did mention something about heirlooms. A diamond brooch, a necklace with green stuff and a ruby something or other. Didn't he keep them in a box under his bed? A bit silly if you ask me. He should keep things like that in a bank.' She fluffed her hair. 'There are five-finger discount merchants everywhere these days.'

Ruddy grabbed Rita's arm and spun her around. But when her friend gave her hand a cold, baleful look, she let her go. Rita was well known for being as talented with her fists as she was on her back.

Ruddy begged, 'Please, Rita. He's a gentleman. He's never done any harm to anyone. Give him his stuff back, he's heartbroken.'

Rita finished her look. 'Has he been robbed then? Why doesn't he go to the law? That's more their department than mine. I'm just a working girl trying to earn a crust.'

Ruddy knew her friend had a hard side but she hadn't seen this level of ruthlessness from her before. 'Yeah, you're a real tart with a heart, ain't you? What do you need his things for anyway? You won't be able to sell them on. Loot like that is way out of your league.'

Rita stood back and admired herself. She was the definition of super cool There was no doubt about it. 'Well, that's where you're wrong. I've got a new job in a place up in Mayfair. You should see the toffs who come sniffing for some action round there. You wouldn't believe who I'm shagging these days. One of them was on the news the other night, an MP! Can you imagine? Me, little old Reet, doing one of them over?

She turned to Ruddy. 'If I had taken the Colonel's collection of tom, which I didn't, I'd have no trouble finding someone to cash it in for me. But even if I had, which I didn't, I wouldn't be selling anyway. I'd store it away for a rainy day.'

'You're a prostitute, Rita. It is a rainy day.'

Rita wagged her finger. 'That's where you're wrong.' She pointed at the ceiling. 'I'm going to the top, my dear. I've had two offers of marriage already from my clients in Mayfair. I'm holding on for the best offer and then I'm getting hitched, horse and carriage, the lot. It's no fun being on the game, it's dangerous. And if the marriage doesn't work out, I'll always have a few choice items of jewellery to fall back on. If I'd stolen any, which of course I haven't.'

Ruddy shook her head with disgust. 'You're a disgrace.'

'Oh, get off your high horse, darlin'. It's dog eat dog out there, it always has been and it always will be.'

Ruddy fixed a stare. 'I'm going to get his property back. I don't care how long it takes or what it costs. I've made my Colonel a promise and I never go back on my word.'

Rita drew up close. 'You of all people should know better than to piss on my chips. That never ends well for the pisser.' She broke into a smile. 'Gotta dash, I'm late for work. See yourself out and shut the door behind you. Oh, and don't bother hunting for the old boy's box of sparkles in my gaff. I ain't stupid.'

The door slammed shut. In the silence that followed, Ruddy repeated, 'I don't care how long it takes or what it costs.'

When Ruddy came to the end of her tale, Brother Bertie looked about ready to storm off on a one-man hunting expedition for the Duchess. 'That woman is wicked. Evil. If I'd known the whole of it, I would've…'

'Exactly. I didn't want no argy-bargy with that she-snake.' A crafty expression twisted Ruddy's features. 'So I bided my time. Waited years. Then Robbie comes along…'

2000

'You all right, young Robbie? Whatcha doing out here at night all on your tod?'

Ruddy was surprised to see Robbie Steele with a smoke

sitting on the old stairs that ran down to the river on the Island. The stairs had once been used by dockers loading and offloading cargo from ships. After visiting Brother Bertie, she sometimes came for a wander down by the river. The peace and quiet here was just what the doctor ordered. Mind you, that expression on Robbie's face didn't look like he'd found much peace. He appeared very troubled, his gaze remote as he stared out across the water.

'Wotcha, Ruddy.' His dimples appeared. 'You out causing mischief?'

'Cheeky sod!'

Not many people knew that Nora Baxter and Robbie Steele had a very close and special relationship. It started when his poor mum, Mini – may the angels keep her safe in their glorious care! – was dying of cancer. Understandably the poor boy had taken it hard. Not that many would know because he'd kept up a strong front for his mum and company that came to pay their respects. That's what was expected of Southpaw's heir. He had to stay upright even when life was left-hooking him dead centre in the face.

Ruddy had come across the broken-hearted lad sobbing his boy's heart out round the back of her prefab in Bethnal Green. Obviously he'd chosen that spot because he thought no one would see him, so he could finally break down about the imminent death of his mother. Ruddy had taken him in hand and got some Milo with plenty of sugar down his neck. After that he'd pop around for a chat, help her with her shopping. From the off she'd made Robbie understand that their little meet-ups were their secret, he mustn't breathe a word to his dad. If Southpaw even got a whiff that Ruddy was near his son there would be hell to pay.

Ruddy narrowed her eyes, observing Robbie more keenly. There was no colour in his cheeks. The poor lad appeared like his world had come to an end. And those shoulders of his that were usually confidently ramrod straight and back were rounded and slumped forward.

Ruddy parked herself down next to him. 'What's up, lad?'

Robbie let out a sigh so heavy it sounded like he had the weight of the world on his shoulders. He said, 'I found out that my ole man's been telling me a load of ole cockle for years. Spinning me a line.' He breathed deeply. 'Because of what he told me I lost my girl years back. She slammed the door in my face.'

Ruddy knew he wasn't referring to his wife. God above! Who could be happy with trigger-happy, motormouth Kristal Steele. Ruddy didn't know her personal, like, and planned to keep it that way. If she was honest, she'd been mightily disappointed when word reached her who Robbie had tied the knot with. Her Robbie deserved better than that. Ruddy had an idea who his lost love was. And about their daughter. The rest of East London might be blind, but she wasn't. Maureen's startling grey eyes were Steel family through and through.

He turned to her, his expression so very unhappy. 'I feel like I don't want to live.'

Ruddy quickly hid her shock and got practical. 'Then don't.'

Robbie was shocked. 'I thought you'd try and talk me out of it.'

Ahh! So she'd been right! Jimmy Southpaw's firstborn had been thinking of doing something stupid. Ruddy cuddled close to him. 'What I mean is you don't have to live *this* life anymore. Turn your back and walk away.' Her brow lifted. 'Or do something drastic where everyone thinks you're dead. Give it a few years then come back and claim, on the sly o' course, the girl you love.'

Seeing his stunned expression, she added, 'Back when I was growing up, some folk who didn't like their life upped and disappeared and started living another one.' Archly, she pointed out, 'I ain't saying whether it's right or wrong. I'm not in your shoes. All I know is a body only gets the one time on this earth and they deserve to be happy.'

Ruddy secretly smiled when she saw that her seed had taken root. Robbie's shoulders were back to their normal straight, and he was thinking. 'There is someone who might be able to help.' Suddenly he hugged Ruddy so hard she lost her breath. 'If, *if* I pull this off, before I go, is there anything I can do for you?'

That conniving, tea-leafing ponce Rita landed in her mind. Ruddy had never forgotten. For years she'd been biding her time for the right moment.

Ruddy looked Robbie directly in the eye. 'Funny you should say that. There's a little job I need doing…'

The light bulb pinged on inside Brother Bertie's brain. 'So Robbie robbed the Duchess' jewels six years ago.'

It all made sense why it had been Robbie who'd rescued them. The expert knowledge of the chimney system at the Duchess' club. His skill with ropes and harnesses picked up by months of practice for the original heist. The gunplay. The bottle you'd need to pull off a stunt like rescuing two people from under the nose of Duchess Rita.

Ruddy clucked her tongue sharply, levelling a razor-sharp glare at him. 'Robbed? More like liberated. That woman nicked them off a man who is a total sweetheart and a dear friend of mine. So Robbie *liberated* them back.'

'My dad was the one who took the Duchess' stash?'

Brother Bertie and Ruddy gasped at the dazed voice that joined then. Mo stood in the doorway looking shell-shocked at the bombshell she wasn't meant to hear. They had been so deep into Ruddy's story they hadn't heard the front door open. Brother Bertie insisted that his granddaughter keep her key to the home she'd grown up in.

Stepping inside, Mo continued, 'I should've figured that out.' The she rushed over to her gramps and gave him the biggest hug. 'Thank God you escaped from the Duchess.'

She pulled away from him, turning to Ruddy. Air sizzled in her throat when she saw the bandages around Ruddy's leg. 'What did she do? I'm so sorry, Gramps and Ruddy. That you got dragged into this because of me...'

The soft tread of footsteps on the stairs stopped her talking. 'Who's that? Who else is here?'

Mo squinted at the sick-looking expressions that her grandfather and his friend suddenly wore. What was going on here?

'Dad.' Precious bounced into the room and came to a juddering halt when she saw her daughter.

'Mum? You all right?' Her mother didn't say a word. Didn't move. 'I thought you were still with your mates up north getting your batteries recharged…' Mo reeled her words back when her mum clamped a hand over her mouth and rocked back slightly on her heels. 'Mum?'

Another set of footsteps came down the stairs. These were heavy, louder.

Scowling, Mo asked, 'Who else is here?'

Mo noticed the other people in the room all held expressions of varying degrees of shock. Appalling shock. Her heart kicked up. Started racing and banging harshly against her rib cage.

That's when she knew what was going on. 'It's the Duchess. Is she here?'

'No, it's not the Duchess.' The voice behind her was one Mo had never heard before. 'It's me.'

MO swung around, never realising her life was about to change forever.

Chapter Thirty-six

Mo could hear the air wheezing in her windpipe as if her lungs didn't work properly anymore. She stared at what she knew must be a ghost. She shook her head, lashes fluttering wildly. She must be more knackered than she thought. The events of the day were finally catching up with her. Maybe that was one of the other symptoms of being pregnant, you started seeing shit. Either that or the bomb at her father's grave had brought him back to life.

Mo sharply shifted her stupefied gaze to her mum. And that's when she knew Robbie Steele was real. Her mother looked like she was on the verge of tears. That wasn't the only thing. The way her mum and dad stood together, something about the positions of their bodies told a story of them having been close and touching many times before. There was the click of the door behind her as Gramps and Ruddy left them alone.

'Robbie?' Dazed, his name dropped listlessly from her lips.

Saying nothing, he gently nodded. Honest to God, Mo didn't know whether to sink in a chair or run over to him, her arms wide ready to hug him to death. She did neither. What she did do was devour him with her eyes. His height and build marked him out as Jimmy Southpaw's son. And that slight tilt of his head to the side was Jimmy all over too. His face… Mo's breath caught. It struck her hard that she was seeing her dad's face in the flesh for the first time. The standout cheekbones, the square jaw, the slightly long nose that she'd been told he'd inherited from his mother, the flop of mahogany-brown hair and beard threaded with grey.

And his eyes. Her eyes. Jimmy Southpaw's eyes. Steely grey.

Feeling her knees shaking, Mo quickly found and fell into Brother Bertie's armchair. This explained the unsettled sensation that had been with her all day. Mo tilted her head at her parents and cried, 'I don't understand.'

After sharing a significant look, her parents calmly sat on the sofa opposite.

Internally, Mo pushed some levers and got back into Big Mo gear and started giving orders. 'First question: how is it you didn't die in that fire in the police station?'

Robbie inhaled and then told her, 'I planned it with Carlson, one of the detectives who arrested me and took me down the nick. We put on a major production in public of him coming into the boozer to arrest me. Me playing dumb like I didn't have a clue why he was doing it. That cop shop had ears, so we still had to keep up the pretence of me not understanding what was going on there too.'

His long fingers skimmed nervously through his hair. 'As with the best of plans, things didn't go according. First off, they slung a drunk in with me. The plan was the cell was meant to be single occupancy. Then the fire got a touch out of hand. It was only meant to do the cell block not the whole bloody station. The cell key Carlson slipped me at first it wouldn't budge the door.'

The shake of his head added fuel to the desperation of his story. 'The flames were licking at the cell door. I thought I was a goner for sure. Finally, I got out. I dragged the drunk out too. I told him I'd see him sorted if he claimed he was in the neighbouring cell. With all the chaos going on, who was going to call him a liar.'

Mo jumped in. 'That was Pockets.' Her mind zoomed back five years. Pockets the homeless drunk she'd met through Sister Aggi's foodbank. He'd 'cross my heart, hope to die', he knew sod all, but Mo had always suspected he was pulling the wool over her eyes. Now she had confirmation her instincts had been right.

Fire lit up her eyes when she recalled what occurred next. 'His body was washed up on the shores of the river right outside here.'

Precious lost some of the colour in her face; she was one of the people who had discovered the body. Breathless with fear and disbelief, eyes widening, Precious point blank asked Robbie, 'Did you do him in?'

'That wasn't me.' Robbie was emphatic. 'Carlson did it. The silly sod heard that the fella was running his mouth. So he organised to meet him on the pretext of giving him a bundle to shut it. Instead, he capsizes him over a bridge into the river.'

'And Birdwhistle?' Mo arched her brow. 'Since we're talking about death.'

Her father's face coloured with suppressed rage. 'I did that. That bollocks solicitor was a menace to good folk and needed to be put down.'

'Because he nicked your documents and tried to sell them on?'

Mo was surprised when it was her mum who answered. 'He was practising the dark arts of blackmail. A nasty business that tears lives apart. One of his victims killed herself.' Mo gasped. 'Both me and Robbie knew her. She was a cracking lady, salt of the earth. Birdwhistle tried to rub her face it in that she had checkered past her family weren't wise to. Robbie came over earlier than me to give that prick what he had coming to him.'

Robbie caught her mum's hand and squeezed encouragement. Precious thought back to her solitary flight to the Ghost Airport and to Robbie mercifully at the other end of her journey waiting for her at the hotel.

Still soaking up all that she was being told, Mo asked, 'Why would one of Her Majesty's boys in blue give you a helping hand?'

Robbie smiled, his legendary dimples grooving deep into his cheeks. Mo was transfixed. His whole face beamed, happy lines crinkling at the corners of his smouldering grey eyes. 'We went back years. Sometimes cops and villains drank in the same places. Anyroads, let's just say, once upon a time I did him a big favour. He owned me and when I cashed in my chips with him, Carlson was near retirement age. We both disappeared. We both stayed on the lowdown for years and then resurfaced in Spain. We each used the name John and variations of it to confuse anyone who might come looking.'

Spain? Spain? Mo's mind whirled a mile a minute. *Hang on! Didn't Nico just come back from Spain?*

He must've read her mind because Robbie confirmed, 'Nico Sinclair turned up. Sticking his beak in, I suspect on the say-so of Dad.'

Mo's mind rewound back to earlier. Inside Granddad Jimmy's. The peculiar stares that her grandfather shared with Nico. Why he'd asked after Precious. Now it all made sense. They had found out that Robbie was alive. No wonder Granddad Jimmy had laughed like a looney tune when she told him that the Duchess had blown up Robbie's grave. The sight of the twisted, mournful expression on his face should've alerted her that something very bad was wrong. Poor Granddad Jimmy. He must be devastated.

'Granddad Jimmy's going to be so hurt.'

Precious exploded. 'Screw! Him!'

Mo wasn't having that. Outraged, she blasted back, 'You don't talk about my grandfather like that. Mine and your relationship has already derailed once over your attitude —'

Precious stormed to her feet. 'My bloody what?' She kissed her teeth, deep long and hard in extreme displeasure. 'Little Miss Lady, you need to mind your business and remember who you're chatting to. I'm the mother in this here yard, not you.'

Robbie raised his hands. 'Let's calm it down, shall we.'

The sound of mother and daughter's ragged breathing dominated the room. Gently, Robbie pulled Precious back down, cuddling her close. Softly, he informed his daughter, 'Dad was the reason all this happened.'

'Don't you get it?' Precious choked out. 'He destroyed my life. Our life.'

A feeling of dread and panic swept over Mo at what she suspected she was about to hear.

Robbie spoke. 'The first time I ever saw Precious she was eighteen and blew me away. I'd never seen anyone so gorgeous in all my days.' He gazed at her, wearing an incredible smile. 'She blew me off at first. And then we started going out.' His smile faltered. 'I took Precious home to meet Dad. He was all sunshine and smiles while she was there. Once she was out the door, he tells me I need to put the kybosh on it, I can't see her no more.'

'He said I was a bad sort with a reputation for putting it about,' Precious finished off.

Mo watched as Robbie lifted her mum's hand and kissed it. Precious ran her free hand with love across his cheek.

Mo asked, 'What happened?'

Robbie picked up the story. 'I convinced myself he was talking rubbish, so we continued to see each other on the quiet. But Dad had planted this seed of doubt in my mind.' His face fell. 'Long story short, I accused Precious of seeing another guy, she wallops me one, I hit the door, and before I know it I've tied the knot with Kristal on the rebound.'

The devastating impact of what Robbie had done was clear to see on them both. Precious looked cut up, and

Robbie's face was ravaged by his life-changing decision.

He shook his head wildly, his expression charged with self-loathing. 'I was so stupid. Don't get me wrong, I will never regret Damien's existence. But to spit in the face of the woman I love…' It was too much for him. He couldn't go on.

Precious pulled his face to hers. Sternly she said, 'What is done is done. All right.' She kissed him lightly on the lips. Quickly, Mo averted her eyes. This was such a private moment between them.

'When I heard Robbie got hitched, I was broken-hearted. Grief-stricken.' Hearing her mother's brittle voice, Mo faced them again. 'Then we kinda bumped into each other. Before you know it we're secretly seeing each other again. Then I got pregnant —'

'The day I cradled you in my arms.' Robbie's chest heaved with the force of his emotion. 'My beautiful baby girl. One of the best days of my life.' A terrible expression gripped him. 'A couple of days later this geezer turns up telling me to stay away from his woman and child.'

'Mum and me,' Mo correctly surmised.

'We had a big row and took it into the street. Dad broke it up. And he tells me the guy is talking the truth. I arrived here shouting the odds, even though Precious swore blind it was a load of ole cockle. Rightly, she told me to piss off outta here. And she wouldn't see me.'

Scowling deeply, Mo shook her head, bemused. 'But how can you lay the blame for that at Granddad Jimmy's door?'

Robbie let go of Precious' hand and ran it across his lips. The strain he was under was evident in the tightness of the skin around his mouth. 'Years on I found out he paid that guy to confront me with that lying crap.'

'Why would he do that?' Mo just didn't get it. No way would it have been because Precious was black. Granddad Jimmy wasn't one of these racist morons. The only colour he cared about was the colour of a person's dosh.

'Over the years,' Robbie resumed, 'I started to put two and two together, hear a word here, a word there. I figured out that there was a mega feud between my dad and Precious' dad.'

'I know that it exists,' Mo acknowledged. 'No one will tell me what it is.'

Precious shrugged. 'We don't know for sure. All we do know is it was the reason Jimmy did everything in his power to keep us apart.' Precious was on the point of breaking down. 'We were made to suffer, our lives destroyed because of what *other people* did in the past. What business is that of ours?'

Robbie wrapped the love of his life in his arms. They looked so right together. The sight of their devotion, the depth of their love brought tears to the backs of Mo's eyes. Her heart was crumbling apart. Mo trembled under the weight of what was being laid bare about Granddad Jimmy. She had big love in her heart for him, nevertheless, how could he have done this to her parents? Wrenched two lovers apart with lies and deception? Granddad Jimmy had given her everything. *Everything*. Mo couldn't just cut out the love she had for him. She didn't know what to do.

Robbie said, 'Jimmy Southpaw is a good man.' Precious let loose with a dissenting kiss of her teeth. 'He is. Whatever went on in the past must've been bad. But it wasn't anything to do with me. Or Precious. I wanted out and took my chance.'

Mo got the distinct impression there was more to his decision. She cast a semi-accusing glare at her mother. 'You knew he was alive all this time? You even came to Robbie's memorial.'

Robbie jumped in. 'She didn't know I was alive. After the fire, I stayed outta the picture for years. I only contacted your mother about six months ago. I wanted to see if she still loved me. If we could make a go of things. Precious only went to the memorial to report back to me.'

Mo levelled a severe look her mum's way. 'I take it all that time you said you were spending with *your mates* up north you were really stopping with Robbie in Spain?'

Precious arched a haughty brow, refusing to look ashamed. 'I nearly dropped when I heard Robbie on the phone. If I'd had my own set of wings, I'd have flown to Spain right there and then. To be given a second chance at love – I snatched it up.'

'Are you planning to stay here? In London?' Mo was afraid of what the answer would be.

Her mother shook her head with regret. 'We can't. Robbie's got to stay dead. If he comes clean, too many people, including the authorities, will ask too many questions. You know the East End, they'll want chapter and verse in weekly instalments. I'm going to live with him in Spain. And we'll take it from there.'

A look of sorrow passed between mother and daughter. Mo was losing not just her father again but also her mum this time.

Precious tried to cheer up the ominous atmosphere that had descended with, 'You can always visit us.'

'What about Granddad Jimmy? Kristal and Damien?'

Robbie didn't hesitate. 'While I'm here I have to face them head-on. Hopefully, Kristal will be up for a discreet and quiet divorce.'

What a mess! Why couldn't families just be nice and simple?

Mo had her own home truths to get off her chest.

'I idolised you, Dad.' Clenching up, Mo spoke her truth. 'Robbie Steele was my father. Since I became head of the family business, do you know what one of my driving forces has been? To impress you.' Robbie was dismayed and tried to butt in, but Mo wouldn't have it. 'Every time I pulled off a deal, I'd wonder, 'I hope Robbie's proud of me.' I tried to steal the Duchess' jewels because I knew that was a job that you wanted to do.' Tears cascaded down her chilled cheeks. 'It ain't right. A child shouldn't have to impress no one but herself.'

Robbie rushed over to her. Crouched down, pulling her into a deep embrace. And feverishly whispered, 'I'm so sorry. So sorry.'

Uncontrollable sobs heaved throughout her body. Mo couldn't stop crying. All the pain and hurt of the years without a father poured its misery and dejection out of her.

Her mum's secure pair of arms joined them.

Mo blurted out, 'I'm going to have a baby.'

Robbie gently eased away from his daughter to stare with wonder at her. 'Honey, that is amazing news. I'm going to be a grandfather.'

Precious was almost jumping up and down too. Suddenly her smiled disappeared. 'Who's the father?'

Mo rolled her eyes. 'Mum!' she wailed.

Face looking fit to murder, Precious scrambled to her feet. 'I wanna know who the father is.' She yanked off one of her high heels and shook it. 'I'll give him what for if he doesn't do right by you…'

Chaos reigned while Robbie and Mo tried to calm her down.

Then reality hit with Ruddy's appearance in the doorway and her quiet statement.

'We need to sort the Duchess out. I've got a plan…'

Everyone gathered around.

Chapter Thirty-seven

Nine on the dot the next morning, Mo walked into Sixes and Sevens Gentleman's Club. The only thing she brought with her was a large satchel hooked over a shoulder. She had no gun, or any other weapons. When she reached the main door, a doorman in the club's regulation red-and-gold livery uniform silently opened it with a smile. Mo stepped inside, and all manner of recent memories assaulted her. Most of them featuring that dickhead, Eddie. Eddie dumping her at dinner. Swinging on a rope in the vertical tunnel of a chimney. Crashing a car into the window of a wedding reception. Eddie again looking at her like she was dirt beneath his shoes.

Mo blanked it all out. *Remain focused.* She spotted the receptionist's desk and walked over. Before she could announce herself, the receptionist was there ahead of her. 'The Duchess is expecting you, madam.'

Mo quirked a curious brow at that. 'Oh, is she?' That put Mo on edge immediately. She hadn't given the Duchess any advance warning that she was coming. What was the other woman's game?

The receptionist spoke into the phone. 'The Duchess'

guest is here. Can you come and escort her up?'

It didn't take long for someone to arrive. And who should it be but none other than the Duchess' assistant, Jane.

Smirking, Mo took the measure of the other woman. And said, 'Dell told me what you tried to do at the club. You thought she would fall into your trap? No chance.'

The other woman made no response. Not one flicker of emotion, so Mo prepared to be searched. Jane ran her hands over Mo's body. Then did it again.

'I'm not wearing a wire, if that's what you're looking for,' Mo taunted.

Jane said, 'Open your bag.'

Mo opened the sizeable satchel she carried. Inside was a small black velvet bag with a gold drawstring. Jane held it up. Whatever was inside clinked as she did so. 'What is this?' she asked.

'None of your business, that's what,' was Mo's tart and tight reply. 'I don't think the Duchess will thank you for poking your beak into her private possessions.'

Jane remained blank-faced. Put the bag back. 'Follow me, madam.'

They took the magnificent staircase to the third floor. The same floor that Robbie had marked out in his plan for the robbery. Mo wasn't surprised when they arrived at the room called The Lady and the Duchess' private apartments. Jane respectfully knocked and opened the door. Inside was the Mo nemesis, The Duchess. She sat ramrod straight on the green Chesterfield with such poise her back wasn't even touching the back of the sofa. Her face was perfectly made up, not a wrinkle in sight and her short grey hair swept back like it had just been professionally styled. She was dressed in a tailored red suit. Mo couldn't resist a twist of her lips. The Duchess might look ultra-elegant to most but to Mo she was the Devil in red. She was delicately eating jam on toast from a silver tray filled with pots of condiments.

Mo noticed that Jane took a seat in the background.

'Please.' The Duchess indicated the chair nearby in her plummy tones. After Mo perched on the edge, the other woman offered, 'You must have some of this fig jam. All the way from Turkey. Sweet and nutty. A delightful combination.'

Mo responded. 'I seem to have lost my appetite this morning.' She placed her bag on her lap and crossed her legs. 'A bit cocky of you to expect to see me at nine.'

The Duchess caught Mo in her beady, watchful gaze. 'I'm never cocky. If you hadn't come, I would have come after you. And hunted you down to the ends of the earth.' The friendly hostess tone vanished. 'I take it you've got my heirlooms. Either that or you've got a death wish.'

Mo considered her long and hard. 'Everything about you is fake, isn't it? From the over-the-top social manners to that phony Bellenden accent you put on.'

'Bellenden?'

'It's a private school, babes. You wouldn't know about that having been only half educated at St Tarts Young Offenders Academy in Mile End.'

The Duchess pursed her lips. 'Don't knock faking it. The art of life is faking it better than the other fakers. And don't knock prostitution either; it's an honourable occupation.'

Mo bit back, 'Stealing an old bloke's family heirlooms isn't an honourable occupation, though, is it?'

The skin around the Duchess' mouth grew pinched. 'The jewels, young lady. Please.'

Mo opened up her bag and took out the velvet black bag, opened up the gold drawstring and spilled the contents on to the table. Glittering jewels sparkled. A diamond bracelet, a ruby ring, a brooch and a set of earrings. Mo watched the other woman's face come alive. Mo had to admit the jewels were an impressive sight. What caught and held the Duchess' attention was a necklace with a large green stone. Transfixed, the Duchess picked it up. Her expression was that of a young woman who had fallen in love for the first time mixed with open greed. *I bet she looked like that when she nicked the stuff.* Mo kept her options to herself.

The Duchess' face was flushed. 'Isn't this one of the most beautiful things you have ever seen?' Her finger caressed the stone like it was the cheek of a baby. 'It's called Imperial Jade. Quite rare I've been told. I have missed these so much.'

Mo burst her bubble. 'But they don't belong to you. They belong to a harmless old man.'

The Duchess cruelly cut in, the flush on her face deepening into a mottled red, 'There are no harmless men.'

'Are you talking about your ole man, the Duke?'

The Duchess' eyes iced over. 'You want to watch your step.'

Mo pressed on. 'They say you killed him. Some say you screwed him until his poor ole ticker gave out. Others say that you poisoned him. Everyone knows you did. Not exactly a big secret, is it?'

'Jane,' the Duchess called, savagely cutting Mo off.

When Jane quickly appeared, the Duchess rose to her full height and slapped the younger woman harshly across the face. 'You stupid girl. I thought I told you to check her for weapons and wires?'

Jane's bowed head trembled as she listlessly replied, 'Duchess, I did.'

By way of a reply, the Duchess snatched the bag from Mo's lap.

Mo stormed to her feet too. 'Oi! Give that back. What do you think you're playing at?'

The Duchess' voice became Rita Evans. 'I'll show you what I'll playing at, you Slaggie Maggie.' In a frenzy, she tore at the insides and the orange lining. Turned the bag upside down and furiously shook it. Out dropped a miniature tape recorder.

'What's that for then? Powdering your bleedin' nose?' She picked it up, chucked it on the floor and crushed and stamped on it beneath her heel.

She turned the full force of her spitting anger to Mo. 'You stupid moo. Did you really think I would fall for the trick of telling you about my husband's death?' She rounded on her. 'Let me guess what the plan was. You give the ole Duchess the jewels, lull her into a false sense of security and then she tells all about how she murdered her husband, which you will just happen to capture on tape.'

Mo said, 'And did you? There's no one recording you here anymore, you've seen to that.'

The Duchess' eyes blazed. 'I killed the Duke, all right.'

She dug her talons into Mo's arm and dragged her across the room, reminding Mo that this was actually a suite of apartments. Mo surprisingly did not resist. Jane followed meekly and very closely behind. They reached a door which the Duchess flung open. In keeping with the rest of the club it resembled something from a stately home, with a chandelier, classic wallpaper and a huge bed in the middle that was fit for a king.

The Duchess, by this stage frothing at the mouth, stabbed her finger at the bed. 'That's where I did him in. Simple enough to put a pillow over his face and press. Keep pressing.' The shape of her mouth was ugly. 'All manner of things can be recorded on a death certificate for the right amount of money.'

Mo inspected her face. 'How could you do that to him? He gave you entry to a better life.'

The Duchess sent her a scornful look. 'You wouldn't be saying that if you had to, night after night, have a man going at you with his fish breath in your face.' She slammed the door shut. 'It was time for me and the Duke to part company.'

The Duchess pushed Mo onto a chair. Her posh tones were back in place. 'Thank you so much for bringing my heirlooms back.' A slow, dark smile creased her face. 'But we wouldn't want you to leave without a parting gift. Oh, Jane!'

Jane was there in a heartbeat. Her employer told her, 'Let's give Big Mo a cracking farewell.'

Jane pulled out one of her snake whips from her pocket.

She twirled it in the air. Cracked it on the floor. Cracked it on the floor again. She looked over at Mo. Raised its wicked length in the air… and brought it crashing down across the Duchess' leg.

Taken completely by surprise, the older woman tipped to the floor, howling in pain. She stared up at her assistant, not believing her eyes. 'What the fuck are you doing?'

Jane crashed the whip down on her again, across her side this time. The Duchess cried out in pain, cringing on the floor.

Mo loomed over her. 'See, that's the problem, Duchess. What goes around comes around. And sometimes it has a sting in its tail.'

Poor Jane was trembling so badly. Mo placed her arm around her to reassure her that everything was OK. After Jane had turned up at Club Class, Dell hadn't thought twice about helping her. So they'd hatched a plan that revolved around having another inside woman, Jane this time. She appeared at work as if nothing had changed and would help Mo with her plan at the same time Jane having an opportunity to enact her revenge against the Duchess. Mo and Jane had kept up the pretence in the reception so that the Duchess' staff didn't think anything odd was happening.

The Duchess bared her teeth, looking daggers at her Mo. 'Take that dim-bat twit, Jane, but leave my bloody heirlooms here. You haven't got nuthin' on me.'

Mo loomed over her. 'I think that's where you're wrong.'

Jane opened her jacket. Inside was a tape recorder. She pressed it on. The Duchess' voice came on. *'I killed the Duke, all right.'*

Mo went, 'Oops! Here's another bit of info for you. I really never stole the loot. Ruddy blagged them six years ago with the help of a certain somebody and gave them back to the Colonel.' Mo frowned. 'I'm surprised you never sussed they were gone. Didn't you check the safe in the last six years?'

A muscles twitched under her eyes. 'Not that it's any of your effing business but I do have lots of other riches and jewels to wear. This collection were going to be a present for my grandson's new wife when they got back from honeymoon.' She said the last with spiteful relish. 'My Eddie would have never married a low life like you.'

Mo ignored her. This evil woman had no power over her. 'It's thanks to the Colonel trusting us with his heirlooms today that we were able to bamboozle you.

The Duchess reared up, lunging for Mo. Jane's crack of the whip against the floor made the Duchess fall back in fear. Mo sauntered over to the jewels on the table and carefully placed them in their soft bag.

She turned back to the Duchess. 'We got back to the arrangement that you had with Jimmy Southpaw. You stay on your side of the river, we stay on ours. You cause any trouble and that tape of your confession will start doing the rounds.'

Outside, in the car, Mo watched Dell embrace Jane. She would make sure that Jane was sorted out. Get her on the pathway to a decent new life. Mo might have put the Duchess in her box but her night was nowhere near over. Now she had to deal with the drama of her family.

Chapter Thirty-Eight

Jimmy sat at the wheel of his 'business' car, the one he used for work. A black coupe with tinted windows. A powerful but understated vehicle that wouldn't attract any attention when he was out on the streets sorting his affairs out. He'd been driving aimlessly, trying to clear his mind before going in search of his son. But the fog in his brain remained. He drew breath, trying to calm down again. He was known around town for his professional behaviour in even the tightest spots. Only second-raters lost their mojo and went mad. Only bottom-drawer boys did stupid things because they couldn't think straight.

Jimmy couldn't manage it this time. Being betrayed was one thing. Double crosses were routine in his line of work, almost expected. Trust no one. Except family. You could trust blood. His own son had destroyed his belief in that.

Robbie! Robbie! Robbie!

To be made a fool of by his firstborn boy? That was one thing he couldn't tolerate. The rules were clear. If your own play Judas they have to die. He examined his shooter in his lap. Glock semi. Would that be enough to put the boy in the ground? He wanted the betraying Robbie's body ripped to shreds. Jimmy got out of the motor and headed to the back. Opened the boot and in a concealed compartment found a sub-machine gun, a model that could be held in one hand like a pistol. He took several magazines and placed them on the passenger seat.

Robbie! Robbie! Robbie!

For a few seconds, Jimmy struggled with his emotions. With the alarmed voice in his head that wailed, *'Kill your son? Are you off your trolley?'* Jimmy steeled his spine and ignored his inner turmoil. He nearly broke the key in the ignition when he turned on the engine and pumped the accelerator. Jimmy took the road at high speed; his foot on the pedal made the car as angry as he was. He drove two short miles to an upmarket gastro pub run by a fella known as 'Clouds' because he was so tall, his head was in them. He'd been one of Robbie's best mates back in the day. After Robbie *died* in the fire, Clouds had gone straight because he felt being on the wrong side of the law was no fun anymore. He'd wept real tears at the unveiling of Robbie's memorial. *Tears that were meant to hoodwink me. Take me for a fucking fool.* Jimmy savagely decided. *Fool me once, shame on you. Fool me twice, shame on me. Nah! Not happening!!*

Southpaw bashed the doors of the pub open with his fists and he strode in. Clouds was behind the bar chatting to a customer. He smiled, although it was touch shaky. Robbie's dad never paid a call on him. Still… 'Mister Southpaw, what a surprise. It's been too long.'

Jimmy marched over and grabbed Clouds by the lapels.

Violently, he hauled him across the counter. The poor guy was terrified. 'Whoa! Whoa! Mister Southpaw, calm down, calm down?'

The pub had gone a deathly silent.

'Where is he?' Jimmy was frothing at the mouth.

Clouds stared back blankly. 'Where's who?'

That earned Clouds two harsh slaps across each cheek. His head snapped back with each blow. 'You know who I'm talking about. Where is he?'

'I don't. I don't. if I knew who you were talking about I'd tell you straight!'

'My son, Robbie.' Jimmy's chest rose high. 'Where is he?'

Clouds looked at him in disbelief. 'Robbie? But Robbie's…' His voice tailed off.

Jimmy had been in the business long enough to know when someone was blagging him. At least, he thought he had. He pulled his pistol from his waistband. Everyone froze. No screams. No noise at all.

Jimmy pressed the nozzle to the guy's ear. 'If I find out that you know something, I'll be back and it'll be no more Mr Nice Guy.' Then he let him go and turned to look at the shocked diners. 'What are you lot gawking at? Eat your fucking dinners.'

Robbie! Robbie! Robbie!

It was the same everywhere he went, first to the long-time associates of Robbie and then on to fringe players. Even the waving of a gun couldn't persuade them to talk. His fury burned so badly it nearly melted his trigger finger. He saw the expressions of pity in one pair of eyes after another and he knew what it meant. Jimmy Southpaw's searching for his dead son? The poor fella's losing his marbles…

He was running out of people. But in a way this made sense. Robbie was far too smart to let anyone know he was back in town. He'd be under the radar, waiting to pull whatever stunt he had in mind. False passports and ID cards? Robbie was probably booked in somewhere out of the way. An anonymous hotel under a fake name. But where? And who would know?

Then it came to him.

He reached into the glove compartment of his car and fished out the envelope that contained the documents Nico had brought back from Spain. He thumbed through the pages until he found a mobile phone bill in one of the names of… of course… John McFly. On it were listed all the numbers that had been called from the phone. Jimmy went down the list. Whenever someone answered he didn't know, he apologised and rang off. But finally he got a voice he recognised. It was guarded. 'Who's this?'

Jimmy relaxed a touch. This was his first break of the night. 'I would advise you not to ring off. That wouldn't be a good idea. I've got a business proposition to put to you and you're gonna wanna hear it.'

'Who is this?'

'You ought to know Carlson, you wanker. It's Southpaw, Robbie's old man. Yeah, I know he's among the living.'

He continued, 'How about me and you wipe the slate clean? I'd never bother you again. All I want is a little bit of info.'

'Listen, Jimmy, I don't want any trouble.'

Jimmy was bitterly cheerful. 'But there's not going to be

in trouble. Not for you anyway. All I want to know is where is Robbie holed up? That's all.'

'Dunno. He never shared it with me.'

Southpaw's voice became almost wistful. 'Just imagine, Carlson, you'll never have to look over your shoulder again to see if I'm in the shadows. Just imagine never having to wake up in the morning wondering if today will be the day when I catch up with you. Just imagine! You could even come back to the Smoke and go public again. I won't bother you. You don't want to spend the rest of your life like a fox being pursued by hounds, do you? You know how close I came in Spain. All I needed was a bit of luck and you'd have come back to my place in the back of a truck carrying tomatoes. Just one bit of information and all that goes away. For good.'

Carlson hesitated. 'He might have asked me to arrange something.'

'I'm listening.'

'He told me to book him and Precious into a chain hotel in the bustle of town. So I did. In the name of Mr and Mrs Roberts. I'll text you the address.'

A grim smile played on Jimmy's cold lips. 'Yeah, you do that. Oh, and Carlson?'

'Yes?'

'Fuck off, you little prick.'

Precious bloody Watson. Jimmy beat his hands furiously against the steering wheel.

Carlson couldn't have picked a better spot for Robbie. The place resembled an office block whose workers all carried suitcases as they went in and out. Jimmy went into reception and tried to cover up his smouldering fury and lust for revenge.

He couldn't have been doing it very well because the receptionist eyed him with suspicion. 'Can I help you, sir?'

'I'm meeting my son here for a chinwag and I'm hoping you'll give me his room number. He goes by the name of Roberts. I believe his wife is staying here too. Lovely woman.'

The receptionist picked up her phone. 'Can I take your name, sir? I'll let him know you're here.'

Jimmy was too close to play games. He took the phone out of her hand and put it back on its cradle. 'Don't do that, doll. I want to surprise him. Now what's the number?'

She was searching for a panic button to alert security. He wasn't stupid. He opened his jacket to show her his gun. 'The number?'

'I'm not giving it to you, sir.'

Jimmy laughed. 'You're a really good employee. I hope they treat you well here. I'll tell you what, I'll look it up myself.' He reached over and took the keyboard from her hand and turned her screen towards him. 'Now, let's see… Mr Roberts. Room four-oh-two?' He gave her back the keyboard. 'I'll just go up and say hello. Oh, and by the way, if the law are here when I come back down, there's going to be some gunplay and I'd hate to see you caught in the crossfire.'

But he didn't care about the law. As long as Robbie was dead, it didn't matter. They could bang him up for the rest of his life after that.

He hurried over to the lifts, pressing all the buttons like

a man possessed. One lift was stuck on the tenth floor while the other was loitering in the basement and didn't seem to be in a hurry to respond. 'Come on, come on.' A staircase was over to his right. He could be up those stairs in a jiffy. He left the lifts and began taking two steps at a time up to the fourth floor. When he got there, he hurried along the corridors 420, 421… He was going the wrong way. He turned and headed back, but the numbers gave out at 410. Then he realised that 409 was tucked around the corner. 408, 407…

The door to 402 was open. Jimmy burst in, sub-machine at the ready. There were lots of personal possessions there but no sign of Mr or Mrs Roberts. He noticed the phone was off the hook. He picked it up and listened.

He heard the receptionist talking to someone. 'He's got a gun, he showed it to me. He's after Mr Roberts in four-oh-two. I phoned Mr Roberts and warned him that someone was coming for him. They just ran out of reception.'

Jimmy let the phone drop to the floor. He stared out of the window which had a grand view of the car park. A sports car had just crashed through the barrier and was heading towards the M25.

Robbie! Robbie! Robbie!

Chapter Thirty-Nine

'Me and your mum used to come here,' Robbie quietly informed his daughter inside Club Class.

They stood on the VIP balcony, staring down at the party people below who were really getting on down and bouncing to Chaka Demus and Pliers' dancehall classic, 'Murder She Wrote'.

In normal times Mo would have looked on with supreme pride as her father surveyed the place at the heart of her empire. Showing off her success to him would have been a highlight of her life. Hadn't that been her dream for so long, knowing it was an impossibility due to his death? But Robbie Steele wasn't dead, and these weren't your everyday circumstances.

Mo had taken him here for a breather. A moment to collect himself before Robbie took the biggest step of his journey back home. To reveal himself to his dad, the mighty Jimmy Southpaw. Mo insisted that she accompany him. God knows what Jimmy was going to do or say. However it played out, Mo was determined to be a rock for both of these powerful men in her life. Nico waited in the car outside first to take Robbie to his dad and then to an unsuspecting Kristal and Damien. She wished he was here by her side now. She could use the extra strength he would give her.

Beneath flickering lashes, Mo observed her father. Outwardly, Robbie appeared as calm as they come, his handsome features settled into an easy-going expression. But Mo saw through his brave front to the signs that showed this was killing him. A muscle pulsed, almost throbbed, in his cheek. The point of his finger tapped against the top of his thigh. His chest quivered in a way that showed breathing didn't come natural to him at the moment.

Robbie continued in his featherlight tone. 'We'd come because it was far away from the East End. Away from our families. Away from all the nonsense. Here we didn't have to pretend to be anything other than what we were. Precious and Robbie, two kids who fancied the socks off each other.' He pulled in a funnel of air. 'On that dance floor we could forget about the world. We'd lean into each other and slow dance. Rocking against each other.'

If Mo had been in any doubt about whether Robbie loved her mother, it disappeared then. His eyes were closed as he spoke, his hips slightly swaying as if young Precious was back in his arm.

His eyes sprang open, glittering with the light of a young man. 'Do you know what tune got your mum grooving like mad?' Mo did but pretended not to. She didn't want to steal the pleasure he would get from telling her. 'Dennis Brown's 'Money In My Pocket'. Your mum could move.'

'She still can.'

Mo bit into her lip, an idea coming to her. She leaned over and shouted across to the DJ. Grinning, he gave her the thumbs-up and seamlessly shifted the song playing into Dennis Brown's classic. Robbie and Mo grinned at each other. So that's where my smile comes from, Mo thought in wonder.

Her dad's smile and relaxed manner disappeared. 'When I found out that Dad had added this club to his property portfolio we couldn't come here no more.' He shuffled his feet, recalling the past. 'We found somewhere else. Then another place. We were always seeming to be on the move. I got tired of it. So tired.'

Her smile dimmed. 'After this tune, we need to make tracks to Granddad…'

A loud crack split the air. Mo knew that sound. A bullet sparked and ricocheted off the chrome railing they stood at. The crowd downstairs screamed. Robbie leapt on his daughter, dragging her down to safety. Mo's anger was back full blast. If this was the Duchess again there was going to be proper ructions. This time Mo wouldn't rest until she drove that lowlife out of town. Mo started to get up, but Robbie held on tight, holding her back.

Frowning, she looked at him in confusion. 'What are you doing?'

'You can't go out there. I won't allow it.'

Mo's face coloured, her gaze fierce. 'You won't allow it?' Anger and resentment swept over her. 'You haven't been here for twenty-four years of my life. You don't get the right to tell me what I can and can't do.'

Mo couldn't escape his stricken and hurt expression. She sucked back her guilt. He needed to know that there was a long journey of healing and understanding to go through before they became true daughter and father. That she made her own decisions, not some man. Her thoughts shattered when another bullet cracked through the air. The panic and chaos downstairs got louder. Robbie loosened his grip, allowing Mo to peer down below. And what she saw nearly broke her in two.

It wasn't the Duchess downstairs. It was Jimmy Southpaw with a gun. Mo's agile mind quickly slotted the pieces together. Granddad Jimmy was here to kill his son.

She stood tall. Stood firm. 'Granddad, you can't do this.'

'Get out of the way, girl. If a member of your flesh and blood betrays you, you don't have an alternative, you've got to put them down. Those are the rules we sign up to in the underground world we live in.'

Mo caught the eye of the head of her security team. She called out to him, 'Everything is under control. Get everyone out of here.' She said more loudly, 'It was just a prank. Blanks. You know what guys get like sometimes. The management will sort you some free tickets for your return visit.' She didn't need to add that everyone was to keep their mouths shut. Come through the doors of Club Class and you abided by its rule. Rule one: No fraternising with the Old Bill.

If Mo thought things couldn't get any worse, she was wrong. She stumbled back when she saw Robbie had made his way downstairs. *Oh my God!* He stood in the pathway of his father's raised, smoking gun.

Father and son stared at each other for the first time in six years. They had the look of each other in the large sizes of their bodies, the way their veins corded in their necks, their bold facial bone structure and something that wasn't visible to the eye. They still held so much love in their hearts for each other.

Jimmy let the pain show, allowed the hurt to glint in his eyes. 'Why did you do it, son? Why did you let me think you were dead all these years? Was I such a wicked father?'

Robbie dared to take a step forward. His reply was rough. 'I'd had enough, Dad. I was tired of the lot of it. Remember how I'd play the piano up the boozer, some days that's all I wanted to do. I hated playing the hardman.'

Ahh! So I was right, Mo realised. *There was more to Robbie's story about leaving.*

'Why didn't you tell me?' Jimmy sounded like he was in the depths of despair.

'Tell you?' There was anger in Robbie's voice for the first time. 'Can you imagine it, your firstborn son telling you he didn't want fuck all to do with business? You'd have probably locked me up until I saw reason.' Robbie shook his head with bitterness and sadness, such sadness. 'From day one you groomed me to be your heir.'

Robbie couldn't stop. 'Do you remember that sports day when I was nine and Harry was eight. You and Mum were there to cheer us on. Me and Harry both ended up in the final of this race. And he won.' Jimmy's face turned white. 'I know what Mum did. Harry never told me, I sorta figured it out. Right after he won, she took him away and smacked him a sharp one across his face. She told him never to do it again. Never to show up his father's heir by taking victory over him in front of others in public.' Robbie's hands came up. 'Dad, we were boys, for fuck sake.'

'I never —' Jimmy tried to intervene, but Robbie wouldn't have it.

'Do you know what? I deliberately let Harry win that day. I hated the way you and Mum favoured me over him. We were both your children. Both deserving of equal love. As we grew older, the way Harry used to look at me...' The words of what that was were too hard for Robbie to reveal. 'That's why I never told you, Dad. Because either you or Mum or both would've slapped me raw until I saw the errors of my way and turned back into the cocksure, swaggering, smart-mouthed top geezer that everyone and their granny loved.'

It was Jimmy's turn to step forward. His shooter remained high and steady. 'Bad-mouth me till the cows come home, I can take that.' The shape of his mouth twisted into an ugly shape. 'But your *son?* Your *wife*? How could you have let them believe you were dead?'

Robbie's fist curled by his side, his breathing coming in short, shallow spurts. 'I love my boy and always will. The truth was, I was in a corner and couldn't see a way out. If I could've taken Damien with me I would've, but the reality was he is and always will be his mother's son.' Tears filled his eyes. 'I couldn't stay in that marriage anymore. Me and Kristal should've never have married —'

'But you did, boy. You should've stayed and respected your vows. Or gone about it the right way and taken it to the divorce courts.'

Robbie's head tilted back trying to set his thoughts straight. He looked his dad squarely in the eye. 'I know what you did. How you lied to keep me and Precious apart.'

'It was for your own good.'

Mo sucked in a shock breath that Granddad Jimmy didn't deny it.

'Bollocks,' Robbie spat. 'It was for *your* good, *Brother Bertie's* good. Me and Precious were a causality of a past we knew nothing about.' Suddenly Robbie's palms covered his head in anguish. 'I lost all those years of being a father to my precious baby girl.'

Mo intervened in the face-to-face confrontation for the first time. 'What happened all those years ago? Between you and Gramps?' She had chosen to remain on the balcony, despite it going against her nature not to do anything. This was father-and-son business, she recognised that. Mo had to allow them to wade through dangerous waters and pray they didn't drown. They had to purge the poison of the past.

Jimmy clamped up at her question.

Robbie jeered, 'Don't waste your breath, he's never going to tell you. Brother Bertie's exactly the same. You know what, Dad? You wanna kill me, go ahead.' He ignored his daughter's horror-stricken cry. Robbie pulled his hands from his head and opened his arms wide. 'Right here, Dad.' His fist thumped his heart. 'Put a bullet right here. If I can't be with the woman that I love and walk the path I choose, then I don't want to be here anymore.'

Mo's frantic footsteps sounded on the steel stairs. Mo flew down them because of what she'd seen in her dad's eyes. Robbie Steele was ready to die. Jimmy and Robbie stared directly into each other's eyes. Neither would look away. Their hearts beat like the pounding hooves of horses running rampant and wild. Jimmy's finger tightened on the trigger. Sweat gathered along the curve of his hairline and trickled down the side of his face. He was caught in a war, a man of two halves. One was a father, the other a feared gangster who ruled by a set of deadly codes and with an iron rod.

Shoot him! Shoot him!

He's your son! Your son!

Robbie! Robbie! Robbie!

The gun slipped from Jimmy's fingers, clattering to the floor. He collapsed to his knees, bowed his head and cried and cried. Robbie's tears boiled over as he rushed forward, got on his knees too and embraced his father. Jimmy did the same to his son, holding with a fierce tightness. Over and over, he chanted his son's name. 'Robbie! Robbie...'

Chapter Forty

Mo found Nico having a smoke inside his sports car outside the club. She eased into the passenger seat.

He flicked his smoke out the window. His smouldering gaze settled hotly her. 'How did it go?'

Her eyes bugged with disbelief. 'You'd have to have no ears not to have heard the gunplay.'

Nico arched his brow. 'I heard it. Suspected what was going on. It was time for father and son to either make death or make peace.'

Mo started; the words clogged in her throat. She couldn't speak. Her face crumbled. Nico open his arms. She fell into them, crying her bruised heart out. His comforting kiss on the top of her head made her sob harder. Mo had no idea how long she stayed in the safety of his arms. Slowly she became aware of the warmth of Nico, the strident, steady beat of his heart. She eased her tear-streaked face back and tipped it up to look at him. Nico was staring down at her. Their gazes caught and held, hot and alive.

Mo stretched up, her hand cupping his cheek. Nico closed his eyes and groaned. Her fingers journeyed to his hair, running through it with a quickness as if Mo wanted to get to know each individual strand. Their mouths met. *I've died and gone to Heaven. This is soooo good. Soooo good.* They kissed and kissed, over and over. Mo couldn't get enough of him. She got her knickers off. Then made quick work of his zipper. Got him out. Crawled over him. And sank down. Merciful heaven! A bolt of electricity took her physically and mentally into another stratosphere. His large hands cupped her bum. They started moving, in total sync with each other. Their harsh, hot breathing tore up the night air. Her lovemaking with Eddie couldn't touch this. This was steamy, sizzling, smoking, spicy, downright saucy… Mo threw her head back, gasping, body shuddering in the most intense orgasm of her life. Nico came too.

A terrible silence came next. Mo stumbled off him to sort herself out. *He won't look at me.* The tears sprang to her eyes all over again. *Suck it up, buttercup!* she warned herself sternly. There were going to be no more tears this night.

Nico finally spoke. 'That shouldn't have happened —'

'But it did,' she countered vehemently. 'I don't do married men, I never have. Maybe that was down to my mum being cast as the other woman in my dad's life.' Mo turned to face him.

Nico's fixed gaze stared out the windscreen. He wouldn't look at her.

Mo sucked that hurt back too. 'Today has been a revelation of truths for me. So I'm not running from our truth no more. We fancy the bollocks of each other and get on like a house on fire. There's a strong connection between us. I know you adore and honour your family and I can't express to you how much I respect you for that.'

Mo heard the quiver of emotion in her voice. 'I'd never, ever ask you to leave them. That's bang out of order. But I don't share. I won't be anyone's bit of muff behind closed doors. I'm probably making a right dog's dinner of this. I'm not going to get all sad about what we did. It was beautiful. Thank you.'

Jimmy and Robbie came out of the club. They walked side by side, in an easy manner. Mo was pleased. She hoped they were on their way to resolving the many issues they had. Jimmy left while Robbie made his way to Nico's car.

Nico got out. Bewildered, Mo watched him move towards her father. When he reached Robbie, Nico decked him with a stunning blow. Robbie went down. Mo leapt out of the car and rushed forward. Nico stood over Robbie, breathing heavily. 'That's for what you did to my sister and my nephew.'

Robbie rubbed his sore chin. 'Fair enough. Now take me to them.'

'How could you do that to us?' Kristal thundered.

Mo heard it all from outside Robbie's one-time home. She sat on the stoop of their front door. The sun was just coming up, bringing the first fingers of light with it.

'My boy deserves better than this.' Mo heard her stepmother gulping, trying to control the shock and the tears.

Mo didn't hear Robbie. Or Nico. And strangely not Damien. She thought he'd be the one kicking off. He'd loved his dad so much.

Then she heard him. 'It's all right, Mum. Everything will be OK. I'm glad Dad's alive. We won't be able to acknowledge that, of course —'

'But Damien —'

'No, Mum, that's how it has to be.' Kristal and Robbie's son would brook no disagreement. 'I can still see Dad. He'll just have a different name.' He paused. 'Besides which, we've been doing very nicely, thank you very much, without him.' Ouch! That must've hit Robbie hard.

Mo shook her head in wonder. Who'd have thought it? Eh? Damien all grown up. It had been a crushing day and night. Why did we hurt the ones we loved the most?

Mo heard the engine and then her car appeared on the driveway. Dell wound down the driver's window. 'You ready, cuz?'

Mo slipped into the back seat. Placed her hand on her tummy. 'Everything is going to be all right, little one. It's all turned out sweet 'n' dandy.'

Chapter Forty-One

No Twinkle. That was the first thing Mo noticed when she strode into Club Class three days later. Scowling, she thought, come to think of it she hadn't clocked her bestie for a few weeks. Her mind dived back. Oh yeah! The last time she saw Twinkle was the day of the pregnancy test. Chatting about being a mummy. Mo felt surprised and heaps uncomfortable that she hadn't seen Twinkle for such a long time.

She called out to the club manager, 'Where's Twinkle? She should be here managing the bar.'

Her manager averted her gaze. As did many of the other staff. What was going on?

Mo slapped her fists onto her hips. 'Whatever's going on here, someone needs to start talking.'

Her manager slowly and cautiously glanced back at her. 'She left.'

Mo staggered back. 'Whatcha mean, she left?'

'She didn't want to trouble you.' That was another voice. A woman at the bar. Josie. Mo remembered the names of all the people she employed. And where you saw Josie you saw her friend, Lindy. They were faves with the punters, men and women alike because they pulled out all the stops, clobber the latest gear and slap contoured to the max. They were close to Twinkle, very protective of her.

Mo reached them. 'If you've got something to say, tell me.'

Mo didn't miss the sour look that passed between both women. Why did she get the impression that the sourness was directed at her? Mo didn't know how their relationship had come about. What she did know was Lindy and Josie wouldn't hear a cross word about Twinkle. Anyone who did would live to regret it. Mo sensed she'd ended up on the wrong side of the pair.

It was Lindy who started filling in the blanks. 'She didn't want to tell you, said to leave you be.'

'Yeah,' Josie popped in. 'You being so busy 'n' all.'

'Though she did try to tell you a couple of times.'

'Mind you, you can't tell someone who ain't much interested.'

A warning finger stopped them. 'Open your lugholes. Where? Is? Twinkle?'

Together, they answered, 'She's in hospital.'

Mo didn't hang around to hear more. She bombed out of the Club at breakneck speed.

Twinkle wasn't up The London, which was the nick for The Royal London Hospital in Whitechapel. Mo instead found her friend in a private wing of a hospital out Kings Cross way, off the Gray's Inn Road. Mo's heart beat so badly wondering what had happened to her best friend. The hospital was calm, purposeful and quiet. The nurse at the reception desk directed Mo to Twinkle's room. What was Twinkle doing in a private hospital?

Even though Mo gathered her composure outside the door she could not hold on to the gasp she emitted when she opened and saw Twinkle. She didn't hear Mo come in because she was sleeping. Mo didn't notice that all she could see was Twinkle's bad leg. It had been elevated for comfort and to help the healing process. Healing from what? The staff had remained close-mouthed about what the issue was due to patient confidentiality. Despite understanding all of that, it didn't lessen Mo's fear. If anything it sent her anxiety levels through the roof.

Quietly, she closed the door and advanced towards the bed. Twinkle looked run-down, her skin so see-through the veins were visible, and there were large smudges of shadows beneath her eyes. A big plus was her red hair was lush and healthy again. Maybe Mo made some kind of noise because Twinkle slowly opened her green eyes. They flashed with alarm when she saw Mo. She started to struggle to get up, but Mo restrained her with her fingers on her wrist.

'What are you doing?' Mo admonished. 'Lie back and think of England.'

That put the cheer back into her bestie, her face transforming with a shy smile. Then it dimmed. 'How did you find out?'

Mo pulled up a chair before answering. She looked upset. 'Why didn't you tell me?'

Twinkle gave it a few seconds before hesitantly answering, 'The truth is our friendship isn't what it used to be,'

'Nah, Twink.' Mo wouldn't have it. Her mate was wrong, wasn't she? 'We're still besties.' Mo didn't like the desperation that she heard lurking in her words.

Twinkle was adamant and held her ground. 'We're not young girls anymore. We're grown up. Got different interests so it's only natural that we'd start to drift apart.'

Shame pushed Mo's head down. Twinkle was so right. Her shame intensified when she recalled one of their most recent convos:

'Actually, have you got a bit of time now. I was hoping to have a word —'

'Time is something I haven't got. We'll sit down and talk soon. Promise.'

She'd broken that promise. Her bestie had tried to talk to her, and what had she done – given her the big brush-off.

Mo's head came up. 'I never meant anything by it.'

'I know.' Twinkle's understanding and gentle nature made Mo feel even worse. In her shoes she'd probably be shouting the odds and showing Twinkle the door. 'You've had a lot on your mind. You're not Mo from the block no more, you're Big Mo Watson who runs a very successful business, thank you very much.'

Mo glanced at Twinkle's leg, biting her lip. 'What happened? Has it got worse?'

'Stop. It. Just stop it right now.' Mo was knocked back by Twinkle's eruption of anger. 'I'm sick to the back teeth of you thinking what happened to me was your fault. I'm tired of it actually. I'm an independent person who doesn't need a friend who pities her.'

'Now hold on one flippin' second there.' Mo's words were heated too. 'I will admit that I feel guilty and nothing you can say will stop that. As for pity – piss off. You're my mate because I care about you and love you. Now tell me what's going on with your leg.'

Twinkle settled more comfortably, some of her tension draining away. 'I've had a right ole time of it with the pain in my hip and leg. Things were getting worse not better.' Mo choked up at the thought of her friend in pain but did not interrupt. 'So I decided to take matters into my own hands. Or my own legs.'

They cracked up at that. It felt so good to be laughing together again.

Twinkle continued. 'I've been putting money aside to have a specialist type of op that might make things better. I'll always have a dickie leg but my limp might not be so noticeable. More than that, the pain might not be so bad. That's a miracle for me. I had the op a few days ago. The doc's happy with my progress so far. Fingers and toes crossed.'

Mo said, 'That's great news. I'm sorry I wasn't there for you at such an important time. It won't happen again.'

Twinkle's face glowed, her cheeks suddenly blooming up rosy. 'Can you imagine it, Mo? Me dancing. I haven't danced in six long years. I might not be able to dance exactly the same as others but I'm going to still shake a leg. Wouldn't that be something? Anyroads, enough chat about me. What's been happening with you?' Twinkle stared at Mo's midriff and cooed to the baby, 'How you doing in there? It's your Aunty Twinkle saying 'hello.''

They eased back into their ole chatty relationship. Twinkle gasped when Mo poured out the story of Robbie's return. The heist. Eddie's wedding. Nico. Mo had missed her best friend's non-judgemental company so much.

What struck Mo was a hard lesson learned. All this time she had been pursuing approval from a father who she believed was dead. So much so that she'd sacrificed her relationship with the bestest best friend a girl would ever know. She had taken Twinkle's love and presence for granted. Mo vowed never to treat her relationship with her bestie as a trivial thing. That's what Mo was going to teach her child. Treat those you love with beauty and care. Friendship and family can be such a fragile thing.

Epilogue

Seven months later

'I'm here to see one of my clients,' Eddie Harvey announced at the gate reception of Highturn Men's Prison. He handed over his ID.

The prison officer was female, so Eddie couldn't resist giving her the eye. Despite being married for seven months gone now, he couldn't stop himself. In his own mind he was God's gift, a platinum-certified babe magnet. All women were hotties who couldn't wait to get their hands on him. His grandmother, the Duchess, had reared him to believe that he was the best. That he could do no wrong. Super successful, good-looking, a wife indoors who knew her place – what more could a guy hope for. Well, one ingredient was missing: he was on the prowl for another bit on the side. The business with Mo hadn't gone to plan. Something had happened after he'd gone off on his honeymoon that grandmother wouldn't tell him about. In fact, she wasn't even here. She'd gone off for a long break to the South of France.

He smiled harder at the female officer who didn't smile back. Her loss!

After she'd done her check, she buzzed him through to security who did their usual body search. Eddie hadn't met this prisoner who he was visiting before. His PA had taken a call from the police asking if he would be present while the prisoner confessed to another crime. They wanted someone from the prosecution team to be present to ensure all the I's and T's were dotted and crossed. Eddie had almost palmed the job off on another colleague; prisons weren't really his scene. Creepy places, full of the stench of overpowering testosterone. Well, that's how he saw it. But there had been no dodging this, the police required his and no one else's attendance. *I suppose that's what happens when you have a reputation like mine; everyone wants a slice of the Eddie pie.*

A prison officer, a large man, was waiting for him beyond the automatic security door to take him to a private visitors' room. He was the silent type which suited Eddie perfectly; the sooner he got out of here the better. All of a sudden Eddie noticed that they seemed to be heading for one of the wing blocks.

'Excuse me,' he enquired. 'I thought we were going to the visitors' suite. The sign we just passed said it's the other way.'

The man's voice was deep. 'They should have explained at the gate that the prisoner has had to be held in the segregation block for his own protection. Even going to the visitors' suite may put him at risk.' His voice dipped. 'I believe that he's implicated other parties which is why your presence was necessary.'

That made sense. They entered the segregation block, which was situated quite a distance away from the other buildings. They walked up the stairs to the first landing. Stopped at a cell door.

'He's in here, sir.' The prison officer unlocked the door.

Eddie strolled in with aplomb, head held high… And then nearly peed his pants. The door slammed behind him. He was trapped in a cell with a man who was not wearing prison-issue clothing. Even though the man was sitting, it was clear he was a big with well-toned muscles. He sat casually with one leg hitched over the other, appearing very relaxed. What had Eddie running scared was the gun in his hand resting on his leg.

Eddie didn't think. He twisted around and banged his fist against the cell door. 'Guard, open up. There's someone in here —'

'I think they like being called prisoner officers these days. This ain't Newgate Prison.'

When it was clear no one would answer his pleas for help, Eddie turned, pressing his back against the cell door. 'What do you want?' His erratic stare fixed on the gun.

The man unfolded himself to his considerable height. 'Me and you, Eddie lad, need to come to an understanding.'

'I don't even know you,' Eddie threw back.

'True. But you know my mate, Big Mo.'

Eddie tried to speak but soon shut it when the gun came threateningly up. 'You're to stay away from her. Stay away from the kid.'

'What kid? I haven't got a clue what you're talking about.'

'That's good. You best keep it that way.' He moved closer

to Eddie, taking the measure of him. 'You're lucky it's me and not her granddad. He'd kill you. Now me, I'm just going to leave you with a little warning. Take off you jacket and shirt.'

'What?' Eddie's voice shook terribly.

Brows calmly raised, the guy waved the shooter. Eddie quickly did what he was told.

'On your knees. Back to me. Hands braced against that chair.'

Eddie knew what was coming and was scared. The only other choice was a bullet. He heard the whoosh sound as the man pulled off his belt. He never saw him double it.

The voice behind him said, 'One for every month that you two-timed Big Mo. On my understanding that's eight.'

He raised the doubled-over belt and laid into Eddie's back with all his power and strength. The segregation block was too isolated for anyone to hear Eddie's screams.

Nico was let out of the prison via a side entrance. A prisoner was already on hand to take the blame for the attack on Eddie. Of course, he was nicely compensated. The prisoner officer and a few other members of staff were known to Nico. He had left Eddie a bleeding mess with the warning that women were to be cherished not used. Mo had no idea what he had done and that's the way he wanted to keep it. Nico was going back to Cyprus with Pam and the kids where they had already been for a couple of months. He needed to clear his head. And leave the temptation of Mo behind.

In the maternity ward, Jimmy Southpaw sat facing Brother Bertie. Neither man acknowledged the other. Or spoke to the other. Or made eye contact. They were both waiting for the birth of their first great-grandchild. The birth of a child was a time for families to bond and unite. These two men had vowed many years ago to never do that.

A beaming nurse came out to them. 'Mother and baby are doing fine. You can both go in now.'

Brother Bertie might have a walking stick, but he was determined that that man was not going to get to see his new great grandbaby before him. Jimmy Southpaw was equally determined.

Suddenly, the nurse turned back to them. 'Mo asked me to escort you both to the door so that you can come in at the same time.'

And that's what happened. Mo was exhausted, but the tiredness didn't even rate. All she felt was an overwhelming joy and adoration for the gorgeous and precious bundle she cradled in her arms.

She looked up at both her grandfathers. 'It's a boy.' She uncovered the blanket to show him off. Brother Bertie propped his stick up by the bed and took the baby in his arms, just like he'd done all those years ago with Mo.

Jimmy softly asked his granddaughter, 'How you doing, girl?'

Mo smiled with all her heart. 'I've never felt better. I'm on the top of the world.'

Brother Bertie asked, 'And what are you going to call this little man?'

Mo answered. 'I did think about naming him after both my wonderful grandfathers but I think he needs his own name.' Brother Bertie placed her precious boy in her arms. 'His name is Tyler.'

Big Mo Crime Series Book 1

DIRTY TRICKS: A Sneak Peek

1992

'Knock her friggin' teeth down her throat.'

'Scratch her eyes out.'

'Rip all that curly-wurly hair out of her head.'

The schoolgirls, baying for blood like a pack of dogs frothing at the mouth, savagely screamed and spewed hate and poison at ten-year-old Maureen Watson. Curly-haired with polished light-brown skin, no one called her Maureen. She was known by one and all as Little Mo because she was a tiny, wee thing, still inches off five feet. And that's why the other girls ganged up on her, classic bullies who used their bulk and bluster to intimidate a much smaller girl. Cowards, every last one of them is what Little Mo's grandfather would have told her. Not that he had told her that, because Mo hadn't breathed a word to him about this spot of bother that was being dished out to her at school.

'Titch.'

'Short-arse.'

'Pint-sized dwarfy.'

The other girls tightened their menacing ring around Little Mo around the corner from the school gates, snarling and abusing her all the way. The other kids, milling out of the school, scented blood in the water. In a flash they encircled Mo and her tormentors, clapping and chanting, 'Fight! Fight! Fight!'

The children loved nothing better than witnessing a proper bashing after being cooped up in school all day.

The boss girl of the bullies was Lulu Lawson, who took pride in her nickname, Loopy Loo. You better believe she was crazy! She was big for her age, broad-shouldered with long arms that ended in hammer-like fists that had been knocking other kids around since the age of four in the nursery. There was nothing she liked better than performing to an audience. It was a reminder to the other children that she was the undisputed Queen Bollocks-Bee of their School. Anyone who thought different ended up with two shiners and a bloody lip.

Loopy's eyes lit up with malicious glee as she went to work with a solid shove that slammed Little Mo into the wall. With all the force she could muster, Mo shoved her attacker right back. The crowd gasped and sucked in their breath with horrified disbelief. Mo Watson must have a death wish.

'You're dead,' the bully barked, a splatter of spit flying from her mouth.

With one of her deadly hands, she yanked a fistful of Mo's blouse, sending a button flying in the process. She lifted Mo to the tips of her toes but before Loopy could deliver a killer blow Mo kneed her in her soft tummy. The other girl staggered slightly back, an audible grunt of stunned air whooshing past her lips. Mo pressed her advantage, swinging and kicking for all she was worth. She was no contest against the much bigger girl who slammed a fist to the side of Little Mo's head. Dazed, Mo wound up face down on the ground. If she'd stayed down, Loopy and her mean-girl crew would've left her alone, no doubt high-fiving each other, congratulating themselves on a job well executed.

But Little Mo didn't stay down. She never did. 'Stay down' wasn't in her vocabulary. Little Mo climbed to her feet, moving her head to shake off the foggy dizziness. Then she tilted her chin with determined defiance, swinging punches left, right and centre. But they missed their mark. The other girls were too big and there were too many of them. The girls steamed in, knocking seven bells out of Mo. So over the pavement she went again.

It was so much easier to stay down. But she got up again. Mo might be small, but she wasn't letting anyone push her around. Never Ever. Sneak over the fence at the back of the school to avoid the bullies was what her friends begged her to do. But Mo's answer was always the same. 'Why should I? I ain't scared of them.'

Mo stood strong and proud despite the wicked pain that pierced through her like the heated blade of a knife. Her school blazer was torn, shoes scuffed, the strap hanging loose from her new bag and her socks marked with the dirt from the kicks she'd taken. Her face was bruised and scraped. She boldly stared Loopy and the other girls in the eye, clenched her fists and gritted her teeth.

As she did so, an angry man's voice in the distance roared, 'Oi!'

The crowd collectively spun round to see who had the brass nuts to interrupt their after-school entertainment. Loopy nastily twisted her lips ready to give the guy a proper, ripe mouthful but when she clocked his face the blood drained from her face leaving her shaken. Her gobsmacked expression was mirrored on the faces of a few of the other kids. The bullies and the other kids scarpered as if a wand had been waved by Mo's fairy godfather.

Surprised, Mo watched them go. When they'd disappeared, she tried to mend the broken strap on her bag. She loved this bag. Her beloved granddad had got it for her down the Leather Market in Petticoat Lane Market or The Lane as everyone locally called the East End institution. And now look at the state of it? It resembled something a dog had mistaken for its dinner.

Mo forgot all about her busted bag when she felt the shade of a dark shadow cast over her. Her head snapped up to find the man who had scattered the crowd standing over her.

'You alright there?' His voice was deep and typically East End. 'What was that row about?'

He was suited and booted, tall, very tall indeed. Muscular and wiry, wearing a baseball cap that shadowed most of his face and shades that hid his eyes. Mo squinted up at him. The guy looked familiar. Then she remembered why. He'd strolled into the chicken-n-chip shop on the High Street, noticed the lengthy line of schoolgirls queuing up, including Mo, and told the guy behind the counter to let them have their lunch on the house. The bloke on the counter didn't argue. The big guy collected his takeaway on the house too.

Mo's mum had warned her, finger stabbing in her face to emphasise her words, not to speak to any strangers, especially men.

Mo didn't heed her mum's advice as she finally gave him an answer. 'They duffed me up because I'm little. They wait for me, regular like a dose of castor oil, at least once a week at the school gates.'

His lips twitched at the corner like he was holding back a laugh. 'What's a young 'un like you know about castor oil?'

Mo's little nose wrinkled. 'Enough to know I'll bite the fingers clean off the next fool who tries to get a spoonful in my mouth.'

He let out a bark of loud laughter. Then quickly composed himself, his expression turning serious again. 'That's not very nice of those girls to be ganging up on you. Why don't you tell your teachers and get them to do something about it?'

'Tell the teachers? You having a laugh?' Mo snorted in disgust. 'I'm not no grass.'

The man nodded. 'Fair enough. Maybe you could just climb over the back fence instead and avoid them that way?'

Mo snapped back with the same explanation she'd given her mates on that account. 'Why should I? I'm not scared of them. I'm not scared of a living soul.'

'You could get some back-up?'

Mo wasn't having that either. 'I don't need back-up. I fight my own battles.'

The man looming over her smiled. 'Hmm, I can see

you're going to go far in life, young lady. What's your name?'

'Little Mo. Coz I'm little and my name is Maureen.'

He folded his arms over his immense chest and sighed. 'Well, Little Mo, why don't you let me help you out? The next time them girls start up on you, tell them I'm a relative of yours. That'll soon put a stop to their little game of soldiers. You'll see.'

Mo folded her arms just like he had. In fact, she shifted her whole body so that she mimicked the way he stood, feet slightly apart. Mo liked the feel of that. It made her feel steadier. Powerful.

'Why should I? Who are you?' Her tone was belligerent.

He seemed to loom even larger over Mo. 'Don't you know who I am then?'

Mo's face screwed up slightly. 'No. Why should I?'

His big hand patted her on the head where her curls were now a tangled mess. 'Don't worry about who I am. Them girls won't be bothering you no more, that's all that matters.'

Grinning, the big guy set off down the street. Little Mo went back to trying to put her bag to rights.

Her new guardian angel was well down the road when he stopped and shouted over his shoulder, 'And another thing, girlie. You'll need to change your name if you want to get on in life. Tell them kids and anyone else who crosses your path that your name isn't Little Mo. It's Big Mo. And if they forget to use your new handle, give them a slap to jog their memory.'

'Change my name?' But Mo was talking to the wind. Her saviour was already gone.

That was the day Little Maureen Watson started thinking big.

Big Mo Crime Series:

Book 1: Dirty Tricks

Book 2: Fight Dirty

Thank you!

Thank you for reading *Wicked Women.*
We hope you enjoyed it! We LOVED writing it!
Checkout Amazon for all our books
The Big Mo Crime Series is also available on Kindle Unlimited.

Reviews: We write for you!
We adore hearing what you think about our books. Reviews help other readers find books. So do please leave a review.

For news and loads more, head off to our website and sign up.
https://dredamitchell.com

We adore hearing from readers, so please do get in touch with me.
Website: https://dredamitchell.com
Facebook: https://m.facebook.com/dredasaymitchell/
Twitter: Dreda Twitter

All About Dreda

Her Majesty the Queen awarded Dreda an MBE in her New Year's Honours' List, 2020.

She scooped the CWA's John Creasey Dagger Award for best first-time crime novel in 2004, the first time a Black British author has received this honour.

Ryan and Dreda write across the crime and mystery genre – psychological thrillers, gritty gangland crime and fast-paced action books.

Spare Room, their first psychological thriller, was a #1 UK and US Amazon Bestseller. Dreda is a passionate campaigner and speaker on social issues and the arts. She has appeared on television, including *Celebrity Pointless*, *Celebrity Eggheads*, BBC 1 *Breakfast*, *Sunday Morning Live*, *Newsnight*, *The Review Show* and *Front Row Late* on BBC 2. Ryan and Dreda performed a specially commissioned monologue on the ground-breaking SkyArts50 on Sky TV.

Dreda has been a guest on many radio shows and presented BBC Radio 4's flagship books programme, *Open Book*. She has written in a number of leading newspapers including the *Guardian* and was thrilled to be named one of

Britain's 50 Remarkable Women by Lady Geek in association with Nokia. She is a trustee of the Royal Literary Fund and an ambassador for The Reading Agency.

Some of their books are currently in development as TV and film adaptations.

Dreda's parents are from the beautiful Caribbean island of Grenada. Her name, Dreda, is Irish and pronounced with a long vowel ee sound in the middle.

Printed in Great Britain
by Amazon

67236965R00192